T0199101

Against the Rules

Laura Heffernan is the author of:

The Reality Star Series

America's Next Reality Star
Sweet Reality
Reality Wedding

The Oceanic Dreams Series

Time of My Life

The Gamer Girls Series

She's Got Game
Against the Rules

Against the Rules

Laura Heffernan

LYRICAL PRESS
Kensington Publishing Corp.
www.kensingtonbooks.com

LYRICAL PRESS BOOKS are published by

Kensington Publishing Corp.
119 West 40th Street
New York, NY 10018

All Kensington titles, imprints, and distributed lines are available at special quantity discounts for bulk purchases for sales promotion, premiums, fund-raising, educational, or institutional use.

Special book excerpts or customized printings can also be created to fit specific needs. For details, write or phone the office of the Kensington Sales Manager: Kensington Publishing Corp., 119 West 40th Street, New York, NY 10018. Attn. Sales Department. Phone: 1-800-221-2647.

Lyrical Press and Lyrical Press logo Reg. U.S. Pat. & TM Off.

First Electronic Edition: October 2019
ISBN-13: 978-1-5161-0849-7 (ebook)
ISBN-10: 1-5161-0849-3 (ebook)

First Print Edition: October 2019
ISBN-13: 978-1-5161-0852-7
ISBN-10: 1-5161-0852-3

Printed in the United States of America

For Tara and Ryan
The family that games together, stays together

Chapter 1

Welcome to THE HAUNTED PLACE. This is a cooperative game. You will win or lose as one. The more in sync you are with the other players the better, so get to know each other. You're going to be spending a lot of time together.

—*The Haunted Place* Player Guide

The guy in front of me shifted from one foot to the other as we slowly and deliberately reviewed every…single…strategy game on the shelves. For an entire hour. "What about this one?" he finally asked. "Do you like this one?"

"That's a fun game, but it's for younger players. Are you buying for a child?"

He blushed. "No."

Usually, I liked my job at Game On!, even if it wasn't what I'd planned to do after grad school. I loved introducing new gamers to old favorites and helping longtime gamers find new stuff. I even enjoyed helping the ordinary indecisive customer. But this guy had no idea what he wanted, and he seemed increasingly unlikely to buy anything at all before we reached retirement age. When he first started coming in, I'd thought he was cute, with his sandy brown hair and blue eyes peering out from behind wire-rimmed glasses. Taller than me, but not too tall, with a bit of stubble in the evenings.

Unfortunately, the more he got on my nerves as a customer, the less good-looking he became. He always lingered and rarely spent any money. He probably only came into the store to compare our prices to Amazon.

An unfortunate hazard of working in an indie game store: We couldn't match big store or online sales.

Behind me, the store's phone rang. I wished I could leave my customer to answer it, but in-person customers came first.

Trying to hide my impatience, I snuck a peek at the clock on the far wall. Three minutes until closing. One hundred eighty seconds until my friends arrived with a brand-new, never-before-played tabletop board game (by anyone—we'd be play-testing this one!). Then I could politely ask this guy to leave.

As if someone heard my silent call for help, the bells on the front door chimed, and one of my best friends appeared in the doorway. Shannon wore a wide grin and about seven coats. It was beyond me how a person could walk wearing so many layers they couldn't put their arms down, but that's what happened when a Florida girl moved to Boston for grad school and stayed to help her nana. Several winters later, my poor friend still never got warm.

Before she hung up her coats, Shannon set a large shopping bag on the ground. My heart started pounding. It was one thing to know what she'd be bringing, but now it was *here*. The game. The game we'd been waiting to play for almost two years. The top secret game we'd heard so much about, but had never been allowed to so much as peek at. Now it sat less than fifteen feet away. I wanted to squeal and race over and scoop it up and rub it on my face. My friends would understand. But unfortunately, my customer probably would not.

With a huge smile, I waved to Shannon and pointed over the customer's shoulder. We couldn't play in the main area after hours because people saw us and knocked to get in. After a few complaints long before I started working here, the owners set a game room up in the back.

"Is the store closing soon?" my customer asked. He pushed a lock of hair out of his eyes.

"In a few minutes." As the face of the business, I should invite him to stay and browse as long as he wanted, but he wasn't going to buy anything.

"Oh, okay. Sorry." He seemed about to say something else, but the bells over the door chimed again, drawing his attention.

Cody and Gwen stood inside the doorway, holding hands and smiling in their "about to be married" way that always brought a big smile to my face and a pang to my stomach. Gwen was one of my best friends, and I was delighted for her. But it was hard not to wish I could find what they had. A couple of years ago, I thought I had it. Until everything crashed and burned so hard, I still hadn't convinced myself to dip a toe back into the dating pool.

I'd never tell Gwen and Cody about my jealousy. They made an adorable couple, and truly, I was ecstatic for them. Given her past, Gwen had never wanted to take a chance on love. After watching her and Cody fumble their way toward each other for months, I knew they were the real deal. They belonged together. It would happen for me someday, when I was ready.

Cody wasn't like my ex. He wouldn't cheat on Gwen, steal her money, then get arrested for running a pyramid scheme.

I called out a greeting to my friends, then turned back to my customer. "Is tonight game night?" he asked. "I could play with you."

"I'm sorry, but tonight's a private event," I said, trying to figure out how to get him out without being rude. "We're play-testing a brand-new game."

His eyes lit up. "That sounds awesome! What is it?"

Behind me, the phone rang again. I ignored it in favor of giving a quick answer. "Do you know legacy games?"

A legacy game was designed to be played as a campaign, which took place over multiple gaming sessions. During each "level," things happened that led the players to discover new rules, additional characters, different obstacles, or other changes. New stickers got applied directly to the rule book or game board, becoming permanent additions. Some pieces were destroyed as the game continued. Players received new goals for each game. The nature of a legacy game rendered the board unplayable after the first time, but they provided so many hours of fun, it didn't matter. Unfortunately, they also required the same core group of players for each session, and some could take a year or more to finish, so you had to be pretty hard core to get into this particular type of game.

"Like *SeaFall*? Awesome! I would definitely play if you needed another person."

"This one is, I believe, sort of like *Betrayal at House on the Hill* meets *SeaFall*," I said. "Shannon hasn't told us much about it. But we're full."

His face fell. "Will you be playing a public game at the store soon?"

"I'm not sure. My boss should be here tomorrow, if you want to check." I stressed *tomorrow*, hoping he would take the hint to leave.

"What if I left you my number?" he asked. "You could call me."

"Sure. I'll tell him you're interested." I didn't mention that the owner should be here any minute to play with us, because my fingers itched to open the new game.

"Yeah, okay. I should go."

I didn't argue, ushering him out as politely as possible and even thanking him for shopping with us.

As I locked the front door behind him, Gwen appeared at my elbow. "What are you doing?"

"Working. Sorry that guy took so long. I was hoping he'd buy something."

She sighed. "He wasn't planning to buy anything. How many times has he come in here?"

I shrugged. "Five or six? I'm not sure. I see him every once in a while."

"Does he ever hang out and talk to anyone else for like twenty minutes?"

"I don't know. I'm usually the only one working when he's here."

"And you think that's a coincidence?"

I didn't see what she was getting at. "I work alone almost every evening."

She shook her head. "Holly, you're hopeless. He likes you. He doesn't care about legacy games or what we're doing. He wants to spend more time with you. That's why he offered you his number. He doesn't want *the store* to call him. He wants *you* to call him, you dope."

Her words made me chuckle. "No way. He's a customer."

"He's a *cute* customer."

That he was, although he'd be even cuter if he'd buy stuff. I guessed what Gwen was getting at, but I still didn't want to date anyone. The fact that I got more excited by a new game's arrival than the good-looking guy flirting with me seemed like a sign.

Gwen said, "Come on. How long has it been since you went on a date?"

I shifted my feet and gazed at my fingernails. It had been more than a year and a half since I found out my ex-fiancé was cheating on me, which Gwen knew since she, Shannon, and Cody busted him. The silence grew until finally I had to say something. "I tried, in the beginning. A couple of parties, a couple of make-out sessions that never turned into anything. You were there."

"Uh-huh. Getting drunk and sucking face at a gamer conference isn't exactly getting out there. What happened to that online profile I set up for you?"

"I went online, and I looked around. They're all cheaters."

"All of them? Every single guy who uses the internet is a cheater? It says that in their profiles."

"I used the notes you gave me. 'Discreet' equals 'cheater.' 'Looking for someone to spoil' means cheater. No profile picture? Married. Likes dogs? Cheater."

She gave me an exasperated look. "I never said that last one."

"Okay, fine. But the others seemed to pop up on every other profile."

"Holly, I know Lucas let you down. It's hard to get back out there after someone betrays your trust. We've all been there. But if you go looking for a reason to reject every guy you meet, I promise, you'll find one. You can't assume everyone is a cheater because of one bad experience." Her tone softened. "Look, I'm not saying you have to marry any of these guys. One day, maybe, sure. All I'm saying is, for now it's time to get back on the horse. Go on a few dates. Meet some people. Get out of your self-imposed isolation. If love develops down the road, great. But that's not the goal right now."

She was right, of course, but I didn't want to admit it. "It's just so hard to tell with guys online."

"Right. It's hard to tell with people online. And cute guys in game stores. And people you meet in bars. Come on, what does a guy have to do to get your attention?"

At her words, a face swam before my eyes, unbidden. Early forties, dark hair, an easy smile, brown eyes, and completely gorgeous. The one guy who monopolized my attention without even knowing it, who made it impossible for me to pay attention to other guys I met. Who I secretly compared every single online profile to on the one night Gwen and I surfed the dating sites. Also the one guy I could never, ever be with. And the one guy Gwen couldn't know I had a hopeless crush on. She'd never understand. Besides, it didn't matter. Nothing was going to happen. He didn't have the slightest interest in me.

A knock on the front door saved me from following that train of thought further. I thought about ignoring it. Our fourth and fifth players should be arriving together, since they lived on the same block, and as owner, John had a key. But since I stood in plain view, hiding wouldn't work unless I froze and pretended to be a cardboard cutout. Of what, I didn't know.

"Sorry," I called without looking up. "We're closed."

The knock sounded again, louder. "Holly? It's me."

Scarves and wind had a way of distorting voices, so I didn't recognize the speaker immediately. It must be one of the regulars. I loved our regulars, and I couldn't ignore any of them. But I had a game to get to, and it was after closing. This person needed to come back tomorrow.

The customer stood with his or her back to the door, a bulky jacket and hat obliterating most of their form. Welcome to Boston in the winter. Everyone looks identical, the stream of people becoming a sea of black coats, hats, and gloves. Except Shannon, who stood out because of her sheer volume of clothing and six-foot frame.

Then the customer turned around, grinning at me, and I recognized him. A wide smile broke out across my face at the sight of Gwen's dad, Nathan. My traitorous body reacted this way every time he was around. Not because we were friends and he'd become my landlord, but because he was ridiculously hot. Also funny, smart, charming...

At first, it had been kind of a joke. Whenever Gwen mentioned her dad, I threw in a "Daddy McHotCakes" comment, and she'd shrug it off. Nathan was forty-four years old, with two successful auto shops and a fully grown child. He wouldn't have the slightest interest in dating someone my age, making minimum wage in a dead-end job. Especially not his daughter's friend. But sometimes, I wished I could find a guy with his rugged good looks and a smile reminiscent of McDreamy from *Grey's Anatomy*.

Ah, well. Maybe Gwen was right; it *was* time to start dating again. My virginity had probably grown back, and I hadn't even considered dating anyone since my ex, if you didn't count the completely inappropriate crush on Daddy McHotCakes here.

Gwen tolerated my comments, but if I ever hit on her dad, she'd be horrified. Not to mention how embarrassing it would be to get turned down flat by the first guy I asked out...in my entire life, actually. My ex and I started dating in high school. He'd made the first move. On me and half the other women in the greater Boston area, it turned out.

Ordinarily, I'd be happy to chat with Nathan, but not when a shiny new game beckoned and his daughter stood behind me. Unfortunately, he was one of the store's best customers, my roommate, and my friend. I couldn't let him in, but I also couldn't be rude to Nathan, of all people. I cracked the door, leaving my foot wedged behind it. "Hey. Sorry, we just closed."

His brow furrowed. "I know. That's why I'm here."

"You're here because you want to talk to me when the store's not open?" My traitorous pulse quickened just a smidgen at the idea.

"No, Gwen invited me to join the game. It's cold. Let me in."

My already-high spirits soared. Oh, goody. Suddenly, the game came with eye candy, the one thing it had been missing.

Chapter 2

Choose your character carefully. This will be your persona for the rest of the game. Unless you die. But let's not talk about that now. You have plenty of other things to worry about.

—*The Haunted Place* Player Guide

Although I'd be happy to have Nathan join our game, his words confused me. *The Haunted Place* played five: me, Gwen, Cody, Cody's friend Tyler, and the store's owner, John. Shannon was here to oversee, watch, and answer any questions about the rules. We'd already warned her that she'd be banished if she got too obnoxious about knowing what was going to happen. This wasn't *Dungeons & Dragons* or *Monopoly*. We didn't need a master to run the game or a banker or anything.

Before I could voice these thoughts, Gwen appeared behind me. "Hey, Dad! Glad you got my message."

I turned to her. "Your message?"

"Yeah, John texted that something came up with the kids, and he can't make it. Rather than delaying the game, he's going to bow out. Said he called the store, but no one answered. I texted you."

"I haven't checked my phone in ages." I opened the door and stepped back. "Come on in. Sorry."

Nathan grinned at me as he brushed past, sending a tingle up my arm. Geez, my hormones were getting ridiculous. We lived together. My pulse couldn't start galloping every time we passed each other in the hall or my hand grazed his while we made breakfast in the morning. This crush needed to be squelched and fast, before it got embarrassing. Nathan could never know the way he made me feel.

I blamed Gwen for planting the seed of finding someone new in my head. Alas, she probably meant finding someone new that I could actually date, like the customer from earlier. I suddenly wished I'd noticed he was flirting. If nothing else, flirting back would give my suppressed hormones an appropriate outlet for release since Nathan was totally forbidden.

Gwen was right, it was time to put myself out there. My extreme reaction to Nathan confirmed that I needed to dust off my online profile and make an effort. Going on dates with nice, safe guys my own age should help me gain perspective. If nothing else, I'd eat a few good meals, meet new people, have interesting conversations. Or maybe I'd spend enough time around members of the opposite sex to at least notice when one of them flirted with me. Baby steps.

With a deep breath, I forced myself to focus. This gaming session wasn't only for fun. We had a job: Shannon was counting on our group to point out problems, errors, mistakes in the directions, omissions, and other issues before *The Haunted Place* went to print. If we messed up, the game could flop on the market, get bad reviews, and it would be partially our fault. Last year, one of our biggest complaints in a legacy game we'd all played was that it felt like no one play-tested it. We couldn't let that happen to Shannon.

With determination, I shoved my personal issues out of my mind and trailed Nathan to the back room. Cody and Gwen sat side by side at the table. Nathan pulled out the middle remaining seat, so I dropped into the empty spot between him and Gwen. From my vantage point, I could see the main area of the store. Not necessary with the door locked, but I liked being able to keep an eye on things. Shannon came over to stand between me and Gwen.

The three of us made an odd trio. Having divested most of her layers, Shannon looked like a much taller version of Velma from Scooby-Doo: curvy, short hair, with glasses. Her frames enhanced the comparison, which I suspected wasn't a coincidence. But she wouldn't be caught dead in an orange turtleneck, wearing mostly vintage-style dresses and some actual vintage dresses passed down by Nana. To her right, Gwen was short and skinny, with the most gorgeous red hair usually hidden in pigtails, blue eyes, and freckles she hated but gave her face character.

Meanwhile, on the other side of Shannon, I was completely average. Average height, average build, wavy medium-blonde hair, medium-brown skin from my Puerto Rican mother, and hazel eyes with mediocre vision. Without my contacts, the world turned fuzzy.

To look at Nathan, you would never know that he and Gwen were related. She must look exactly like her mom, but I didn't know. Dr. Connors—who never changed her name—left when Gwen was a kid. There wasn't a single picture of her in their home. While she went to medical school, Nathan worked to provide for the family—and then she ditched them both after getting her degree. Poor guy. He deserved better.

According to Gwen, her father barely dated in the years since. It broke my heart to think he pined for the woman who treated him so badly. Especially when any number of women out there would love a chance to make him happy. Like me.

No, not me. *Focus, Holly.*

Shannon placed a box in the center of the table, slowly, almost reverently. Since this was a play test, the box hadn't been printed yet. The plain white cover provided a stark contrast to the dark wooden table. A blank slate, not a hint of what we were about to experience. "Is everyone ready?"

"We've been ready for *years*," I pointed out. "Ever since you started making this. Stop stalling. We're dying to play."

"Shouldn't we wait for Tyler?"

"If you don't open that box now so we can set up, I will take it from you," Gwen said. "We won't start until he gets here."

With an evil grin, she lifted the lid an inch at a time, slowly revealing the contents. Cody hummed the *Jeopardy!* theme song. A board sat on top, which Nathan removed to find the rest of the pieces. He also pulled out a few cardboard sheets. Underneath, the box was filled with compartments, covered so we couldn't see what was inside, all marked with numbers or letters.

"Issue number one: There aren't any instructions," Gwen said.

Shannon held up a sheaf of papers. "I was going to read them to you."

"Nope," Nathan said. "Let us play. As if we were five strangers who pulled the box off the shelf and don't know you from Adam."

She started to protest, but the rest of us agreed. Play-testing gave the game designer valuable information, sure. But if she read the rules, self-editing and guiding us as she went, we wouldn't be evaluating the game so much as Shannon's explanation of how to play. That didn't help her or future gamers.

Part of the nature of a legacy-type game is that things change. Certain events would tell us to open sealed packets in the box, read cards, or take other actions. Cards read at the beginning and end of each game revealed rule changes. Players made choices based on the information available, but we wouldn't know until later whether those choices panned out. A seemingly good idea early on could lead to disaster after a plot twist. No way to plan, no way to know. So much fun. And impossible to play as intended with the creator hovering. The tiniest flinch or smile could alter our choices, impacting the course of the game.

"Go read out front, or hang out in the staff room," I said. "We've got some new comics. Just read carefully. Let Tyler in when he gets here."

Begrudgingly Shannon handed the instructions to Nathan. She then gave him a second booklet, with strict instructions *not* to open it until the game directed us to. She would, after all, be listening from the other room.

Cody unfolded the board onto the table. I held my breath. The tone in the room was quiet, almost reverent. We were hard-core gamers, all of us. We loved the smell of a new game, the feel of cards that haven't been played, the excitement of finding out what an untouched box contained. After waiting so long for this one, I could hardly believe the time to play had finally arrived.

Lines crisscrossed the surface of the board, creating a grid. The squares themselves were blank, except for three. One on the left side said "Front door." One on the right side said, "Upstairs." And one near the bottom said, "Basement." According to the rule book, the remaining room stickers came in a stack. We were prohibited from looking through them until the time came to place each new room on the board.

Nathan bumped his knee against mine under the table to get my attention. A thrill went through me. "You okay?"

As I gazed up into his dark eyes, I nodded. "I'm just excited."

And not only about the game, I added silently before I could stop myself.

Something flashed in Nathan's eyes at my words.

"Tyler's going to be a few minutes late. He said we could read the introduction and fill him in," Gwen said. "Let's do this!"

I forced myself to drag my gaze away and focus on Cody, who held the Player Guide.

Opening the instructions, he started to read. "It is a dark and stormy night. Your car breaks down by the side of the road. You see a house in the distance, and you approach, seeking shelter."

"Is this the *Rocky Horror Board Game*?" Gwen asked.

"You wish!" Shannon's voice came from the other room.

I yelled back. "We can't hear you!"

Cody continued reading, keeping his voice low and spooky. "This house isn't like other houses. For one thing, it's got some…unusual rooms. Strange things keep happening. Some of you might not make it. For now, each of you chooses a character. This will be your role. There are more roles than players, and each has unique attributes. Choose wisely."

"Do you think Tyler will mind if we pick characters while we wait?" Nathan asked.

"Even if he did, we can trade once he gets here," I pointed out.

"Good point." Gwen waved a stack of cards. "Here are the role cards. Looks like there are six characters. We've got your fairly standard horror movie roles: the Virgin, the Jock, the Flirt, the Geek, the Skeptic, and the Nice Guy. Does anyone have a preference?"

Cody snagged the Geek instantly, naming his character Noah after the horror movie fanatic in MTV's *Scream*.

"Well, you know me," Gwen said. "I'm the Skeptic."

"Shouldn't there be a couple?" Nathan asked. "In horror movies, there's always two people who get killed making out."

At the thought of making out with him, even as part of the game, my face grew warm. I'd happily volunteer to be part of the couple. To feel his lips against mine. To…stop fantasizing about my best friend's dad.

Shut up, Holly.

"There's no couple character." Cody gestured at me and Nathan, presumably since we hadn't picked yet. "Unless the two of you want to team up."

It was as if he'd read my thoughts. I shifted in my seat, then pulled out my phone to cover my discomfort. Luckily, my naturally dark skin would hide some of my flushing face, if anyone noticed. I could blame a little redness on the warmth of the room.

"Half of that couple is usually the Virgin or the Flirt," Gwen said. "You're far more virgin than flirt these days, Dad. Go with it."

Most people would've been shocked at the way Gwen spoke to her father, but I'd long since become used to the fact that they had an unconventional relationship. More like the Gilmore Girls than any father/daughter pair I'd ever met. Considering how my own father faded from my life after marrying the stepmonster, I did my best not to envy them.

"I'll be the Jock," he said. "The jock's always hooking up with the pretty ladies. Maybe the role will give me some real-world practice."

Gwen rolled her eyes. "You can only dream."

"Let's be honest, guys," I said. "As Gwen pointed out not five minutes ago, I haven't been on a date in so long, it's embarrassing. I'll take the Virgin."

She shook her head. "Nope. You need to get out of your comfort zone. Be someone you're not. Get your groove back. Be the Flirt."

I hesitated. The Virgin felt appropriate. But part of this game was playing a role, and I got tired of always being who everyone thought I was: Quiet Holly, Meek Holly, Holly-Who-Doesn't-Notice-When-Her-Boyfriend-Steals-Half-a-Million-While-Cheating-on-Her. Maybe Gwen was right. Time to flip the script, get out of my comfort zone. I'd experienced a lot of trouble trusting my instincts over the past year or so; maybe listening to Gwen was the way to go.

"Okay, fine," I said with more conviction than I felt. "I'm the Flirt."

"Are you sure?" Cody asked. "Don't let her bully you."

"No, she's right," I said. "I've been sequestered since Lucas and I split up. It's time to live a little. Broaden my horizons."

"Exactly," Gwen said. "You may not be the Flirt now, but there's no reason you can't learn to be."

"Maybe Holly just needs to practice," Nathan said.

"Okay, fine. Practice." She looked from him to me and back. "But not on my dad. Ew. You can practice on me, Tyler, and Cody."

So much for allowing my fantasies to spin out during the game, since I couldn't explore them anywhere else.

Trying not to look disappointed, I took my character card and reviewed the stats. Players could make their character any gender they wanted or no gender at all. My character possessed high movement, high sensitivity, low intelligence, low strength. I also got a special power: my character got one extra die when rolling for sensitivity. I guess because she was so attuned to people or something. Since I generally sucked at dice rolling, I'd take it. Some people might say you can't be bad at rolling dice, but they'd be wrong.

A voice sounded from the doorway. "Not to state the obvious, but I do have mad flirting skills. Who am I practicing on?"

Our fifth and final player stood watching us. I groaned to have a near total stranger overhear this conversation. I liked Tyler well enough, but I barely knew him.

Then again, he would certainly be easy to practice flirting on. Tall, which I liked. Close-cropped black hair, beautiful white teeth, flawless dark skin, and a heart-stopping dimple. A little skinny, but what did you expect of an accountant who gamed with all his free time? Yes, a girl could flirt with Tyler easily, and enjoy doing it.

Unfortunately, he wasn't my type. Maybe he would've been, with his quick laugh and classic good looks. Too bad he'd had an enormous crush on Shannon since the day he met her. Being second choice didn't do it for me.

This conversation increasingly made me want to crawl under the table and hide. As Tyler settled into the final empty chair, I said, "It's cool, I can flirt online. I swear, I'll work on it. Let's play."

Gwen handed him the remaining character cards, and he did a double take. "Hold up. I hope y'all don't think I'm going to be Dead Body Number Two."

"Hey! That's not what the card's called," Shannon called from the other room. "That's the Nice Guy."

He read from the description printed on the index card. "'Smart, liked by everyone, wears glasses, reads sci-fi.' This character is never going to make it through a haunted house. It's cool. I'll be the Virgin. Sorry, Hol. No flirting for you."

"I'll live," I assured him.

Once we'd named our characters, Cody read the next set of rules. To start, we were learning the game mechanic, since we'd use it for each session of the campaign. We'd explore the ground floor, finding rooms and determining the layout for later plays. Upon entering a new room, we'd draw a card. Some of the cards referred us back to the book or to draw cards, and we'd go from there. If we lost the first game, we'd reset, leaving the previously explored rooms on the board. That way, we'd have a better shot at winning the second go. Shannon made special room stickers for Game 1, presumably to ensure we found the most important rooms early on. Or maybe so we didn't put the game into an unwinnable state from the first session. It would suck to spend a year playing a cooperative game only to realize at the end you'd never had a shot at beating it due to an unknown mistake early on.

Cody pulled out an app on his phone to determine a random starting player, and I wound up with the first turn.

The instructions didn't tell us how to win the first game, so I figured we'd start by exploring the house. But I couldn't resist trying out my new character before getting started.

"This house looks so scary!" I batted my eyes at Nathan and put one hand on my chest. "Wherever will I find a big, strong man to help protect me?"

Nathan smiled, but I couldn't read his expression.

Gwen snorted. "Your role is 'the Flirt,' not 'Scarlett O'Hara.'"

"Valid. I can do better."

"You're not using those lines with real guys, are you?"

Although she obviously suspected, I didn't want to admit I hadn't met anyone yet, online or off. Largely because I failed to look. I'd never even checked for messages after setting up my profile. "Uh. No."

Thankfully, Tyler came to my rescue. "We don't know how long this game will take, so maybe we can work on Holly's love life after?"

Cody quirked an eyebrow at him. "We? You helping?"

He shrugged. "If Gwen has any say, we're all helping."

At this point, I wanted to crawl under the table and die. I thought about excusing myself and hiding in the restroom, but that would only encourage them to talk about me until I got back. Better to change the subject. Grabbing my character's pawn, I moved through the house to an open space. "Give me a room."

The sticker I placed on the board told me to draw a card, which directed me to roll to see whether zombies attacked. The mention of zombies surprised me, but well, it *was* a horror-themed game.

"What do you need?" Nathan asked, passing me the dice.

Our fingers brushed, and a spark shot up my arm. My eyes darted to Nathan, searching for any hint that he felt the same thing.

Still holding the directions, Cody answered for me. "She has to roll equal to or above the total number of players and revealed rooms. We've only got one room on the board, so that means six or better."

"With five dice?" Gwen asked. "Easy peasy, even for Holly."

I grinned at her. We both remembered how poor dice rolling got me eliminated from the *Explorers of Islay* tournament last year. After playing about a zillion games, I'd come to accept my bad dice karma. It was a running joke. Usually in cooperative games, I never touched the dice. But this game didn't allow us to pick who rolled.

"Well, not completely easy," Nathan said. "These aren't standard dice."

He took one back from me, holding it up. The die had six sides, a regular cube, as expected. But the pips didn't range one through six. Three of the sides were blank. The others sported one or two dots.

"And look!" I held up another die. "They're all different. This one only has twos and zeros."

"We're doomed!" Gwen's smile took the edge off of her words.

I blew her a kiss and reached for the dice. Tossing my hair in the most flirtatious manner I could, I shook my arms and waved my clasped hands a bit for show, shaking both the dice and my boobs. They'd all see I could flirt. And I almost managed to avoid sneaking a peek at Nathan to see if he noticed.

The dice clattered onto the board, and we all watched as they rolled to a stop. Zero. Zero. Two! One. Zero. Zero.

Oh, no. See where flirting got me? In trying to attract Nathan, I'd managed to catch the attention of some zombies.

Chapter 3

Pay attention to everything. The most inconsequential events could turn out to be of monumental importance.
—*The Haunted Place* Player Guide

Now that we had a problem to solve, the game began in earnest. Every turn, the zombies advanced based on rolls of the dice. As a team, we needed to avoid the zombies long enough to gather weapons and fight back. Players could freely transfer objects back and forth as long as they stood in the same room, so anyone who found what we needed could share.

Finally, only one zombie remained. It started with twenty hit points, and none of us could inflict more than five damage, so we gathered together to attack as one. Gwen drew a card at the end of her turn and read aloud. "The zombie advances. He pushes a button on the wall. Shutters slam into place over the windows. The doors begin to close. It's a trap!"

"Not so fast. I've got dynamite." Cody waved a card. "I can throw it through doors, even as they're closing."

"The dynamite could explode, fail, or boomerang back on you," Tyler said, taking the card and reading it. "If you roll at least a five, we're safe."

We stood to watch the action, as if our intensity could affect the roll. For two hours, everything we'd done came down to this moment. With a five or above, we'd win the game. But if Cody rolled zero through four, we'd not only lose, we'd suffer a setback that could make the next game more difficult. Not exactly the way we wanted to start a long-lasting campaign.

Four dice hit the table. Each die moved in slow motion before coming to a halt. Two…one…zero. Collectively, we held our breaths as the final die tumbled toward the edge of the board. Finally, it stopped. Two black pips stared up at us. We won!

At seeing the results, I squealed with joy. Cody let out a whoop. A cheer went up around the table. Nathan threw his arms around me, sending warm-fuzzy feelings down my spine. I hugged him back before remembering how many other people stood in the room. Our eyes met awkwardly. He pulled back, moving to hug everyone else, leaving a rush of cold air where he'd stood. A moment of excitement, nothing more. I high-fived Gwen, Cody, and Tyler, ordering myself not to think about Nathan's spontaneous move.

After we put the game away, Cody and Gwen left for their apartment, less than five minutes from the store. Tyler, who also lived nearby, went with them. Shannon had managed to get a parking space directly in front of GameOn!, so after trying unsuccessfully to convince her to leave the game here "for safekeeping"—it's not like I would've peeked ahead!... much—Nathan and I waved good-bye to her, too.

In what seemed like an instant, we stood alone in the dark store. My body wanted to think about all the possibilities, but my mind slammed that door shut. The only possibility that truly existed was me embarrassing myself and pissing off my friend. No thanks.

I busied myself at the register, shuffling papers and pretending to look for my keys until I could be sure my traitorous thoughts didn't show on my open book of a face.

"You ready?" Nathan asked, waiting near the door.

"Just a sec," I called.

Since I'd been crashing in his spare room, the two of us took the T together when he happened to be at the store near closing. He often worked past midnight, but I usually saw him once or twice a week, either after visiting Gwen and Cody, buying games, or playing at the store's public game nights. I didn't mind riding home alone, but since it would only take about four minutes for me to double-check everything and lock up, I appreciated him sticking around to give me the company.

Slipping into my coat, I grabbed my keys off the counter and turned down the thermostat. I wrapped my scarf around my neck, swung my arms a few times to get the blood flowing, and motioned toward the door. "After you."

"Ladies first," he said with an exaggerated bow and a smile that shouldn't have gotten my heart racing, but I'd just spent half the night playing the Flirt.

Darn you, Gwen, for trying to help.

"You have to go first so I can lock the door," I pointed out.

"Fair enough."

He moved onto the sidewalk while I pulled the door shut behind us, wincing at the touch of the cool metal. "No gloves?"

"Can't."

The forty-plus-year-old lock stuck. This happened all the time. After many failed attempts when I first started working here, I'd worked out the trick. To engage the lock in cold weather, you needed to: (a) grasp the handle as if water-skiing, (b) jiggle it counter-clockwise, (c) put your entire weight into it, and (d) swear like a sailor while (e) turning the key. If my freezing flesh wasn't seared to the knob, it didn't work.

One of my feet slipped on the snow and ice near the door. I gripped the doorknob and scrambled at the frame with my free hand.

"Careful." Nathan lunged forward to steady me with a hand on my hip.

A wave of sparks...was studiously ignored. This was getting ridiculous. It was fun to play the Flirt for one game, but I couldn't keep getting excited by every little interaction. Nathan thought of me as his daughter's friend, no more. We were two adults, who would remain good friends. I would find someone else to date as soon as I got home and picked up my tablet. It was the only way to preserve my fragile emotional stability.

Once I stopped mentally berating myself, I thanked him. His handprint still burned my flesh, as if he'd branded me through his gloves and my coat.

"Do you need help with the door?"

"Nah, I got it. There's just a trick to it."

"Yeah. When I worked here, John's dad used to have us lock it from the inside."

What? In the eighteen months since I started working here, no one ever made that suggestion. More importantly, "You used to work here?"

He nodded. "Right after I dropped out of high school. Needed money, loved games, didn't know what to do. I worked here for about a year before I started at the garage."

I'd had no idea. I wanted to talk about this more, swap stories, but also, my hands were going numb. Opening the door, I reached around to lock the knob from the inside.

"Hold the handle up when you close it," he said.

Nodding, I obeyed. The door slid shut, easy, as if it was brand-new. I jiggled the handle. Locked. I rolled my eyes at how easily Nathan solved a problem I'd been dealing with since the first freeze.

"My hero," I teased, rubbing my hands together for warmth as I fell into step beside him.

As we walked toward the subway station, I peppered him with questions about working in the store twenty years ago. He answered easily, not seeming to mind that our leisurely walk slash game postmortem had turned into an interrogation.

By the time we reached our stop and exited the train, the conversation turned back to every Bostonian's favorite topic this time of year: the weather.

"You would be warmer with gloves, you know," Nathan pointed out.

"Probably. Unfortunately, after losing about fifteen pairs, I decided it was easier to just keep my hands in my pockets."

"Or...you could buy more gloves."

"Maybe when we get back from Mexico."

To no one's surprise, travel-blogger extraordinaire Gwen—and holder of about a billion frequent-flier miles—had decided to have her wedding in Cancún. Considering that the average low in Cancún when I checked was literally five times the temperature in Boston, I bowed to her wisdom and decided not to complain about the cost.

Jetting off to foreign countries wasn't part of my budget on a game store employee's income, but I'd convinced my dad to cover my hotel room as my Christmas present. Guilt at largely ignoring his oldest child sometimes worked miracles. The resort wasn't terribly expensive, considering it was all-inclusive, and I would be sharing a room with Shannon. Dad agreed to pay, and I agreed to skip the guilt trip for never seeing him. We both made out on the deal. I couldn't wait to cut loose for a few days.

Especially in a foreign country full of (in my mind) unattached men who were dying to flirt with me. No strings attached vacation flirting could be the best kind, at least for the type of confidence boost I needed.

"Speaking of Mexico, how long are you staying?" Nathan asked.

"Not long," I said. "I can't afford to take time off, so I'm flying in two days before the wedding and leaving early the morning after. You'll find me on the beach most of that time, soaking up the sun."

"Can't wait. I'll be right there with you."

My pulse pounded again, as I reminded myself that many people enjoyed sunbathing, and an old friend sitting next to me didn't mean anything. The fact that I was reading into everything was another sign that I needed a vacation. Or a date.

When we got to the house, Nathan let us in and went straight to the living room. "You up for some action before bed?"

"That's what she said," I replied automatically, borrowing a joke from our favorite TV show.

He chuckled. "You're getting better at flirting. But that's not what I meant."

My face grew warm as I realized he stood in front of his impressive collection of entertainment consoles. Right. That kind of action. Maybe beating things up for a couple of hours would make me feel better, but what I most needed was a cold shower and time to calm down.

It was one thing to move in when Nathan broke his leg and needed help, especially since I'd been living on Shannon's couch and Gwen traveled all the time. When she moved in with Cody, my staying seemed perfectly natural. But the longer I lived here, the more my crush grew, and the more I needed to distance myself from Nathan. Staying up playing video games late into the night didn't help. Plus, I needed to go online and set up a date or two before Gwen stole my phone and did it for me.

"Not tonight," I said, searching for an excuse he'd understand. "I'm beat, and Terri sent me a copy of the questions for my deposition."

Another memento from my ex: I'd developed a close, personal relationship with the assistant United States attorney prosecuting him for running a pyramid scheme with money stolen from our business investors. Not entirely out of spite. Mostly because they'd wanted to charge me, too, and I very wisely agreed to help them in exchange for immunity. Since I'd had no idea what Lucas did behind my back, I refused to let him drag me down with him.

That was why I started working at Game On!: In addition to pleading guilty to a misdemeanor (which would be expunged once I fulfilled the terms of our agreement), I wasn't allowed to work with computers until my eighteen-month probation ended. When John's wife, Maria, told me they wanted to hire help, I jumped at the opportunity. It wasn't why I went to school, and it didn't give me the same thrill as programming, but at least I felt like a contributing member of society.

As much as I loved the store, it would be nice to use my master's degree again when this ended. And make some real money. And have a real computer, instead of a tablet that was subject to being searched or reviewed at any time. It contained nothing except Netflix, a few games, and the dating app Gwen installed. I didn't even use it for email.

"Ugh. Legal jargon." Nathan laughed. "Have fun with that. I'm here if you get bored."

"If I get bored, it'll put me to sleep." I flashed him a grateful smile. "But thanks. I'll see you in the morning."

"Sweet dreams," he said.

"You, too," I said. What I wanted to say was, "You have no idea."

* * * *

Although I did need to read and review my deposition questions, I had a couple of weeks before the scheduled interview. Telling Nathan my plan to find someone online to practice flirting/dating on was too embarrassing. But as soon as my bedroom door shut behind me, I flopped down on the bed and picked up my tablet. My friends were right. I'd spent enough time feeling sorry for myself and hiding.

My former fiancé and I had started a business from the ground up, which excited me almost as much as our impending wedding had. If only I'd realized he was embezzling the investors' money; that the cash "wedding gift" from his parents had disappeared. But I didn't. Like a fool, I let Lucas handle the money, believing whatever he said to me. I never once thought to double-check the books or ask to see receipts. Why would I? I trusted him. A mistake I never intended to repeat.

Still, even after I found out the truth about the company, my life had gone okay. A recruiter friend from college—who couldn't stand Lucas—helped me set up some quick interviews, in hopes of finding a new position before Lucas's misdeeds went public. Thanks to Rob, I'd found a job in Providence and had been on the verge of accepting an offer when the U.S. attorney came knocking on my door. The reality of my situation sank in when they told me I couldn't accept any of the jobs I'd interviewed for. No fiancé, no company, no money—and suddenly, I faced years in jail unless I gave up my job prospects, too. Such a change from the high life I'd been living only months earlier. That was when I put dating on hold indefinitely. The type of guys who got turned on by a woman facing felony charges didn't exactly appeal to me, and events had turned my normally sunny demeanor inside out. If I didn't like myself, how could I expect anyone else to?

More importantly, after being so very wrong about Lucas, I didn't trust my instincts. Without being able to tell the bad men from the good, dating appealed to me about as much as taking a bath in a vat of jalapeños.

The stark bedroom walls reflected my mood perfectly. When Gwen lived here, she papered the room with glossy photographs: pictures of places she'd been, magazine spreads for places she wanted to go. A huge corkboard once held pictures of her friends. It still hung in place, the emptiness reminding me of a college dorm room on move-in day. I couldn't even look at the spot on her wall where her master's degree hung before she moved. The condo I'd shared with Lucas held a framed degree on the wall, too. I'd been so proud of it, before the federal prosecutor prohibited me from using my education. Now the document was buried in a drawer in the bottom of Gwen's old high school desk so I didn't have a constant reminder of what I'd lost.

Either I needed to get out more or I needed to decorate. Sitting in this sad little room wasn't doing me any favors, as much as I appreciated Nathan allowing me to stay here where the rent was dirt cheap, especially for Boston.

Finally, I turned on my tablet and opened an app. Not the same one where Gwen found Lucas cheating on me. I didn't know if his profile was still up, and didn't want to know. Last I heard, his parents had bailed him out of jail, and he'd moved into their basement.

A page of potential matches appeared before me, with a thumbnail, name, age, and basic stats. At the risk of sounding old, I couldn't believe how much dating had changed over the years. Lucas and I met in high school. Since we were only fifteen, even if I'd known about online dating, I wouldn't have dreamed of trying it.

I loved the idea of being afloat in a sea of men, able to reel in anyone who caught my eye and toss back the duds. It was so easy, with everything posted right there, in the profiles. Part of me couldn't believe people would post so much personal information on the internet. On the other hand, when trying to find a person to date, it was nice to see right away if there were any deal breakers. Alas, no one's profile opened with "I'm engaged and secretly using the venture capital business I opened with my fiancé to defraud people." I'd have to find another way to avoid the Lucases of the world.

In the corner of the screen, an icon flashed. A new message! Someone called RandyBuddy69 wanted to chat. No picture, but it couldn't hurt to say hello. Chatting led to flirting, which led to confidence building and eventually regaining my ability to trust, not just in men but in myself.

Randy needed to learn to flirt, too, apparently. His first message didn't give me much to grab on to. *Hey.*

Before responding, I navigated to his profile to see if we had anything in common. He was twenty-nine, worked in IT—cool, although I didn't want to open our communication by discussing the degree I couldn't use.

I was still scrolling down when the icon flashed again.

u there?

Before my eyes, a slew of messages popped up, so fast, it was all I could do to read, much less respond.

u know i c u online, right?

fine, don't answer.

bitch.

Wait, what? I double-checked the first message. It had been approximately two minutes since RandyBuddy69 first said hello. Sure, the internet gave us instant access to almost anything we desired in a heartbeat, but to get angry that I didn't respond in two minutes or less? What if I'd been replying to someone else? Or, I don't know, gone to the bathroom?

Part of me was poised to tell him just that when another message popped up. *whatever u ugly an-e-wayz. no one will want to screw you. i was going to do u a favor. nice life, bitch.*

Nope. Sorry, Randy, you're not even worth a reply. Without another second's hesitation, I hit the "block" button. His hateful words vanished, and I breathed a sigh of relief. Bullet dodged.

Back to the list of potential matches. Parker31 was pretty cute. Longish red hair, blue eyes, a friendly smile. Worked in construction. Lived in Cambridge, which put him near the store. I wondered if we'd crossed paths. His profile said he liked dogs, which seemed like a good sign, despite what I'd said to Gwen earlier. I didn't trust men who hated animals. Part of me wanted to send him a message, open up communication, but I'd never in my life approached a guy. Wasn't even sure how to do it. So far, my only interaction online had told me how *not* to talk to a potential date. Thanks, Randy.

As my fingers hovered, I noticed a button on the side of the screen. "Smile at Parker!" Okay, I could do that. Send him a smile, leave the ball in his court. With a tap and crossed fingers, I sent off my first attempt to open up communication with a potential date.

Triumphantly, I texted Gwen. *I am trying this online dating thing. Be proud of me.*

Her reply came a moment later. A slew of celebratory emojis followed by, *You're brave for doing it alone. I would have gone through it with you.*

Me: *Thanks, but I'll be fine. Time to pull on my big girl panties.*

My tablet showed me that another message had popped up, so I tapped quickly to see if Parker had already replied. Nope. It was someone named GoodTime42. *Hey, there. Isn't it a bit late to be up?*

He used complete sentences and punctuation, which put him miles ahead of Randy. Also, the message had been sent three minutes ago, and he hadn't gotten openly hostile with me for not replying yet. With a deep breath, I typed a quick response. *I just got home. Out late with friends. You?*

Oh, I'm always up. An insomniac? How unfortunate. I had trouble sleeping when Lucas and I first broke up, but things had been easier since I started working at Game On!. I was halfway through typing a sympathetic response when another message popped up.

A very close-up, blurry picture of...No. It couldn't be. Except the object was flesh-colored, with curly hair at the base. I'd never seen an uncircumcised penis, so it took an embarrassingly long time to figure out what this guy had sent me. In my defense, I never expected someone to randomly send me a picture of their genitals. But as I gazed at the picture, mouth open, it became very clear to me what GoodTime meant by "always up," and it wasn't a sleep disorder.

And...blocked!

Then I picked up my phone again. *OMG. Some guy just sent me a picture of his penis!*

Gwen: *You got a dick pic on your first time out? Way to go!*

Me: *I am not excited by this turn of events.*

Gwen: *Sorry. I wish I could say you didn't get used to it, but...One thing that may help is setting the program so it doesn't show when you're online. You'll get less horny guys late at night looking to cyber.*

Me: *Thanks.*

Quickly, I found the setting before I got any more horrifying messages. Parker hadn't responded to my smile yet, but if he was anything like these other two guys, that was okay by me. Then I glanced at the clock. Or maybe he was asleep at one o'clock in the morning and not online looking to hook up. I decided to take his lack of response as a positive sign.

Before signing out, I forced myself to find another interesting-looking profile. Andre, age thirty-one, a veterinarian living in Brookline. I sent another smile, still not feeling confident enough to start a chat with a total stranger. Tomorrow, I'd ask Gwen for more advice/moral support. For now, the day's events left me exhausted. I should just ask out my shy customer next time he came into the store. If I invited him to play a game, he'd say yes even if Gwen was wrong about his interest.

Leaning back against the pillows, I finally pulled up the deposition prep from Terri. On the other side of the wall, muffled thumps told me Nathan had finished playing video games and was getting ready for bed. I bet *he* never sent a woman an unsolicited dick pic or insulted her for not immediately responding to a message. Of course, they didn't have the internet when Gwen was born, which probably helped. But still.

Hearing him move around brought me some hope. There was at least one good single man out in the world. Even if I couldn't have him, he couldn't be a unicorn among men. There must be others. Surely, I'd meet one soon.

Chapter 4

Sometimes, you've got to roll the dice and take your chances.
— *The Haunted Place* Player Guide

The following week found me once again speaking with my indecisive customer moments before closing, after about an hour discussing the pros and cons of every deck-building game in stock. And four we didn't carry.

"But which is your favorite?" he asked, shifting from one foot to the other.

An excellent question, but never a good one to face as a gamer. I once spent five full minutes listing my "favorite" games without pausing for breath. And I still needed to close out the cash register. Still, I remembered what Gwen said before and decided to cut this guy some slack. If he kept coming back because he liked me rather than because of the game selection, I wanted to encourage him. Not only was he cute, nice, and a gamer, but it took courage to put yourself out there. Talking to someone in person was way more nerve-racking then sending them a smile via an app, which was all I'd managed.

I thought for a moment before pulling two games off the shelves. "This was my first deck-building game. I still consider it my 'gateway' game, because it took me from casual party game player to the more hard-core stuff. Which I love."

"Good to know."

Holding up the other game, I said, "I like this one because it's cooperative. Some of my friends can be pretty competitive. For a change of pace, I like a game where we win or lose together. Anyone who plays more for the fun of the game than the thrill of victory will love this."

Behind us, Gwen, Cody, and Tyler entered the store. Gwen saw who I was talking to and shot me a huge grin with a thumbs-up. I kept my expression blank, but as my customer studied the games, I studied him. I'd been waiting long enough for this guy to make his move. Maybe it was time to take a chance. Or at least give him a solid opening. He was cute, after all. Better mannered than anyone I met online. Maybe he was my unicorn.

"By the way," I said, "my name's Holly."

"I know." He pointed at my name tag. Right. "I'm Marc."

"Nice to meet you." I gave him an encouraging smile. He went back to studying the games, and my smile dropped.

Maybe Gwen was wrong. Or maybe I still sucked at flirting. I desperately needed to find my groove.

The bell over the door jingled, and Nathan appeared with takeout from the wings place nearby. I waved at him before he disappeared into the back with the others. Suddenly, this geeky mating dance with Marc exhausted me. If he wanted to ask me out, he'd had plenty of opportunities. I was being polite, friendly, and encouraging. Yet he showed less enthusiasm in talking to me than in the games in his hand, which I'd long since given up on him buying.

Gwen would tell me to just ask him out, take uncertainty out of the equation. But my shaky confidence wouldn't allow me to say the words. Getting rejected by a guy I only sort of wanted to go out with, while standing fifteen feet from the guy I *actually* really liked, would only ruin the good mood I struggled to maintain.

As my customer mulled the games in front of him, I glanced at the clock pointedly. "I hate to do this, but we're closing. Did you want to get one of these?"

He finally met my eyes. "These are two of your favorite games?"

I nodded.

"If I brought them in for the open games night sometime, would you show me how to play?"

His words brightened my mood considerably. Finally, a hint even I could pick up! I grinned back at him. "Absolutely."

"Great!" For the first time in all the weeks he'd been coming to the shop, Marc seemed animated. He'd been cute before, but that smile transformed his face. For the first time, I noticed a dimple in his left cheek. "I'm going on an extended business trip in a couple of days, but I'll come by when I get back?"

He seemed so eager and earnest, I decided to help him out. "Sounds good. Why don't you text to make sure I'll be here? I'll give you my number."

I took his phone and entered the digits before handing it back. He glanced at it, then typed something. A moment later, a beep sounded from the counter where I stowed my phone while working. He blushed. "Check that after I leave?"

A brief wave of dread hit me. If he sent me a dick pic saved on his phone, I was giving up this game forever. My instincts said he wasn't the type, but I'd been wrong before. "Sure. Did you want to buy these?"

Marc took both games, which I considered a personal triumph. He left, promising to be in touch soon, and I locked the door behind him. Before heading back to my friends, I bolted for my phone to read the text.

Marc: *Or maybe we could get a drink sometime? If that's okay?*

A huge smile split my face in two. I was really doing this, getting back on the horse. Getting over Nathan and moving past what Lucas did to me. Gwen would've been so proud of me, even without knowing about my crush. I didn't even hesitate before shooting back a response. *I'd love to.*

"Good news?" Not realizing anyone else had left the back room, I jumped at the sound of Nathan's voice. "Sorry, I just came to tell you the food's ready and I saw that smile."

"Thanks. And, yeah. Well, maybe good news. I have the possibility of a date."

He smiled thinly. "Excellent. Who's the lucky guy?"

"One of our customers. He's been hanging around a lot—you may have seen him."

"That's great. Do you like him?"

I shrugged, trying to play it cool. "Maybe? He seems more normal than any of the guys online, he's cute, and he's interested."

"You deserve better than 'more normal than the other guys.'"

"Thanks. But it's too soon to tell. At least he listens while I talk incessantly about games. Maybe it won't go anywhere, and that's fine. I'm not looking to get married. Just go on a couple of dates to get out of my shell."

"Fair enough," he said. "Just promise me you won't attach yourself to the first 'okay' guy you find. Hold out for someone who's worth it."

His words warmed my heart. "I just hope he's half as awesome as you are," I said. "You're one of the good ones."

Nathan frowned. "I'm a little concerned about your bar for 'awesome.' It should go deeper than wanting good things for your friends, especially someone going through a rough time. After Lucas, you deserve happiness. If not this guy, with someone."

Shannon knocked on the door, ending our conversation. But as we let her in and went to start eating, a little voice inside my head questioned Nathan's sudden interest in my dating life.

When we sat, Gwen pounced, asking me all about Marc. Nathan cheerfully told her I'd given him my number, which sent her into squeals of excitement. That's why he cared. He knew how happy his daughter would be at seeing me put in the effort. Of course.

I turned my attention to the game board lying on the table. At the end of the first game, all five characters had sealed ourselves into a room to defeat the zombies. We started this session still trapped in the library.

The instruction manual gave a series of hints for moving out of this room and returning to the rest of the house, our sole aim for this round. It also directed us to open a new packet of cards, but not to shuffle or read them. The game would refer us to numbered cards within the deck when the time came.

According to the book, each of the cards depicted either half of a pair of items we'd need to escape the room (like a key and a lock) or a device to defeat before moving to the next stage.

"How does the game know we're doing things right?" I asked.

"With most of the cards, we add the numbers together and go to the card with the result on it. If we're wrong, the card will tell us." Cody pulled his phone out of his pocket and tossed it on the table. "But there's also an app."

"Shannon! You designed an app without me?" I tried to sound like I was joking, but it stung. Even though I wasn't allowed to code right now, I could have helped.

Her reply came instantly. "Nope. You did most of the work. Remember my secret project our second year?"

Gwen chuckled, and after a moment, so did I. We both remembered when Shannon asked for help designing an app to pass one of her classes. I'd never thought twice about showing her what I knew.

"Can Holly play if she designed the app?" Tyler asked.

My stomach twinged at the question. I didn't want to miss a single level, but how could I play-test part of a game I'd helped create?

"It's not exactly her design," Shannon said. "I made some changes."

"Yeah, I never coded an escape room app."

"Should be fine," Nathan said. My heart warmed at him coming to my defense. "She didn't know what the app was for, and if there are bugs, she's the best person to find them, right?"

I smiled gratefully at him. The others thankfully agreed, especially since Shannon recoded the app herself.

We had one hour to defeat the puzzle for maximum points. If we failed, we would be allowed to move on, but our overall score for the campaign would be reduced. As soon as we started the level, the app would begin counting down. After that, every second counted. Not wanting to mess it up, we called a five-minute drink refill and bathroom break before starting.

I took advantage of the downtime to check my phone. Marc had already texted me back. *I can't wait! It was great talking to you today. Thanks for the game suggestions.*

Me: *You're welcome! Let me know what you think.*

Nathan pulled out the chair beside me and sat, drawing my attention away from my phone. "You going to play or text?"

"I can't do both?"

"Not when we're on a timer, no," he said, a little sharply.

"Touché." I put my phone away, but not before checking it one last time. Nathan rolled his eyes, but said nothing.

For the first time, I understood why this game could only be played once. Before we'd started, I assumed the end result would be a board used to play some kind of basic haunted house–themed game. But as we resolved the hints and beat this room, we'd know exactly how to defeat this level next time, and the play value would lose something. Even if we could reset the entire board to what it had been before we started and replace all the stickers (no small feat), I wouldn't be able to forget the details of this level.

When I first heard about legacy-type games, it seemed like a waste to me. Board games could be expensive, and part of the appeal was playing over and over. But when you thought about it, a game cost about the same as going out to the movies a few times. Each level took at least an hour to complete, and the campaign could take up to twenty sessions. So we got our money's worth, and we also got a personalized playing experience. Only the five of us would ever play this exact game, solve these exact puzzles.

Speaking of puzzles, Nathan seemed less chatty than usual. When I asked him about it, he said he was tired from another long day going back and forth between the shops.

"Maybe Dad's jealous that my twenty-eight-year-old best friend got a date before he did," Gwen said. "Want to give him pointers on picking up strangers?"

I snorted. "Yeah. Um, apparently, the secret to getting asked out is to be totally oblivious until your friends hit you with a clue-by-four. Then stand awkwardly and drop hints until the guy in question figures out what you're doing. Marc's got more game than I do, and that's not saying much."

"Well, at least his game worked," Gwen said. "But don't put all your eggs in his basket. You're still going out with other guys, yes?"

My eyes darted to Nathan, a gesture I hid by lowering my head to study the board. A pang of longing hit me. He was the only other person I wanted to date, and he was off-limits. If only he'd come across as less caring earlier. Or if he didn't fit in so well with our group. The more time I spent with him, the more I worried about my feelings for him. Obviously, I could never date my best friend's father. But I wished I didn't feel so drawn to him.

Marc seemed nice enough, and I really was looking forward to our date. Unfortunately, he didn't give me the same warm, fluttery feelings as the guy sitting beside me. Of course, he hadn't had nearly the same number of opportunities. He deserved a chance. And so did the myriad guys left to meet who might be infinitely more appropriate for me than Nathan.

I'd find someone. The internet provided tens of thousands of dating options. Even though the thought scared the crap out of me, I'd put myself out there. Go on dates, meet lots of guys, and show my friends that I wasn't some sort of sad sack, sitting at home all the time. More importantly, I'd find someone to take my mind off the one man I couldn't have.

To Gwen, I said, "Absolutely. I'm still one hundred percent open to meeting other guys. But I can't wait to go out with Marc."

Chapter 5

Although the game is ultimately cooperative, there is some individual
strategy involved. Choose wisely; all actions have consequences.
—*The Haunted Place* Player Guide

After that night, I started dating like my life depended on it. The crushing
pace probably wouldn't last forever, but I needed to throw myself into the
fray or I'd keep making up excuses to put things off. There were too many
reasons to say no, so once I decided to go ahead and get back out there,
I needed to really throw myself into the experience. Otherwise, it would
be too easy to give up.

Only a week and a half passed before my determination started to
wane. I'd tried online dating, mobile dating, and even some app where
you swiped to meet people who happened to be nearby. Such a genius
idea to find casual sex, but I wanted more. The one guy I'd agreed to meet
insisted on his hotel room rather than a bar or a coffee shop, so I cancelled
immediately. I'd been to breakfasts, lunches, brunches, drinks, dinners,
and dessert. I'd eaten my weight in free bread.

Some of the guys were utter creeps, some too cocky, too obsessed with
work, too uninteresting. Some were perfectly interesting and polite. Some
were utterly fine in every way, but bored me. Most of my dates didn't
spark any interest in me, but at least I was getting better at making polite
conversation. Baby steps. Dating was a numbers game, right? Surely, if I
went out with enough guys, I'd find someone I wanted to get to know better.

During the day, I texted Marc regularly. We'd progressed from polite
conversation to overt flirting, but his hectic work schedule meant we hadn't
been on our date yet. The fact that he hadn't sent a dick pic or asked me

to sext with him both inspired me and made me worry that Gwen had misread his intent. Maybe he was just looking for a friend to play games with. Until I saw him again, I couldn't tell. Meanwhile, I kept meeting new guys. I couldn't let the promise of a date that hadn't happened yet keep me sitting at home every night. The dating practice might even help once the big day arrived. Unfortunately, this process exhausted me. Thank goodness Cancún was coming up. I needed a vacation from casual dating.

The most recent of these nice-enough, somewhat-interesting guys gazed across the table at me, watching a waiter grate Parmesan cheese onto our appetizer. His wavy dark hair and the set of his jaw reminded me of Nathan, which was an unfortunate distraction from the date. No chin dimple, though.

Focus, Holly. Dinner. Nice guy. Talk to him. He could be the one. Nathan is not the one.

He thanked the waiter, so I mentally gave him a bonus point. I couldn't believe how badly some people treated servers. Often the ones with the most money or who seemed extra eager to impress with their fancy clothes and cars.

Before I could ask my date to remind me what he did for a living (or his name), he took a long gulp of wine and leaned forward as if we were about to share a secret. "Would you ever consider wearing a mermaid tail? For me, I mean."

My fork hovered in midair, a strand of marinara-covered calamari swinging dangerously close to my white boob shirt. I was grateful he'd posed the question before I'd taken a bite. Choking on overcooked fried squid wasn't the way I wanted to die.

He didn't really say that. He must have asked something else.

I cleared my throat delicately. "I'm sorry. Did you say—?"

My date leaned in even closer to the table and locked his gaze on mine. His gleaming brown eyes examined me intently. His pupils dilated, telling me that if he'd asked what I thought, the idea excited him. Silently, I cursed myself for being taken in by a couple of good photographs online and a profile free of typos. We should've gotten to know each other better before I agreed to meet him. If only I'd thought to send him a sexual kinks questionnaire.

"It turns me on when a woman wears a mermaid tail. During sex. I'm not saying I expect sex or that you have to sleep with me because I'm paying for dinner." He laughed nervously as I told myself to hand the waiter a twenty before slipping out the bathroom window. "But if that weirds you out, I'd rather know now."

Not knowing what else to do, I stuck my fork in my mouth before the food landed in my lap. At least now I had a convenient excuse for stalling.

I'm going to kill Gwen. Why did I listen to her? I was doing great on my own, pining over her d— okay, fine, I wasn't. But if lusting after thy BFF's father is a crime, surely this punishment is excessive.

My heart ached as Nathan's face superimposed itself over this guy's. I shoved it aside. Allowing myself to get hung up on someone so wrong for me was what led to this pleasant Friday evening taking a rather disconcerting U-turn in the space of about thirty seconds.

I cast about frantically for something to say. At a total loss for words, I delayed by completing what was about to become the most thoroughly chewed bite of calamari in history. One hand motioned toward my mouth to indicate I'd respond after I swallowed. Meanwhile, I prayed I'd think of something to say without sounding overly judgmental.

Oh my God, I should've known. All the men online are so messed up. What was I thinking?

When I finally swallowed the massive bite, I choked. It took several minutes of sputtering into a napkin before I regained control. I sipped water to clear my head, wishing I'd thought to order something stronger.

My date's eyes widened. "Are you okay?"

"I'm sorry. I have to go to the restroom."

The corners of his mouth twitched, and he eyed me with the knowing look of someone who'd been in this position before. "Are you going to come back?"

"Yes, of course," I lied. It would be polite to come back, make conversation, suffer through the end of the meal. The Holly who spent most of her twenties with Lucas would have. Holly the Flirt wasn't in the mood to waste any more time on this nonsense.

A wad of cash and a quick word with the waiter convinced him to wrap my dinner in a to-go box. Then I hid in the ladies' room, leaning against the wall next to the tampon/condom/aspirin machine so I could text Gwen comfortably without taking up a stall.

OMG OMG 911. I'm calling you in five minutes. Worst first date ever.

I smoothed my hair, pulled it back into a ponytail since I no longer cared if it looked messy, and reapplied my lipstick, giving the waiter time to get my doggie bag ready before I went back out there. My phone beeped.

Gwen: *Worse than the guy who insisted you watch* The Bachelor *with his mom?*

Much, I typed. *Will call once I escape.*

Gwen: *Need a fake emergency? I may be about to get violent food poisoning...;-)*

For a minute, I considered it. But it took a lot of courage for my date to tell me what he liked so early on. At least he asked. When I was with Lucas, he never cared what I wanted. We ate at his favorite restaurants, I wore clothes he picked or bought for me, I styled my hair the way he liked, I used a lot of makeup because he wanted me to look "polished" for our clients. The clients he secretly swindled. If Lucas got excited by the thought of me in a mermaid tail, he'd have tossed it on the bed and started calling me "Ariel." No discussion, no questions. And I would have gone along with him, because that's who I let myself become. Luckily, he'd never been a terribly adventurous guy in bed. At least not with me.

I'd been growing since the night we started *The Haunted Place*, becoming more confident. I felt more attractive and desirable than I had since finding out about Lucas's cheating. What would Holly the Flirt do?

This date wasn't going anywhere, and I'd wasted enough of my time on bad dates at this point. Nothing could save this evening. Not when I just wanted to go home and shower. Sitting back down to finish the meal wasn't an option, even if the waiter hadn't finished packing it up yet.

Still, I felt bad sneaking out. This guy seemed earnest, and he couldn't help that I didn't like the same things he did. He deserved better than me faking an emergency or slipping out the window. He didn't deserve a whole date, of course, but an explanation. Telling him why I needed to go was the right thing to do.

After this consideration, I replied to Gwen. *No thanks. This guy needs to know why I'm leaving.*

My phone buzzed again almost immediately. *Good for you! Let him have it.* ☺

The clock told me I'd only been hiding for three minutes. I checked my email and my Instagram feed while deciding what to say. Then I spotted a text from earlier in the evening, confirming our plans.

Carson? So that's his name.

Finally, I inhaled deeply, threw my shoulders back, adjusted my purse on one shoulder and walked back to the table.

A white box sat where my plate had been. I didn't touch my chair. Carson looked up when I approached, and a tentative smile crossed his face. He started to say something, but I didn't give him a chance.

"Look, Carson, you seem like a nice guy. Or, you did, until about seven minutes ago. Here's the thing, though—you gotta ease a girl into something like this. You can't bust out with 'I want to put you in a mermaid tail and smash it out' before the main course arrives. First, you see if we hit it off. We take things slow, go on a few dates, maybe we sleep together, then down the road, you know me well enough to ask these things. This isn't the way."

"Are you saying—"

I cut him off by patting his hand before picking up my white Styrofoam box. "I'm saying, there are women who'd prefer to know up-front if they're wasting their time with you, but I'm not one of them. Maybe if you'd presented your request a little differently, we could've had a more productive conversation about your needs and how I could meet them.

"I'm going to walk home. Thanks for the stories."

* * * *

As I walked toward the T, I texted furiously, the plastic bag containing my dinner swinging from one wrist. Before I even sat down, Shannon and Gwen got the entire sordid story.

Gwen: *I can't believe you didn't ask him how mermaids have sex when they have fins covering their genitals.*

Shannon: *Gwen, don't help.*

Me: *Sorry. I needed to get out of there.*

Gwen: *You missed a once-in-a-lifetime opportunity!*

Me: *Let's hope so. Some conversations don't need to be repeated.*

Shannon: *Sorry your date didn't go well.*

Me: *Thanks. It's fine. There are good men out there. Gwen found one.*

Gwen: *And so will you.*

Shannon: *What about that guy from the store a couple of weeks ago? You still texting?*

Me: *Extended business trip. A couple of Snapchats. Plans for dinner in a couple of weeks. Seems normal so far.*

Gwen: *Fingers crossed!*

At least any other first date had to be an improvement. The dating app sent me new matches all the time, and while I was starting to get pickier about who to meet, I might still find someone. Parker, the first guy I smiled at via the app, messaged me a few days ago, and we chatted a bit. We still hadn't set up a date, so maybe it wouldn't go anywhere, but we got along pretty well. And there was Marc. I liked Marc. Those two prospects gave me hope.

My forced positivity sustained me all the way home, until I changed into jammie pants, wondering why I'd bothered to wear cute panties on this date. I hadn't had sex in almost two years; not even Patrick Dempsey was going to see my panties on a first date. Then I reheated my dinner and sat down on the couch to watch *The Office* reruns.

I'd ordered spinach and cheese ravioli. In my hurry to get out of there, I hadn't checked the contents of the bag. This was tortellini, so I didn't immediately pay attention to the difference, but at the first bite, I choked. Coughs racked my body. Barely able to breathe, I flailed for my water glass with one hand while fanning my face with the other.

As I examined the container, my date's earlier words rang in my ears. "Tortellini arrabiata. The spicier the better, please." Well, they'd done it. He would have been happy, had he known. Unfortunately, I hated spicy food. There was nothing else to eat. The food in the fridge had to last until my next paycheck, and there wasn't much. Unless I wanted to eat mustard for dinner, I was stuck with these way-too-spicy, inedible leftovers.

A wave of sadness hit me. Two years ago, I'd been on top of the world. Living in a luxurious penthouse with the man I loved, planning our wedding. Some of the things he wanted seemed extravagant, but he said his parents would pick up the tab, and I didn't want to argue, so I gave in. As usual. I should've asked more questions. Or any questions. Now I was sitting on my friend's dad's couch in dirty clothes, forcing myself to choke down disgusting, lukewarm takeout on a Friday night. I'd given most of my spending money for the week to the waiter because I hadn't wanted to accept a free meal from Carson.

Before my breakup, I'd been a pretty upbeat person. But sometimes life handed you lemons, mocked you, handed you more lemons, then threw them in your face while still laughing. To call the past couple of years overwhelming was an understatement.

The front door slammed behind me. If I'd heard Nathan's key in the lock, I might have gone to wallow in my room, but too late now. He'd see me cross the hall and wonder what was wrong. I sniffled and wiped away the telltale signs of my misery, then focused intently on my food.

Nathan appeared in the doorway a moment later. "Hey, how was the big...oh, no."

"Hey. I thought you were working late."

"That was the plan, but things slowed down enough to take off early. The staff can close up without me for one night," he said. "Are you okay?"

I forced a big smile onto my face, but my voice wobbled. "It's fine. I'm fine. Just...the 'big date' turned out to be another dud."

"Do you want to talk about it?" He settled on the couch beside me, barely an inch between our thighs. I should've moved over to make room, but I didn't. "I know Gwen thinks I'm basically a monk, but I do have a couple of decades of dating experience on the two of you."

I raised an eyebrow at him. "Really? Do tell." A story about a great love affair or a secret girlfriend might temporarily distract me from my own pain. At least I could live vicariously.

"Hold on a sec. Whatever you're eating smells really good, and I was planning to order pizza when I got home."

I held the container out. "Want it?"

"You don't?"

"It's not what I ordered. They gave me my date's food by mistake. He didn't eat any of it. The waiter boxed up our entire meal before it hit the plates. I only took one bite."

He took a bite, chewed it slowly. "And you don't like it because it's so spicy. A shame, because it's delicious."

"It's all yours."

"Don't be ridiculous. We'll share a pizza."

I hesitated. "I can't."

"It's on me. If you need to contribute, I'll eat the leftover pasta for lunch tomorrow."

A small smile crossed my lips. Why couldn't the guys I met online be as thoughtful and sensitive as Nathan? You know, *attainable* guys? "Thanks."

He placed the order without needing to ask what I wanted. Funny, it used to bother me when Lucas ordered for me, because he expected me to eat whatever he wanted without complaint. Which, sadly, I'd done, because I hadn't known any better. But Nathan asked for a barbecue chicken pizza, my favorite. Exactly what I requested every time.

A moment later, he put the phone away and settled back onto the couch. I still hadn't shifted, but he now sat even closer than before. If I moved at all, my leg would brush against his. "Now, let's see. I didn't date when Gwen was in middle school, because I was learning how to raise her on my own and figuring out how to support us. But once she started high school, I became well versed in online dating. There was the woman who professed her love to me on our first date."

"Oh, that's nothing," I said. "From what Gwen tells me, you have women throwing themselves at you constantly."

"My devoted daughter exaggerates. Plenty of women want to *set me up*, but that's not the same. You must know by now how frustrating it is to go on a bunch of dates with someone who doesn't interest you."

I nodded. "That's twenty-plus years of online dating?"

"Oh, God no. I gave up online dating more than a decade ago. Not for me at all. I still meet women and go out. Mutual friends, bars, at the grocery store, wherever. But things can always go wrong. I caught one woman trying to steal a used condom out of the trash."

"No!"

"Swear to God."

"That's disgusting!"

"You're telling me. Apparently, it happens," he said. "She wanted a baby and didn't care how she got it. A guy at work told me he puts hot sauce in them before he throws them away. At least I haven't become that paranoid."

I laughed. "That's so bizarre. Glad to know I'm not the only one suffering."

"You are very much not alone." He got up, brought back two beers, and sat down, offering me one. "To terrible dates."

"To finding better dates," I countered, taking a sip. "But Gwen's mom left ages ago. Surely someone has piqued your interest in all these years?"

"A few have." He glanced over at me, sending my world careening upside-down. Then he turned his attention back to the TV, and everything returned to normal. "One woman bailed when I asked her to meet Gwen. There were a couple of others I liked well enough, but it never went anywhere. And sometimes you feel a spark with someone, but it can't work for reasons beyond your control."

"I'll drink to that."

"At least we have each other." He draped his free arm across the back of the couch. A friendly, comforting gesture. I shouldn't have, but I leaned in, nestling against him. He picked up the remote and pointed it at the TV. "*The Office*?"

"You know it." The show had been my favorite since junior high. When I discovered Nathan loved it, too, I'd been delighted. Lucas made fun of me for watching sitcoms, so I'd done it in secret, on my old laptop with headphones. It was nice to see my old friends on a normal-sized screen.

The long, emotional day caught up with me. Nathan rested his head on top of mine, and we watched the show together. I wondered who he was thinking about, the woman he wanted but couldn't have. I didn't ask. Instead, a comfortable silence stretched between us. It was enough, for now, to enjoy this moment.

By the time the pizza arrived, I'd fallen fast asleep.

Chapter 6

Breaking character won't ruin the game, of course, but you may enjoy
yourself more if you let go.
—*The Haunted Place* Player Guide

My long-awaited date with Marc finally arrived the night before my
flight to Mexico. We'd texted back and forth so long, it seemed like I'd
met him more than a handful of times. My nervousness ratcheted up at the
idea of this feeling more like a third or fourth date than a first one. What
if he expected me to sleep with him, like so many other guys? We might
eventually get to that point, but I had zero intention of doing anything
more than a goodnight kiss on our first date. I'd be horribly disappointed
if Marc expected more. Still, I'd enjoyed our conversations so far, and I
wanted to give him a chance.

He was, after all, the guy who sparked this whole "rebuilding my
confidence" journey. More importantly, he didn't insult me or send a dick
pic within minutes of initiating contact. A low bar, sure, but, well…not
everyone managed to clear it.

These thoughts swirled through my head while I waited outside the
Harvard Square T stop for Marc. He'd offered to pick me up at the store
after my shift, but I felt more comfortable on neutral turf. Where I wouldn't
have to answer questions from my absolutely lovely and very-interested-in-
my-welfare bosses. The longer I stood there, though, the more I regretted
this decision. Game On! had heat. At the very least, I should have suggested
meeting at the nearby comic book store or the restaurant, so hypothermia
wouldn't set in before my date arrived.

Luckily, he emerged from the underground stairway just as I started to contemplate texting an alternate place to meet. A huge smile crossed his face when he saw me, which made me feel good about taking the extra time to look nice. Sure, he liked what he saw in the store, but a real date was different.

"Hey," he said. "It's good to see you."

"You, too." I fell into step beside him. "Ready for dinner?"

"Absolutely. I've been looking forward to this all day."

How sweet. Suddenly, I was glad Gwen pushed me to give Marc a chance. I'd have been too oblivious to encourage him without her help. "Me too."

"I brought you something," he said, holding out a small bag.

His shy smile and the way he kept his gaze low warmed my heart. After going out with so many arrogant, overly confident guys, I found Marc's sweetness refreshing. Plus, he'd brought me a gift! I couldn't remember the last time a guy brought me a gift, not counting the stuff Lucas bought with stolen funds. Most of which he got in order to mold me into his image of the perfect future wife: expensive perfume, cashmere sweaters, jewelry. All stuff that suited his tastes, not mine.

Curiously, I took the bag and peered inside. A handful of small objects lay inside, in a variety of shapes. A smile broke out across my face. "You bought me dice?"

"Well, a corsage seemed cliché."

"Absolutely. Dice are perfect! Thank you. I love them." These weren't all normal dice. They ranged from four- to twenty-sided, from what I could see, in a variety of colors. Impulsively, I leaned forward and kissed his cheek. He turned bright red. Then a thought hit me. "Hold on. I didn't see you buy these at the store."

"I went in on your day off. Don't worry, I didn't buy from a competitor."

"That's good, or this date might end awfully early." I smiled to show I was teasing before changing the subject. "My best friends said this is their favorite restaurant. Good thing, because I'm starving."

"Awesome. How's the play-testing going? That new game?"

"Oh, it's so much fun!" I said. "Of course, it's hard."

"That's what she said," he replied smoothly.

I giggled. He sounded just like Nathan. I wondered if Nathan ever showed up on a date with dice as a gift or quoted *The Office* to a girl. Not that it mattered. I wasn't thinking about him, even if we both loved "that's what she said" jokes. So did Marc, after all. My date.

Pasting a smile on my face, I vowed to give this guy a real chance. It wasn't his fault he wasn't Nathan. He was cute, nice, and we clearly had the same taste in television shows. Successful relationships had been based on less. For all I knew, Marc could be my soul mate.

The rest of the way to the restaurant, we spoke animatedly about *The Haunted Place*, although I carefully avoided spoilers. When Marc expressed interest in joining one of the other tester groups, he seemed sincere. If I'd thought he was doing it to suck up to me, I'd have told him Shannon didn't need the help, but instead promised to have her text him.

At the restaurant, Marc stepped in front of me to open the door. I bristled for a second before he stepped back and held it open for me. The first of all my dates to do that. Maybe chivalry wasn't dead. When we got to our table, he pulled out a chair, then stood behind it, hands resting on the top rung.

"Is something wrong?" I asked.

"No." A look of confusion crossed his face. "This is your chair. Have a seat."

"You pulled out my chair for me?" My whole life, I couldn't think of a single time anyone had done that. Such a small gesture, but so sweet.

His face turned bright red. "I know it's old-fashioned. Sorry."

"Please don't apologize." Putting my hand over his, I squeezed it briefly before taking the seat. "It's sweet. I like it. Just unexpected. Most guys don't think about that stuff."

"Maybe you've been dating the wrong guys."

"Maybe I have."

We slid into a comfortable silence as he took his seat and the waiter filled our water glasses. Once we were alone, I asked how he liked the games I picked out for him, and the conversation took off. When the waiter came to take our order, we hadn't even opened our menus. It was the most comfortable I'd felt with a man since, well…Since hanging out with Nathan.

By all accounts, Marc and I shared a perfect first date. He was a nice guy. We'd probably have a lot of fun playing games together. The conversation flowed easily, and he made me laugh. We could be good together. We could hit it off and probably date for a while. He wouldn't try to control me the way Lucas had. He didn't bat an eye when I ordered a cheeseburger instead of a salad. He didn't give backhanded compliments. I really liked him. Marc was safe, comfortable. A smart choice. He wasn't Nathan, but that wasn't his fault.

Why was dating so difficult? There had to be some way to shake my feelings for Nathan. Unfortunately, I didn't know how. Gwen would have told me that the fastest way to get over one guy was to get on top of another, that wasn't my style. I'd only ever slept with Lucas, even more than a year after our breakup. I liked Marc, but needed more time to see if something real developed before we got physical.

These thoughts consumed me on our walk back to the T after Marc paid for dinner, so much so that I missed whatever he talked about on the trip. Thankfully, his story didn't require input from me beyond the occasional nod or sound of agreement. If he noticed my distraction, he didn't comment. Maybe he thought I was nervous about the inevitable good-night kiss. Which, now that I thought about it…Not counting drunken hookups at gamer conferences, my last first kiss had occurred during the second Bush administration. What if I'd forgotten how?

"I have to catch a bus," he said when we arrived down the stairs, gesturing to the tunnel across from us.

Uh-oh. With those six simple words, he brought the end of the date from a vague down-the-road idea to an immediate, concrete concept. Which meant the end-of-the-night kiss was coming sooner than expected.

A million thoughts whirled through my mind. Why did I have garlic mashed potatoes with dinner? Why didn't I brush my teeth before leaving the restaurant? WHY hadn't I said anything in response to Marc's comment about leaving? This silence grew weirder by the second.

Coming to a halt, I turned to face him with a smile that hopefully looked encouraging rather than constipated. "Thank you for dinner. I had a really nice time."

"Me too. I'd like to see you again, if that's okay."

"I'd like that," I said.

He leaned forward and kissed me gently. His mouth felt warm and soft against mine. Vaguely pleasant. Before I could wonder whether to part my lips, it ended. A perfectly nice, if unexciting first kiss. From a perfectly nice, not-terribly-exciting guy. But first kisses could be awkward. Things could get better in time.

The announcer informed us that Marc's bus was pulling into the station. As he jogged toward his stop, I watched, one hand to my mouth. After a string of terrible first dates, I couldn't believe things had gone this well. Part of me almost expected Marc to be a serial killer, or a nose picker, a racist, or a guy who made fat jokes. But I was glad my inner optimist had talked me into going on the date. While I didn't feel sparks flying yet, I liked Marc. I couldn't wait to see him again. Surely, once the initial awkwardness passed, the passion would come.

* * * *

The next morning found me at Logan International Airport, wrapped in about seven sweaters and carrying a bag not large enough to hold any of them once I arrived. For the next four days, I intended to wear nothing but bikinis, shorts, tank tops, and an enormous smile. Average high temperatures during the day in Boston in February hovered around 37 degrees. In Playa del Carmen? Seventy-five. As much as I loved Boston and ice-skating in the Common and hot cocoa and giant sweaters, winter lasted a long time. By the time Valentine's Day rolled around, my thoroughly chilled blood welcomed the opportunity to embrace the sun.

My flight left at six-twenty in the morning, so the international terminal remained fairly quiet. Many people slept in the uncomfortable plastic chairs. Not for the first time, I silently thanked Gwen and Cody for getting married on the eastern side of Mexico and not, say, Hawaii. Both excellent places, but I'd definitely pick a four-hour direct flight over twelve-plus hours with connections. Especially when I'd only gotten a few days off. Spending half of that flying didn't sound awesome, but as one of Gwen's BFFs and co–maid of honor, I'd have been there.

Shannon was supposed to fly with me, but switched to a later flight at the last minute because her nana needed to see her doctor. Part of the reason Shannon got such cheap rent on the two-family she lived in was that Nana gave her a huge break in exchange for helping out when needed. Besides, the rest of their family lived in Florida. The appointment was probably nothing serious, but she wanted to be safe. She planned to join me soon.

I'd offered to take a later flight, too, but Shannon wouldn't hear of it.

"What if the doctor finds something serious?" she'd asked.

"Then I'll be here to support you," I'd pointed out.

"Don't be silly. You need to be with Gwen and Cody. They can't lose both maids of honor. If anything goes wrong, I'll text you."

My gut instinct had been to keep arguing, but she made an excellent point. On top of that, I couldn't afford the flight change fee, and the later flight cost over a hundred dollars more. Begging money from Dad to cover the flight had been humiliating enough, even though he could easily afford it. I couldn't ask for more, and there wasn't much in my bank account. The assistant U.S. attorney had confiscated my credit cards until my probation ended, so I had limited options. All part of my ex's lovely parting gift.

So there I sat, alone, bored, and only about half awake, waiting for my flight, wishing my friends were with me. Gwen and Cody went out early to make sure everything was in place for the ceremony, check out the resort, and enjoy some alone time before everyone arrived. Nathan flew out yesterday morning, along with Tyler and John, the groomsmen. As I sat in the gate area of the airport, drinking stale coffee and wishing I'd bought a muffin instead of a low-cal breakfast wrap, they were probably just starting to think about going to bed after a night of partying.

My vision blurred too much to focus on the book I brought. My eyes grew heavy; my head started to droop to one side. Then a beep from my phone caused me to lurch awake, nearly falling out of my seat in the process.

Marc: *Good morning! Hope you're already awake and at the airport. :-)*

Me: *Do I get credit for 1/2?*

Marc: *Only if it's the airport.*

Me: *Boarding soon. What are you doing up so early?*

Marc: *Conference call with London. Just wanted to wish you a good flight.*

My heart warmed at his words. Gwen had been right; there were still some good guys if you looked for them. As I tapped back a thank-you, the gate agent started the boarding process. Since I didn't have Gwen's airline status, I stood with boarding group six. It would be a long while before I could even see the Jetway. Ah, well. I put in my headphones and prepared to wait.

Someone poked me in the back. For a split second, I thought Marc had booked tickets on my flight. Which would be cool, but a little weird after only two dates. No such luck. The Poker was a total stranger: about my height, blond hair, blue eyes, orangey spray-on tan. In February, he wore board shorts, flip-flops, and a muscle shirt.

Really, dude? I know we're going to Mexico, but it's currently 25 degrees in Boston, and the Jetway isn't heated. Instead of offering my opinion on his wardrobe, I figured he'd poked me by mistake and turned back toward the front of the line.

Again, a finger jabbed me in the back. This time, I spun faster, removing my headphones. "Did you need something?"

"I said 'hey.' You didn't answer."

"I'm listening to music," I said. "Do I know you?"

"Not yet, but you're going to want to." He winked at me.

Ugh. What did he think, he could poke me in the back, say "hey," and then I'd beg him to join the Mile High Club with me? Lucas was never a great romantic, but at least he'd never jabbed me with a finger—twice—when he wanted something. The fact that this guy made me look at my ex in a positive light only made me less inclined to talk to him.

"Thanks, but I'm not interested."

"Maybe not yet, but we've got a long flight ahead of us," he said.

"Please don't take this the wrong way, but I intend to spend the entire flight sleeping." This guy deserved a stronger put-down, but it wasn't in my nature to be rude, even when justified.

He chuckled. "Sweet! Then I guess you could say we'll be sleeping together."

I rolled my eyes. "Sure. You, me, and the two hundred other people on this plane."

As if I hadn't said anything, he asked, "Do you like to party?"

Thankfully, the gate agent called my boarding group. The line shuffled forward. I shrugged before turning away yet again, allowing him to interpret the gesture however he wanted. Replacing my headphones, I started toward the door leading to the plane and freedom from this jerk.

On such a full flight, with any luck, he'd sit far away, next to someone else he could bother for the rest of the flight. Or, um, he and his seatmate could fall in love and have babies or something. As long as it didn't involve me, whatever.

The Poker fell into step with me when the Jetway widened.

"You didn't answer my question," he said. "Do you like to party?"

"I like hanging out with my friends, playing games. Sometimes we'll go to a party, sure, but it's mostly smaller, more intimate gatherings."

Immediately, I regretted using the word "intimate" when talking to this Neanderthal. His eyes lit up. "I'd like to play some intimate games with you, if you know what I mean."

The entire flight knew what he meant. At that crude comment, my patience snapped. "Does this act work for you? Are there women who find you charming? Go talk to one of them."

"I'm talking to you," he said. "You'll come around. They always do."

I rolled my eyes at him, put my headphones back in again, and blasted the music before turning away. I knew this guy's type. He was hot enough to get most girls, and he didn't want a real relationship. He didn't put any effort into making a connection. According to Gwen, these guys tended to be terrible in bed because they figured their good looks should be enough to get any woman off.

No thanks, for a thousand reasons. I preferred my men less crass, more polite...completely the opposite of this guy. Thank goodness I'd met Marc.

When the line finally reached my seat, I shoved my bag into the overhead bin and threw myself into the row.

"Excuse me."

I sighed heavily. For the past nineteen rows, I'd been pretending the Poker didn't exist.

"What?" My voice came out shorter than intended, but I couldn't even with this jerk.

He motioned toward the middle seat. "That's me. Earlier, I asked the stewardess to put me next to the prettiest girl flying alone. There weren't a lot of empty seats, so it came down to you and this grandma. I picked you, although I prefer girls who spend a bit more time on themselves in the morning."

"Gee, I'm so flattered."

My sarcasm was lost on him. "You should be. Anyway, so here we are."

Groaning, I silently cursed Shannon for rescheduling at the last minute. It was going to be a very long flight.

Chapter 7

Don't be afraid to take chances. Nothing ventured, nothing gained.
—*The Haunted Place* Player Guide

Six hours later, I arrived at the resort, excited to watch my friends get married and enjoy the first vacation I'd had in years. Also glad to leave the dudebro from the plane behind and never see him again. At least he gave me enough material to send Gwen a hilarious message using the airport's wi-fi while waiting for the resort shuttle. She always appreciated my stories.

A porter carried my bag to a third-floor room with a stunning view of the beach. The room faced east; I imagined how much more beautiful it would look with the morning's rays bathing everything in soft light. The resort lay in an earlier time zone than Boston, and I tended to be a morning person, so I expected to catch the sunrise.

After hanging my bridesmaid's dress in the closet—a short, pale-blue sundress perfect for a beach wedding and equally well-designed for getting frostbite in Boston—I pulled out a map of the resort. Pool with swim-up bar down the stairs to the left, food pretty much anywhere, and beach down the stairs, then straight ahead. It took no time to change into my swimsuit, don a rashguard, grab my e-reader, and throw a bottle of sunscreen into my bag. The wedding-related fun started with tonight's rehearsal dinner. My plan for today involved lying on the beach and doing nothing until then.

A quick text to Gwen and Shannon let them know I'd arrived safely. Shannon replied with an apology for missing our flight and a note that Nana's appointment went seamlessly. She'd be on the next flight, as expected. Gwen replied with emojis of hearts, beach, bikini, and drinks.

Although Boston sits on the coast, we didn't go to the beach much. North Atlantic waters stayed cold most of the year, plus work and other responsibilities tended to take priority. Swimming in the ocean in February felt downright decadent.

At the edge of the sidewalk, I took off my sandals, reveling in the sand beneath my toes. Glittering beach spread out before me in all directions. A couple hundred feet away, the waters of the Caribbean beckoned to me. Before finding a place to lie out and read, I dipped my toes into the water, letting the cool waves nip at my ankles. The sun beat down, warm but not too hot. Ahhh, paradise. I could stay here forever.

The only thing that could make this moment better was someone to share it with.

I frowned at the intruding thought, shaking my head to make it go away. People *were* here to share this weekend with me. If I didn't want to be alone, Nathan, John, and Tyler were around somewhere, probably in the pool. Shannon's flight would land in a few hours. No reason to be alone.

In the distance, someone yelled a warning. I ducked as an object whizzed over my head. A bright yellow discus landed in the ocean a couple of feet away. Seconds later, an enormous black dog charged past me, scooping it up in his mouth. I moved out of the surf to give him space, but he followed.

The dog poked the toy at me, tail wagging. I looked around for an owner, but didn't see anyone. It shook the toy again and whined. This time, I took the disc, moving slowly, just in case. Way down the beach, a guy waved at me. As hard as I could, I flung the toy at him.

The wind picked up the disc and whirled it around, bringing it back to me. With a laugh, I handed it to the dog. "Sorry, I'm not good at that."

He (she?) gave me a withering look. Somehow, I felt like I'd gravely disappointed the poor animal.

The dog's owner approached, looking like he stepped off the pages of a magazine. Long and lean, naturally brown skin, gleaming white teeth, and dimples that flashed, probably because he'd seen my pathetic attempt at throwing. I tried again, this time managing to get it about halfway between us.

The dog took off, but the owner continued his approach. "Sorry about that."

"No big deal. It didn't hit me. Thanks for the warning."

"*De nada*," he said. "I couldn't stand the thought of injuring a beautiful woman on my last day in paradise."

His words sent a thrill through me. Beautiful, me? He probably said that to all the girls, but after the beating my self-confidence had taken the past couple of years, it was nice to be complimented. My immediate instinct was to look down, mumble a disagreement, and wander away, but I didn't want to be that Holly anymore.

Gwen's voice echoed in my head: *Flirt with this guy. He's cute. Cut loose. Enjoy the interaction. It doesn't have to mean anything.*

Here I was, in a foreign country, over a thousand miles from home, talking to a very good-looking guy who was smiling at me. If I couldn't enjoy myself here, what was wrong with me? I tossed my hair back and forced myself to grin back. "Leaving so soon? I hope it wasn't something I said."

"As if meeting someone so fascinating could push me away."

He laid it on thick, but he didn't bother me. At least he wasn't crude or crass. I could get used to a guy peppering me with compliments, after Lucas picked at everything I did. Besides, this conversation wasn't going anywhere. It was just nice to talk about nothing with someone charismatic. "I'm Holly."

"Alejandro. And this is Blanca." I glanced at the black dog and raised an eyebrow at him. "It is, what is the word? Ironic."

"Well, I like it," I said. "It suits her. Where are you from?"

"I live in Texas, but my parents were born and raised in Mexico City."

"Really? My grandparents lived in Puerto Rico. On my mother's side. I never met them, though. Mamá moved to California when they died, before I was born."

"*Lo siento,*" he said. *I'm sorry.*

At his words, I switched to Spanish. "Thank you. I'm sorry I never got to visit Puerto Rico before the hurricane."

We headed back up the beach, toward a line of beach chairs. Blanca padded along at Alejandro's side. I couldn't wait to order a drink, lie back, and chill in the sun. Maybe a one-time hookup in Mexico was just what I needed, after all. It wasn't my style, but my style hadn't exactly been working for me thus far. I was about to invite my new friends to join me when someone called my name.

Nathan. He wore a pair of board shorts with sandals, a towel casually slung over one shoulder. My eyes glued themselves to the expanse of his chest, following each line and plane, trying not to linger on the trail of dark hair starting at his belly button and heading beneath his shorts. It wasn't fair for him to look so good when he didn't have the slightest interest in me.

"Who's that?" Alejandro asked, breaking me out of my trance. He also reminded me of the need to get over this stupid crush and focus on a guy I *could* have. Like this charming, super-hot guy who would be ridiculously appealing if only I could stop fixating on my best friend's dad.

"A friend." I answered too late, realizing that the silence had become awkward.

Nathan arrived at my side, putting one arm around me and kissing my cheek. My face burned where his lips met my skin, as if the small act branded me. I tried not to think about those same lips touching me other places. "There you are! I've been looking for you everywhere."

"Hi?" It came out more as a question than a statement. "I got in about an hour ago."

"You should've called me, sweetheart. You know how much I miss you when you're not around."

In fact, I knew no such thing. Was Nathan drunk at eleven o'clock in the morning?

Beside me, Alejandro said, "Are you…"

"Hi, I'm Nathan," he said, wrapping one arm around my waist.

Under ordinary circumstances, I'd be thrilled at this contact. I'd be thinking about leaning in, snuggling up against him the way I dreamed about late at night. Now I wondered if I'd passed out on a beach chair without realizing it. None of this made any sense, and I didn't even know what to say or do. Play along? Ask Nathan if he got high after breakfast?

"A friend, huh?" A shadow crossed Alejandro's face.

"Yes, we're very good friends," Nathan said. "Holly's been living with me for the past several months."

My mouth fell open. What was going on? This behavior was 100 percent out of character. Whatever it was, though, my new friend didn't want any part of it. Ignoring Nathan, he turned to me. "Well, it was nice to meet you. Sorry again about almost hitting you with the disc."

I wanted to answer, but he was gone. As soon he'd moved back into the crowd, Nathan dropped his arm from around my waist and stepped backward. "You're welcome!"

"I'm…. what?"

"You're welcome! Gwen told me some creep wouldn't stop hitting on you, so I came down to save you."

This couldn't be happening. I took a deep breath, forcing myself not to lash out. After all, that cheek kiss and fake hug were the most thrilling action I'd gotten in a long time, even considering my first kiss with Marc. Nathan meant well. He couldn't know what he'd done.

I chose my words carefully. "The creep was on my flight this morning. I haven't seen him since leaving the plane. With luck, he'll soon be a distant memory."

"Then who was that guy?"

"A very nice, friendly man I didn't need saving from." A welcome distraction. I sank onto the chair beside me, head in my hands. It figured that the guy whom I'd felt both a mental and physical connection with would be accidentally chased off by the man I needed to forget.

Nathan sat beside me and put his hand on my shoulder. The touch did nothing to lessen my confusion. "Hey, I'm sorry. Want me to go after him and tell him the truth?"

He didn't know the truth, that sometimes I wanted him so badly, I couldn't breathe. That I'd give anything to make his comments a reality, but I couldn't.

Something in his tone made me wonder at his sincerity. I glanced up, noticing just how close his face was to mine. The air between us grew heavy. He didn't look remotely inclined to stand up and go after Alejandro. And while I'd been enjoying that conversation, it would have taken a meteor to get me to walk away from Nathan.

Maybe this whole situation was as innocent as he claimed. Maybe he heard some creep was bothering me and came to save me, not realizing I was talking to someone else. But maybe, just maybe, he got jealous when finding me flirting with another man. The thought made my breath catch in my throat.

I still felt the imprint of his arm around my waist, the softness of his lips against my cheek. I couldn't help wondering what they'd feel like against my mouth, what it would be like to let my tongue tangle with his. If I leaned forward, I might find out. Would he kiss me back? Was he really "saving" me from Alejandro, or was he jealous? Could I convince him to take the act a teeny bit further?

As I stared at him, my tongue darted out to moisten my lips. His eyes followed the movement briefly, almost imperceptibly, then moved back up to mine. As if he looked in spite of himself. The silence grew, and the rest of the world faded away. He swallowed, and for a moment, I couldn't move.

We'd entered a dangerous area. He was my best friend's dad. She'd never be okay with me lusting after him. Nathan only approached me because he thought I needed help handling a creep. It was sweet, a friendly thing to do. He never would have touched me otherwise. He didn't want me for himself. Or to make out with me on the beach. He didn't need to waste his time on some twenty-eight-year-old girl when he could have any woman he wanted. If I leaned in, closed the gap, all I'd do would be embarrass myself. With restraint requiring the strength of Wonder Woman, I forced myself to pull back. "No thanks. We were just chatting."

Something flashed in his eyes. Disappointment that I'd moved away, or relief that he wouldn't have to chase Alejandro down the beach? "Okay, then. Well, I should go shower and get ready for dinner."

"Yeah. I'm going to lie out for a bit longer. I'll see you later."

He hesitated, as if he wanted to say something else. If so, he decided against it. A moment later, I was alone.

After applying my sunscreen, I leaned back in my lounge chair and picked up my book. It was no use. My thoughts kept returning to Nathan. The words swam together, sending my thoughts tumbling back to what just happened. I tried to nap, but when I closed my eyes, his face swam before me. The look in his eyes when he saw me talking to another man. A look I desperately wanted to believe was jealousy, not chivalry.

One thing was clear, though: This crush didn't seem to be getting any easier.

Chapter 8

Actions taken may have a significant effect on other characters. Some objects affect everyone in the vicinity. Consider when making a choice not only the ramifications for yourself, but for the rest of the game.
—*The Haunted Place* Player Guide

The next morning, Shannon and I met Gwen bright and early, as directed, wearing workout clothes and sandals. Since most exercise classes wanted some type of shoe, I assumed we were about to engage in some sort of pre-bridal yoga. So I stopped dead in my tracks when I spotted the sign in the window behind Gwen.

Shannon saw it at the same time I did. "Unleash your inner diva?"

Suddenly, I had a very bad feeling about this. The woman on the poster wore sky-high heels, the tiniest shorts I'd ever seen, a bra, and a feather boa. She didn't look like she was about to engage in any sort of fitness routine. This poster looked a lot less like "Let's have a fun day celebrating Gwen and Cody" and a lot more like "Project Get Holly Laid," which wasn't why I'd decided to start dating again. I mean, sure, sex would be nice, but that wasn't the point of regaining my confidence.

"It's not as bad as it looks," Gwen said. "It's a fitness class. We're going to learn to spin and twirl and get in touch with our inner confidence. We should leave here feeling like a million bucks."

"Is that a million bucks in dollar bills?" Shannon asked.

I snorted. The woman in the picture did look like a stripper. Which was fine, except I didn't need to learn how to be one, too.

"Ha-ha," Gwen said. "Yes, they teach fitness with a pole. But we'll be fully clothed, and there's no audience."

"I suppose it could be fun," Shannon said doubtfully.

If either of them noticed my silence, they didn't comment.

"I swear you'll love it," Gwen said. "And, hey, you never know, Holly might learn some sexy moves to try out on all those lucky guys she's meeting online."

After the Poker's comment about preferring women who spent more time on themselves, I couldn't handle any "Holly needs to be sexier" comments. Hearing how not-sexy everyone found me didn't help my self-esteem. Adding in the frustration of not clicking with any of the guys online, no sparks with Marc, and Nathan chasing away Alejandro, I was done. My feet ground to a halt. As much as I loved Gwen, I simply couldn't go in there.

"I'm sorry, but no," I said. "I know it's your weekend, Gwen, but I'm not up for this. It's not my thing."

"You don't know if it's your thing until you try it," Shannon pointed out. "It might be fun. And even if it blows, at least we'll all hate it together."

"You won't hate it!" Gwen insisted. "Have you hated the other things you're doing to get out of your shell?"

"Well…." I didn't want to say yes. I mean, flirting with Nathan was fun. I liked hanging out with Marc. My other dates so far had been disasters, and that was the primary thing I'd tried. It might be time to do something else outside of my comfort zone. But this?

"I want to do a girls' day out to celebrate my wedding. Shots or a club aren't the way to go, not for me. And, okay, sure, I could have set up a spa day, but those are expensive. I didn't want you to have to spend a lot and can't afford to pay for all of us, even if I thought you'd take my money."

"You're right, I wouldn't," I said.

"What are you so afraid of?" Shannon asked.

I hesitated, not wanting to reveal the truth. I was afraid everyone would see my "moves" and realize I had no sex appeal whatsoever. Afraid I'd feel even more inadequate and awkward after the class than before. Afraid it would take the fragile tendrils of self-confidence I'd managed to rebuild and crush them to bits.

At the same time, Gwen would be pissed if I didn't go in, and I still wanted the three of us to have a great day together. She tended to get angry quickly and cool off just as fast, but as a friend, I preferred not to unnecessarily upset her.

Gwen turned to Shannon. "Can you give us a minute?"

"Sure." She went inside to sign in and make sure we didn't lose our reservation, while Gwen pulled me over to a bench placed beside the doors so we wouldn't be in the way. Part of me felt like a jerk for messing up

the fun day she'd had planned, but I'd spent so much time doing things I
didn't want to do and containing my true feelings. The effort exhausted me.

"You know I only push because I love you, right?" she asked. "You do
your best to act positive, but you forget how well we know you. You're
not happy."

I tried to paste a smile on my face, but it failed. "You're right, I'm not.
But I'll be okay."

"Of course you will. But as your BFF, it's my job to refuse to allow
you to sit around and mope forever. Like how you and Shannon wouldn't
let me write Cody off as another gamer who only wanted to get laid. We
wouldn't even be here if it weren't for you two."

"I doubt that. You would have figured it out eventually." She raised
her eyebrows at me, and I giggled. "I mean, it might have taken a really,
really loooooong time...."

"See? I owe you. It's not about finding a guy. We both know life isn't
about being in a relationship. But you need something that will make you
happy, and I want to help."

"Seeing Lucas get sent to jail at the end of his trial will make me happy,"
I said. "Getting off probation and starting my career. Finding my own
place to live so I'm not mooching off your dad."

"I know," she said. "I get it. But you can't do those things yet. Do you
want to spend the next several months being miserable and lonely?"

When she put it like that, the answer was obvious. "No, I don't."

"Excellent!" She clapped her hands several times. "Then let's have
some fun."

"Okay, I'll do it."

With great trepidation, I entered the room. It looked like any other open
fitness room, similar to where I'd done Zumba back when I could afford a
gym membership. The primary difference was that mirrors lined three of
the walls, not just the front. And that metal poles stood every six or seven
feet, connecting floor to very high ceiling.

The woman on the poster strode to the front of the room. "¡Buenos dias!
I'm Yasmine, and I'm your instructor for Finding Your Inner Diva. I'm
not a stripper, but it's cool if you are. When I'm not teaching here, I work
as a bartender. In my free time, I'm going to school to get my MBA. Pole
has given me the confidence to pursue the things I want in life, and I hope
you can say the same. What would you do if you knew you couldn't fail?"

Unbidden, an image swam before my eyes. I didn't have the courage to
go for the one thing I wanted most. What would Gwen say if this worked,

and I told her she was the one who gave me the push I needed to take a chance on dating her father?

Gwen's voice interrupted my thoughts. "I want a long and happy marriage, unlike my parents."

Shannon said, "I want to venture out on my own and create a successful game business. To show the guys I work with that a woman can make games as well as they can."

Everyone turned to me. Wiping my palms on the back of my pants, I chewed my lip for a moment before responding. "I…I want to stop feeling trapped by circumstances beyond my control."

"Worthy goals, all of them," Yasmine said. "By the time I'm done with the three of you, you'll be ready to take over the world."

* * * *

As promised, the class turned out to be a huge amount of fun. By the end, I was glad I'd let Gwen talk me into it, and I apologized profusely for doubting her intentions. She didn't say another word about me dating or hooking up or anything, and the three of us had a blast. By the end, I decided to find a place offering similar classes in Boston…just as soon as I found some spare pennies to rub together.

After class, we spent the afternoon lounging by the pool, just the three of us, until it was time to get ready for the rehearsal dinner. The resort planned and executed the entire wedding, so there wasn't much to "rehearse" in the traditional sense. Gwen and Cody had already gone to look at where their ceremony would be held, we checked the weather report for rain clouds, and that was it. In the morning, the wedding planner assigned by the resort would meet with everyone and tell us where to stand, when to walk, etc.

Since we didn't need to spend a lot of time going over readings or song choices, Gwen and Cody invited the bridal party to dinner at one of the resort restaurants. It wasn't covered by the all-inclusive package, and therefore wouldn't have been within my budget, but Cody's parents offered to pay for everyone. They said the groom's family traditionally paid for the rehearsal dinner, so it was only right for them to cover this meal.

Shannon and I arrived early. I wouldn't mind so much being stuck next to Cody's drunk uncle, but after a day spent not thinking about He-Who-Shall-Not-Be-Lusted-After, the last thing I needed was to wind up seated beside him for an entire two-hour meal.

Thankfully, Cody's sister Tessa arrived at the same time we did. The three of us went to the bar for pre-dinner drinks.

"How's Preston?" I asked Tessa. She'd brought her one-and-a-half-year-old to the resort, but she'd also wisely brought a sitter to help. We hadn't seen much of them, probably because Tessa didn't bring her child to pole-dancing classes or the adults-only pool with a swim-up bar.

"Great! He loves the kiddie pool. Cody and I spent about three hours over there earlier so the sitter could have the afternoon off."

"It's great that he helps so much."

She nodded. "Even though I fought him at the time, I'm lucky he moved to Boston. And look how it worked out for him! He and Gwen will probably be having their own babies soon."

Shannon laughed. "Don't let Gwen hear you say that."

"She doesn't want kids?"

"It's not that," I said. "But she's not ready, especially with just coming to terms with her relationship with her mother and not being married yet. Plus, her blog is taking off. She may not want to take maternity leave right when she's starting to land some big sponsors."

"Fair enough. The whole thing with her mom was tough. Luckily, she has an amazing parent and role model in her father."

The last person I wanted to talk about was Nathan, so I made a noise that sounded sort of like an agreement and sipped my drink.

"Maybe we should change the subject." Shannon nodded to the door. "Here they come."

Behind me, Gwen entered with Cody and Nathan on either arm. My heart skipped a beat, noting how his dark green shirt complemented his coloring. Did absence make the heart grow fonder so fast? I'd only been avoiding him for about twenty-four hours. Not even enough time for him to have noticed. And yet, I couldn't deny the way the room brightened when he appeared.

The three of us joined the group and headed for the dining room. Tyler showed up while we were still figuring out the seating, so I maneuvered a spot between him and Tessa, with Shannon on Tyler's other side. Gwen wasn't the only one who could meddle in her friends' private lives. Once Shannon got to know Tyler better, she might develop an attraction for him. Nathan sat on the other side of Gwen and Cody, far enough away for me to nod hello and then pretend I couldn't hear him over the din of the restaurant.

Once the rest of the family members arrived, I didn't have to pretend. Tessa told me all about Preston's development while Tyler and Shannon talked game design on the other side of me. He loved *The Haunted Place* and had a lot of ideas for her next game.

By the time everyone finished eating, I'd almost forgotten that Nathan sat less than ten feet away from me. I stayed for the toasts, then slipped away to the ladies' room, figuring everyone would be gone by the time I got back.

Instead, I found Nathan lounging on the wall outside the exit. My traitorous heart skipped a beat at the sight of him. "Hey. Waiting for someone?"

"Yeah. You." He fell into step beside me. "Is everything okay?"

No.

"Sure. Why?" I asked.

"I don't know. You seem different. I haven't seen you all day, and then you barely said hello. I thought you were still mad about yesterday."

Mad that you chased Alejandro away? No. Mad that you didn't kiss me and declare your love for me? Yes.

"Why would I be mad? You thought you were helping. Besides, that guy was leaving today and lives three thousand miles away. It's not like we were going to start a passionate love affair."

As soon as the words left my mouth, I wanted to snatch them back. Nathan was the last person in the world I wanted to discuss my love life—or lack thereof—with. But he didn't seem the slightest bit fazed.

Expression inscrutable, he said, "Okay, good. I really am sorry."

"I know. Thanks."

"Are you coming to the after-party?" he asked.

"After-party" might be a bit of an overstatement, but we'd reserved a table near one of the outdoor bars where everyone could drink and hang out. My normal cautious self might have passed, considering the half dozen or so drinks I'd already consumed over the course of the day, but I barely felt a buzz. One drink per hour, watered down by the resort, wasn't enough to impair my judgment. Besides, after tapping my inner diva, I couldn't wait to shove Old Holly aside and let the Flirt out to play. "Definitely. You?"

"Looking forward to it. Especially now that I know you're not mad at me."

I beamed up at him. "How could anyone possibly be mad at her knight in shining armor?"

"I hear it's easy," he said. "Gwen may have some tips."

Turning the corner, we arrived at the tables where the rest of the wedding party already milled around. A waiter would eventually come take our order, but I didn't want to wait. Bolting straight for the bar, I ordered two shots of tequila. Ordinarily, I didn't love tequila, but when in Rome...or Mexico, as it were.

Maybe it was the alcohol talking, or the class, or whatever, but my conversation with Nathan sparked a wild rush of emotions that needed to be tamed. I wanted to throw myself into his arms, confess my crush, and let him reject me so I could move on. I wanted him to ask me to dance so I could press my body against his and feel his strong arms around me again.

At the same time, I wanted to avoid him so I could finally focus on finding something real. It was easy to focus on the one man I could never be with, because then I wouldn't risk getting hurt again. A harmless crush might sting a little, but he could never cheat on me, never cause me all the pain Lucas had. Not getting attached to anyone else made everything easier. I wanted…everything to fade away, for just a few hours.

So when the bartender brought my shots, I tossed them both back and ordered a margarita. And when a guy at the bar gave me a big smile and said hi, I flipped my hair and introduced myself.

Chapter 9

Each character has their own individual goals. These should not be shared with the other players. If you achieve your secret goal, you'll receive a character bonus at the end of the game—as long as the group wins.
—*The Haunted Place* Player Guide

It's amazing what a difference a few drinks makes. Soon enough, I found myself having a splendid time at the after-party. Much better than at the rehearsal dinner. The group all hung around and chatted for a bit, but Gwen and Cody went to bed early. His parents and Nathan took off at the same time.

As it got later, our party disbanded but the bar filled with people. The bartender pumped up the music. This wasn't a bar for deep conversations. Anyone who wanted quiet could sit at the tables outside, where our party started. But I didn't want to sit under the stars with a drink and my thoughts. I wanted to sway to the beat and have a good time.

Now that my greatest temptation was gone, I let myself go. Not having to worry about embarrassing myself around Nathan, I flitted around the bar, chatting with everyone. Older men, younger men—Holly the Flirt came out in full force. At some point, Shannon vanished. Weird that she'd go to bed without telling me, but maybe she wasn't feeling well. After my fourth or fifth drink (hey, they were really watered down), I sent Marc a dirty text.

He read the message but didn't reply, and suddenly I wondered what was wrong with me. Here I was on vacation with my best friends. A great guy waited for me back home, but I'd let myself get so oddly fixated on Nathan that I wound up drunk, alone, sending highly inappropriate texts for the first time in my life. Probably freaking Marc out, since he didn't strike me as the sexting type. Especially considering we'd only exchanged a fairly chaste kiss in public. We hadn't even made out yet. In my mind, we were at least four dates away from Netflix and Chill-ing. My mouth fell open in horror when I realized my mistake.

Great. On top of everything else, jet lag plus alcohol had made me forget how to behave, and I had to pee. This night sucked. The bar shared a bathroom with the club on the other side of the courtyard, and a line zigzagged back and forth between the two buildings. No thanks. I could pee in my room. I looked around the bar for the remains of the wedding party, but didn't see anyone. No one to walk back with. Ah, well. Guess I'd strike out on my own. As per usual.

Might as well grab a drink for the road. Or two. Why not? Once I got to my room, I could weep and pee and drink until the cows came home. What did that even mean? Whose cows? Where did they go? How did they know when to come home or how to get there?

Whatever. I needed Shannon. Tell her how stupid I was for messing things up with Marc and hopefully not spill my love for Nathan. Not love. Affection. Attraction. A crush, a nothing. Whatever. Alcohol made my head spin.

With a margarita in each hand, I'd walked about a quarter of the way back to my room when the cupcake shop lights blazed ahead of me. A sign in the window proudly declared twenty-four-hour cupcakes. Amazing. The only thing better than margaritas were cupcakes. Or cupcakes with margaritas. Also, they had a bathroom.

Since I couldn't pee while holding a drink in each hand, I downed them both. Immediately, I regretted that decision. More alcohol, I did not need. Carbs, that was what I needed. Also, *el baño*. Sitting down made me a little dizzy, but emptying my bladder made the extra swaying worth it.

A few minutes later, I stood at the counter, surveying the available options. Everything sounded amazing. I wanted fifteen cupcakes. I wanted not to have to make any decisions. "Give me the two best ones you have. Surprise me."

"Hey, sexy lady."

At the sound of the familiar voice, I felt light-headed. Spinning on my toes, I prayed the speaker was talking to someone else.

Lady Luck did not have my back. The Poker from the airplane stood behind me with a couple of friends. I wondered what he'd do if I smashed my cupcake into his face. "Accidentally," of course. I didn't have time for this guy. "*No hablo inglés.*"

Unfortunately, he answered me in flawless Spanish. "You spoke English on the plane, remember?"

If only I could forget. "What are you doing here?"

"I'm staying here. Small world, huh?"

"Too small." I started to walk around him, but he grabbed my elbow. My phone beeped, but I ignored it.

"Are you okay? Do you need someone to walk you back to your room?"

The words seemed caring, but the leer in his eye reminded me that the worst guy ever had uttered them. Well, the worst after Lucas. I'd rather sit in this cupcake shop till morning than let him know where I slept. "I'm fine, thanks."

He stayed between me and the door. "Come on. I'm a great guy. Don't you want to get to know me better? There are better things you can do with your night than eating cupcakes alone in your room."

The desire to smash one in his face grew stronger. But the reminder that I held two pastries gave me a convenient lie. "I'm meeting someone."

Behind him, the bell over the door jingled. Two familiar faces walked in, and I almost sagged to the floor in relief. "Nathan! Cody! There you are."

The two of them glanced from me to the Poker and must have immediately grasped what was going on. Cody took long strides to my side. "Hey. Sorry we're late."

Nathan hung back, avoiding my gaze. I wondered if he was thinking about the last time he "rescued" me from a conversation with a man. That had been a very different interaction, but of course he wouldn't know that this time I wanted his help.

"No problem," I said loudly. "I'm just glad to see you."

The Poker looked from me to Nathan to Cody and back, then swore under his breath and took off. My shoulders sagged with relief.

"Are you okay?" Nathan asked.

"Fine. That's the creep Gwen told you about the other day. From the plane. I didn't know he was staying here. I'll hang around here for a few minutes. He should be gone by the time you leave."

"If you're remotely concerned he might hang around, one of us should walk you to your room," Cody said. He stepped up to the counter and placed an order.

Nathan stared at me, pupils dilated, and I wondered how much he'd had to drink. Not that it mattered. I felt safe with him, even drunk. He tilted his head in an unspoken question, and I knew he was thinking about how I'd avoided him all day. In answer, I moved my head in the tiniest fraction of a nod and offered him a small smile to let him know that I'd be happy to walk with him.

"I'll go," Nathan said. "We're headed in the same direction."

"Thanks." Cody held up a white cardboard box. "I've got to get some sleep. Besides, Tessa's waiting for her cupcakes."

He left while Nathan stepped up to the counter to place his order. I vaguely remembered that I had a text, probably from Marc, but checking it seemed like too much effort. Instead, I turned the device off and shoved it to the bottom of my bag.

A few minutes later, Nathan and I strolled under the moonlight, headed toward our respective rooms. We walked slowly, holding each other upright. Then we got to the elevator and I stopped dead. "Thanks for the walk. See you tomorrow."

"Are you on the first floor?"

"No. I don't do elevators."

"Right." He glanced at the steep staircase beside us, then at the ground, back at me. "I am way too drunk to climb those stairs."

"Men." I took a step toward the staircase and stumbled. Nathan caught me before I fell. My cheeks grew warm. "I'm fine. Just need to take off my shoes."

"You're holding your shoes."

A glance at my bare feet and the objects clutched in my right hand confirmed his statement. In response, I burped, then started giggling uncontrollably. Plopping down on the cement, I laughed and laughed until hiccups consumed me. A moment later, Nathan joined me. By the time I got control of myself, my sides ached. "What do we do now?"

"Let's go to the pool. They have chairs. And a bar. We probably shouldn't go to the bar."

"A bar!" What a wonderful idea. "Let's go."

He helped me to my feet, and we walked in silence. Finally, Nathan spoke. "Do you want to talk about it?"

"Talk about what?"

"Whatever it is that made you drink so much you forgot you're not wearing shoes? Because, I mean, I'm drunk. I can't believe I'm still standing. But you're a special kind of drunk."

I groaned. "Why do you have to be so observant?"

"Because I care. What happened?"

"I practiced flirting with everyone in the bar. I still suck at it. No one interested me. I drunk-texted Marc, and he didn't reply. And then I ran into that douche from the plane. He likes me just fine. No nice, non-creepers like me, but icky guys, I've got coming out of my ears."

"That's what she said." The joke didn't even make sense, but we both cracked up. "I'm sorry."

"What's wrong with me?" I moaned, coming to a halt. "I don't know how to talk to guys. I'm the worst flirt in the world, and I've been working on it."

Nathan stopped and faced me. "Nothing. Nothing at all is wrong with you. You're smart and kind and caring and beautiful. You're an amazing woman. A knockout like you should have guys lined up around the block, begging to take her out."

"You have to say that because you're Gwen's dad."

"No, actually, I shouldn't say that because I'm Gwen's dad." He took a deep breath. "That doesn't mean it's not true."

My heart skipped a beat, then quickly settled. I would give absolutely anything to believe he meant what he said. But he was drunk, I was drunk, and he was just trying to make me feel better. Normally I'd let it go, but being drunk made me rather truthful. "Liar. You're just trying to make me feel better."

Something flashed over his face, so fast I couldn't identify the emotion. "You don't believe me?"

"We've been hanging out almost every night for a year, and you've never shown the slightest interest. If I'm so irresistible, why don't you want me?"

He took a deep breath and stepped backward before returning to the same spot with a groan of frustration. He gripped my forearms with an intensity that made my eyes widen. "I want you so badly, sometimes I can't see straight. And I can't believe I'm saying this, because I'm going to feel like a fool tomorrow when I remember how you shot me down."

All the air rushed out of my lungs. "I'm not going to shoot you down."

In the back of my mind, a tiny voice asked what was happening, but I squashed it. I don't know who moved first to close the gap between us, but it didn't matter. We moved in slow motion until, finally, his lips pressed against mine. I sighed against his mouth, and he wrapped his arms around me. Desire shot through me as I leaned into the kiss. God, he felt amazing. His tongue darted into my open mouth, tasting me, shocking me back to reality.

We stood out in the middle of the resort. Anyone could see us.

I pulled back. "Wait. I changed my mind."

He stepped back. "Of course. I'm sorry. I—"

"No, I changed my mind about the pool. Take me to your room."

* * * *

A thousand drums beat out a chorus inside my skull. Pinpricks of light
dug into my brain like fingernails. In my early morning haze, it took longer
than it should've to realize that I could roll over and put a pillow over my
face to make everything go away. Silently, I cursed myself for not closing
the blinds before going to bed.

When I'd first checked in to the hotel, I'd said something about how
beautiful it must be to wake up to the view of the resort outside. Dumb.
The only thing I wanted more than the drumming to stop was the light
to go away.

Unfortunately, that wasn't going to happen. My phone buzzed on the
table beside me, reminding me of why I'd woken up in the first place—and
the reason I needed to get up and out of this bed faster than you can say,
"Tequila is the devil." My friends were waiting for me.

I'd only had...four margaritas after dinner? Six? But they were the
crappy resort ones made of 80 percent water because they came included
in the all-inclusive resort fee. Maybe I should've stuck to beer. Or possibly
downing two shots before starting had been a mistake.

My phone buzzed yet again. Why did I turn it back on before going
to sleep? With a groan, I pulled it under the covers with me to read the
screen. Loads of missed texts.

From Gwen to Shannon and me: *I'm getting married
today!!!!!!!!!!!!!!!!!!!!!!!!!!!!!!!!!!!!!*

The number of exclamation points made me smile until the movement
escalated the throbbing in my head. I was ecstatic for my friend, and very
happy to be here in Mexico celebrating her big day, but I needed painkillers
and a giant glass of water before properly displaying my enthusiasm.

Before doing anything else, I slammed the drapes shut, with a bit more
force than necessary. Then, tripping over discarded clothes and shoes on
the floor, I made my way to my purse on the dresser.

Except my purse wasn't on the dresser. The dresser wasn't on the right
side of the room like it was supposed to be. And what I'd failed to notice
when waking up was that I hadn't been sleeping in one of the two double
beds in the room I shared with Shannon. Shannon wasn't here at all, which
explained the number of texts from her.

This wasn't our room. A giant king-sized bed filled the center, with a
nightstand on either side. To my left, a massive TV hung over the dresser.

Suddenly, the previous night came rushing back to me. Dinner, the bar,
the beach...Nathan. Lots of Nathan. Me and Nathan. My turning into a

drunken hot mess. His confession that he wanted me. That kiss. Oh, that kiss. And all the amazing things that happened after. The memory brought a smile to my face until my brain kicked into overdrive, reminding me what a mess this could turn into.

Oh, wow. What had I been thinking? How could I? What was I going to do? I'd never had a drunken one-night stand before. Panic flowed through my veins. I needed to get out of there, ASAP, before he returned from wherever he'd gone.

After a bit of searching, I located my purse on the floor next to the nightstand. No idea how I thought to fish my phone out and leave it by the bed, but apparently Drunk Holly still wanted to wake up in time for Gwen's pre-wedding breakfast. Pouncing on my bag, I dug until finding my prize.

Yay for painkillers. Sweet, wonderful things. After shaking four onto my palm, I turned toward the bathroom to get some water. And stopped dead.

The bathroom door was closed. A light peeked out from under the door. When I woke up, I hadn't heard the rushing of the shower over the rhythm beating in my head, but now it seemed obvious that Nathan had gotten in the shower without waking me. I didn't have any idea what to do.

Lucas had been my first everything. First boyfriend, first kiss, first love, first lover. Only lover, until a few hours earlier. Plenty of people had no trouble hooking up with strangers, but I'd never been one of them. After my breakup, I'd made out with a few guys, but never wanted to go all the way with someone I didn't care about. For the first time, I was about to experience a first without Lucas. My first awkward morning after. Although I'd heard plenty of stories from Gwen, I didn't have the first clue what to expect.

Would he be annoyed I hadn't left? Would he want to have sex again? Or would he say, "Thanks for a good time," and show me the door? What did I want? I couldn't believe I'd slept with Nathan, of all people. That I'd gotten to touch and taste him and hear his sex noises and see his face.

The memory made me smile so much, I winced at the added pounding in my head. It had been everything I'd dreamed about for the past year and a half. But...

Looking down, I realized that I stood in the middle of the room, completely naked. Funny, since with Lucas we always put our pajamas on to go to sleep after sex. I couldn't remember ever sleeping with no clothes on. But I hadn't even thought about getting dressed after, and even if I had, all the rest of my clothes were back in my room.

My phone buzzed again, reminding me that, in addition to not knowing how to talk to a naked, showering Nathan, I didn't know what time it was, or how soon to be at the restaurant. Gwen made a hair and makeup appointment for all three of us at eleven, so I needed to get back to my room, shower, and eat before then.

From Gwen to Shannon and me: *Are you two still meeting me for breakfast? Girl time? You know it's bad luck for me to see my intended groom before the wedding.*

From Shannon to Gwen and me: *Didn't you two share a bed last night?*

From Gwen to Shannon and me: *No. He crashed on Tessa's couch. With Preston waking up at the crack of dawn, poor guy probably didn't sleep a wink.*

A glance at the phone's display told me I had plenty of time to shower—depending on whether I wanted to face Nathan before I left and how much longer he spent in the bathroom. The logical solution was to knock and at least say good-bye. After all, we were friends. Or we had been. I didn't know what we were now. For some reason, the thought of facing him froze me in place.

My phone buzzed again. This time, it was Shannon, but she only texted me. *Hey, are you OK? I can't help but notice that you never came back to the room last night. Please reply so I know you weren't axe-murdered and left on the beach for the seagulls.*

Her text made me chuckle. *It was Miss Scarlett on the beach with the wrench.*

Shannon: *Too bad. I was hoping you'd gone off to have a good time.*

Me: *Yeah. Um...how much did I have to drink?*

Shannon: *You were veeeeeerrrrrrryyyyyy happy when I went to bed. You feeling it now?*

Me: *I guess you could say that.*

Shannon: *Where are you? Are you okay?*

Not really. Sort of. Probably. Feeling too many emotions to unpack them now via text. Incapable of telling my best friend where I slept or what I'd done the night before. Too hung over to deal with any of it. I decided to be brief and technically truthful.

Me: *I'm fine. Woke up in this guy's room.*

The reply came instantly, with about fourteen emojis. *GOOD FOR YOU!! I need all the details.*

Me: *Not right now. I need breakfast. And please don't say anything to Gwen. I don't want her to think I'm stealing her thunder.*

Her response took a few minutes, during which I glanced repeatedly from the door to the bed to the pants on the floor. The shower still ran. I was still naked, albeit under the covers again. Should I get dressed? Would that make things more or less awkward when Nathan came out? What if he was naked, too?

Since Shannon was drawing out the torture, I texted Gwen back to assure her that I was ecstatic about her big day and couldn't wait to meet her for breakfast. Then I got up. With no other clothes, I put my dress back on, slipping my dirty panties into my purse. Hopefully this room wasn't too far from my own, because I needed to change. Then I turned to the mirror over my dresser. Thankfully, I didn't use a lot of product in my hair, so while it wasn't exactly wedding-ready, it went back into a short ponytail easily enough. They said not to wash your hair before getting it professionally styled, anyway. All I had to do was rub at the mascara under my eyes with a spit-covered tissue, and I looked almost normal.

The water turned off, so my questions were going to be answered very soon. Unless I was prepared to run, I needed to face him. Of all the things planned for today, none of them involved running naked down the hotel hallway. I checked my breath. Not that it mattered. No kissing Nathan. Last night had been a horrible mistake.

My phone buzzed again, but I ignored it. Shannon or Gwen, it didn't matter.

The bathroom door opened, and he stepped out, naked from the waist up. Despite my near-panicked state, my eyes feasted on his toned, tanned chest. Not a lot of hair, but not waxed. On his muscular arms. I couldn't quite bring myself to meet his eyes.

"Hey, you," he said.

"Hey."

Here we were. Having an awkward, naked morning after. I should be ecstatic, considering how long I'd wanted this. Would be, too, except for the all-encompassing dread. We could never, ever repeat what happened. As wonderful as it felt at the time, we made a giant mistake.

The kind of mistake I'd been wanting to make for over a year. The kind of mistake that Gwen would never, ever forgive me for, if she ever found out about it. Even Shannon would have a hard time taking my side, and she was one of the most compassionate people I knew.

He sat on the bed next to me. "Are you okay? I know we drank a lot last night."

A hysterical bubble of laughter escaped me. I didn't even know what to say. How could I possibly be okay? How could anything be okay, ever again?

"Shhh," he said. "I'm sorry. I didn't mean to freak you out."

"I'm not freaked," I lied. He gave me a skeptical look. "Okay, I am. But not about what happened. I've had a crush on you for a while. Part of me has been secretly hoping for this, even though I didn't think it would ever happen."

"The feeling is definitely mutual." He leaned over and kissed me softly. His words thrilled me all the way to the tips of my toes. Until last night, I'd never suspected he had the slightest bit of interest in me. Part of me couldn't believe I was so lucky. And the kiss—I'd never dated an older man, but if they all had this sort of mastery with their tongues, I'd seriously been missing out. After a few seconds, I was fully prepared to abandon my maid of honor obligations, skip the wedding, and beg him to show me all the things he'd learned in his extra fifteen years on earth.

But something nagged at the back of my mind. While I savored the feel of his lips against mine, it had to be for the last time.

"I honestly thought I never had a chance," I said when we parted. "Especially when you said you had feelings for someone else."

"I never said I had feelings for someone *else*," he said. "I said I was interested in someone, and it was complicated. Which it is. Because we live together, and because I thought you'd never be interested in an old man like me."

"You're not old," I said. "Age isn't the issue. But it *is* complicated. And not just because we're living together. Gwen's never going to forgive me. How am I supposed to tell my best friend I slept with her dad?"

Chapter 10

No one knows what's in your character handbook. Give peeks into your
character through your moves and in-game conversations.
—*The Haunted Place* Player Guide

Beneath his tan, Nathan's face went pale at my words. "I hadn't thought
about it that way."

"It's her wedding day! I have to eat breakfast with her and...oh, no.
What if she stops by to see you?" I lunged for my phone, dashing off a
quick text to confirm we'd all be meeting at the breakfast buffet. I couldn't
imagine what would happen if Gwen showed up to talk to her dad before
the wedding and found me in last night's dress and him wearing nothing
but a towel.

A towel that clung to his hips, making him look so, so tempting. I wanted
to lick every inch I could see, and those I couldn't. Silently, I cursed the
towel for covering part of the glorious flesh on display.

Focus, Holly.

It had been hard enough to keep my crush under control before I saw
him naked. Now I didn't know how I would ever temper the flames.

"You know, my daughter's been bugging me to start dating again for
years."

"Really? Because she's been telling me for ages to stay away from her
dad."

He grinned at me, flashing a dimple that would've made my knees weak
if I hadn't already been sitting. "For how long?"

My face grew warm. I looked at my fingers, mumbling. "It's possible
I've had a crush on you for a really, really long time. Like, years. But in

my defense, I mean, you're Patrick Dempsey hot. And you're not that much older than me."

He laughed, taking my hands in his. "Hey, relax. You're preaching to the choir. I like you, Holly. We're both consenting adults. We didn't do anything wrong."

Technically, I couldn't argue that. Both adults, both unattached. And yet...somehow, I doubted Gwen would see it that way. "It feels wrong."

"We were both drunk, but I'm not sorry. I've been wanting to be with you for a while. I just figured you thought of me as Gwen's old dad, and if I told you how I felt, you'd get awkward and stop being my friend."

When I glanced into his eyes, saw the earnestness written there, I was lost. "I've been feeling awkward because I kept having all these feelings for you, and I figured you'd never reciprocate. I don't care that you're Gwen's dad if you don't.

"I like you. You're smart, you like games, and you're kind. You're comfortable with who you are. That's incredibly sexy. The guys I meet online mostly come across as jerks or obsessed with sex. Or worse, both. I've been on dates with guys who spent more time talking about how much their manicures cost than asking me a single question about myself. I like that you're not obsessed with impressing other people. I didn't realize it at the time, but Lucas was like that. Also, I know I said this already, but you're incredibly hot."

"So are you," he said, his eyes raking up and down my body in a way that made my heart flip-flop. "Especially in a dress I know is wrinkled from spending the night on my floor."

Once upon a time, I'd have turned my gaze to the floor at those words, arguing that no, I wasn't that pretty. With Lucas always telling me what to wear, how to do my makeup, and what to eat, he had made me question everything about myself. But Holly the Flirt was getting more comfortable in her own skin and going after what she wanted. Especially now that I knew my attraction wasn't one-sided. Maybe that Inner Diva class really did help me find my confidence.

Leaning forward, I kissed him. His lips were so soft. The kiss was tender, sweet, but passion hinted beneath the surface. It wouldn't have taken much to get him to remove the towel and join me under the covers if I wanted. I very, very much wanted. But I couldn't. Darn it. I almost forgot.

With regret, I pulled my lips from his. "I'm sorry."

"Don't be."

"It's just...how did we let this happen?"

"Sometimes, when you're drunk, it's easier to do things you've been afraid to do sober."

"I guess so," I said. "And it was absolutely amazing. I'm very sorry we can never, ever do this again."

"What are you talking about?"

It killed me to say the words, but he had to know the truth. "We can't be together. Last night has to be a one-time thing. It would destroy Gwen. Her best friend and her dad?"

He made a face. "When you say it like that, it makes me sound old. I prefer 'George Clooney-esque.'"

"George Clooney may be hot, but he's still pretty old," I pointed out. He winced. "I mean, compared to me and Gwen. Your daughter. Oh, hell. This is all coming out wrong. I'm sorry. You're more of a Patrick Dempsey. I never thought of you as old. And now I can't stop talking because I'm totally freaked out right now."

My thoughts and emotions swirled together until I didn't know where one ended and the next began. To calm myself, I jumped off the bed, pacing back and forth. Nathan perched on the edge, watching me. Part of me wanted to climb into his lap and kiss him and forget the rest of the world. Part of me wanted to pretend I'd forgotten how to speak English and run away. And all of me had to be coherent and intelligent and excited and not conflicted when I met my friends for breakfast in less than half an hour. I needed to leave if I didn't want to appear that I'd stumbled into the restaurant at the end of a Walk of Shame. Exactly what I'd be doing.

"I should go," I said, grabbing my purse and digging for my room key. "This was a mistake. I'm sorry."

"Then why did you kiss me a minute ago?"

"I wanted to make sure it wasn't a dream."

He stood, coming to meet me in the center of the room. "Look, we don't have to decide anything now. I like you. You like me—I know you do. We had a good time last night. We're on vacation. No one has to know. When we get home, we'll figure out the next step."

At his mention of "home," my heart stopped. In the hysteria of morning, I'd forgotten that I was still renting a room in Nathan's house. Gwen's old bedroom, to be precise. Sleeping in her old bed.

Now on top of everything else, I was going to have to find another place to live sooner than I'd planned. Every day staying with Nathan was one day closer to the end of my probation, one day closer to getting a job that used my MBA. Living there gave me time to save for a new place. But now? I couldn't continue sleeping so close to temptation, not after giving in once. I wouldn't be able to go to bed at night, knowing Nathan lay on the other side of the wall, wondering if he was thinking about me. Wondering what would happen if he threw open my door and joined me, or if I took off my clothes and crawled into bed with him.

I mean, sure, I'd wondered before, more than once. Nearly wore out the batteries in my vibrator wondering. But I never would have done anything. Until, apparently, the worst possible moment and the right amount of tequila.

"What's wrong?" he asked.

"My mind is swirling," I said. "There's so much to think about. You, me, Gwen. What happens now? Will it be too awkward to live together?"

"Everything will be fine. Calm down," he said. "One thing at a time. We'll figure this out. First, go shower. Meet your friends for breakfast. I'll see you at the wedding. We'll watch a woman we both love get married. Everything else, we worry about later. No need to start mentally checking apartment listings."

One thing at a time. I could manage that. Then I leaned in and hugged him, savoring the feel of his bare skin against my cheek. Inhaling as if I could imprint the missing memories from last night and save them forever. His arms came up around me, and I never wanted to leave.

Not trusting myself to say anything else, I finally pulled myself away and headed for the door. Maybe once I showered and woke up, once I got some food and coffee, things wouldn't seem so confusing.

* * * *

By the time I made it to breakfast, Shannon and Gwen sat at a table, Gwen with a diet soda (ew!) and Shannon having ordered coffee for me, tea for her. I sipped gratefully, then thanked her before turning to Gwen.

"Today's the big day. Congratulations!" I wrapped her in a huge hug, hoping she wouldn't realize I was overcompensating.

"Thank you! How are you? Really." Her eyes searched mine, and I stiffened, wondering what Shannon told her before I arrived.

I turned to shoot her a questioning look but now that I'd gotten my coffee, something about her appearance made me pause. Shannon generally looked like she stepped off the pages of an old-time magazine. Flowing, flowery vintage dresses, high heels that left her towering over the rest of us even more than her natural five-foot-eleven-inch frame, and red lipstick that popped against her pale skin and hair. Many women in tech preferred to blend, going to work in little to no makeup and the same jeans and geeky T-shirts as the guys. Shannon wore her dresses and lipstick like armor.

Never letting the guys forget who she was while kicking ass left and right. In several years of friendship, I'd never seen her without makeup.

Until now. She wore a scarf tied over her hair, which wasn't completely unusual, but the strands peeking out stuck out in all directions. Face completely clean, not a trace of makeup. Shadows under her eyes. That might seem normal to most people, especially considering we planned to get done up at the spa after breakfast, but Shannon once stopped to reapply lipstick in the middle of a 5k.

When I couldn't find her last night, I'd assumed she'd gone to bed. Now I remembered why they say not to make assumptions. I should've sent her a message, gone looking for her.

It was on the tip of my tongue to ask if *she* was okay, but she spoke first. "We were just talking about how it must be weird for you not to be the first of us to get married."

Oh, that. The excuse seemed perfect. I started to grasp at it, but didn't want Gwen to think I wasn't 100 percent on board with this wedding. I settled into my chair with a genuine smile. "Oh, not at all. I'm so glad I didn't marry Lucas. What a snake. I got over him ages ago."

"You keep saying that, but I can't help noticing that you haven't dated anyone since. It's been a long time," Gwen said.

Shannon shot me a questioning look, which I ignored. "I'm trying to date. The guys online are absolutely miserable."

"What about Marc?" Gwen asked. "You seemed pretty excited about your date with him."

"I was," I said, "and it was perfectly nice. But...that kiss."

"Yeah," Shannon said. "But you said yourself, first kisses can be awkward. It might get better."

"Maybe. Also, I sent him a sexy text last night and he never replied."

Gwen's eyes grew large. "You sent a sexy text? I'm so proud of you!"

"Don't be," I said. "I might have blown it. Like I said—no reply. And his phone says he read it."

"So maybe Marc's not the one," Shannon said. "And that's okay. No one else piques your interest? For a relationship, or even maybe just to have a good time?"

She obviously wanted me to spill the details of my night, which wasn't about to happen. Still, this might be a good opportunity to test the waters, see if Gwen was remotely open to the idea of me and Nathan. With an overly broad smile, I flipped my hair, trying to seem casual. "I don't know. Daddy McHotCakes looked pretty good at dinner last night."

Shannon's eyes widened, and I realized instantly my mistake. Now I'd have to throw her off the track.

Gwen shuddered and gagged, heaving over her empty plate. "Please. Are you trying to ruin my wedding day? And I don't believe for a second you can't find someone better to date than my dear old dad. Don't sell yourself short."

"She wouldn't be selling herself short," Shannon said. "He's a good-looking guy. And he's still young."

Gwen glanced from one of us to the other, suddenly serious. "What's going on? You can't be serious. That's one of the golden rules of friendship. You don't hit on your friends' dads."

"I think that's exes and brothers," Shannon said, still keeping her tone light.

"Well, if it's not a rule, it should be," Gwen said. "Come on. You're freaking me out. That's so messed up."

My face flamed, but I forced myself to keep my tone light. "Calm down, sweetie. I was kidding. Just trying to change the subject. I didn't mean to upset you. Maybe Marc will text back today."

"I hope so," she said.

"Thanks. We'll see. I like him, but I want someone who gets me excited."

So excited, I betrayed my best friend. First last night, then again this morning with that soul-searing kiss. I closed my eyes against the memory, but both friends still watched when I opened them. Gwen seemed slightly mollified by my backpedaling, but I suspected Shannon wasn't fooled.

"Sorry," I said. "Maybe all the wedding stuff is getting to me, after all. But I'm here to support you, whatever you need. As soon as I get some food."

Thank goodness for buffets, offering the perfect excuse to jump up and leave the table when the conversation got awkward. Gwen went straight for the omelet station, but Shannon followed me to the array of baked goods.

"Okay, spill," she said. "What was that?"

"What was what?"

"Why didn't you tell Gwen you hooked up last night?"

"It was nothing. A total stranger. I'll never see him again."

"Who cares? Gwen would still appreciate the story." She squinted, pulling her glasses down on her nose as if that would help at all. "Was it a girl? You know we won't care."

I rolled my eyes at her before grabbing a muffin. "No. That I would tell you. This was nothing. Some guy named Juan. He's flying home to Texas today."

"Mmm-hmmm." She didn't believe me, but she wasn't going to push for more information now. Shannon was the most sensitive of the three of us, and the last thing she'd do was make Gwen's wedding breakfast about me.

After I filled my plate and returned to the table, she followed quietly. Gwen showed up a moment later with an egg-white omelet roughly the size of Texas. We dug into our food.

Thankfully, my hangovers never lasted long. The combination of painkillers and greasy breakfast food made me feel normal enough to fulfill my maid of honor duties. The rest of the morning got lost in a blur of preparations, until the next thing I knew, I stood back in my room. Shannon needed to pick up the flowers before the ceremony, so I stayed out of her way, listlessly deleting dating app messages until she left. None of these guys did anything for me.

Marc had sent me a message after I turned my phone off last night, letting me know he couldn't wait for our next date. Nothing about the dirty text. Just seeing his name made me want to throw up, before even reading the message. Poor Marc. We were supposed to get dinner next week. Until about ten hours ago, I'd looked forward to seeing him again. Now I didn't know what to do. Should I cancel? Should I go, knowing that Nathan and I had no future? No idea. Even if he wanted to keep seeing me, did he want to be exclusive? I didn't want to see anyone else, but he might. I didn't have time to figure it out, so I put my phone away, wondering how I went from crying into inedible leftovers over my lack of dating prospects to trying to figure out which awesome guy to choose.

Going to the closet, I pulled out my bridesmaid dress. Short and gauzy, the blue dress was perfect for a beach wedding. And theoretically, I might wear it again. Shannon could help me find the right wrap when we got home.

Slipping it off the hanger, I undid the zipper and stepped into the dress before moving back to view my reflection. The sweetheart neckline accentuated my breasts nicely, showing a hint of cleavage. My long, naturally brown legs looked great. Nathan would…no. Full stop. I couldn't let those thoughts in.

He was so nice, so sincere, so down-to-earth. We both liked games, tabletop and video. We got along, sharing many long, easy conversations while he'd been laid up with his broken leg. When I found out I'd have to testify at my ex-fiancé's trial, Nathan was the one who talked me through my panic. Sure, I'd had a crush on him since we met, back when I dubbed him "Daddy McHotCakes." But that had largely been a joke. Now my feelings ran deeper. This thing between us wasn't purely physical. I cared about him.

The nickname now made me shudder. I didn't want to think of Nathan as a father figure, hot or not. In fact, I didn't. Never really had. My own parents were in their late sixties, waiting to have kids until they were well-established. At forty-three, Nathan had much more in common with me than my parents' generation. Heck, Gwen's grandmother would be about my dad's age if she were alive.

With a sigh, I finally admitted to myself that I didn't want my night with Nathan to be a one-time mistake. More than anything, I wished he was some guy I'd met in a bar, hit it off with, gone on a date with. I wouldn't have thought twice about going out with him under any other circumstances. But he was Gwen's dad, and nothing would change that. She hated the idea of us being together. Even if I'd been unclear before, her reaction at breakfast said volumes. Telling her what happened, or asking for permission, would ruin her wedding day. Not to mention our friendship.

My phone dinged a reminder to leave for the ceremony. I dragged my thoughts away from the mess my life had unexpectedly become and turned back to the mirror. Dress, check. Hair, check. Makeup, check.

White wedge-heeled sandals completed the look. These I'd definitely wear again, having taken them from my closet. Thankfully, Gwen didn't see the point in making us buy shoes to stand in the sand for twenty minutes.

Nothing to do now but push Nathan out of my mind, think about how happy Gwen and Cody were going to be together, and head down to the beach. I could do it. Everyone would be waiting. I didn't want to be the reason the wedding started late.

Don't think about him. Don't think about him.

An excellent plan, foiled as soon as I walked out of my room. There, leaning against the railing, I found Nathan.

Chapter 11

Players shouldn't lie to their fellow explorers, but not all situations call
for absolute truth. Keep your character's goals in mind. You want that
bonus at the end of the game.

—*The Haunted Place* Player Guide

My stomach flip-flopped at the sight of Nathan waiting for me. As
always, I couldn't stop the smile from spreading across my face when he
appeared. But now I recognized the same expression mirrored on his face.
He'd always been polite and friendly, greeted me fondly. But last night,
things between us shifted. This look was more than polite or friendly.
This look made me want to drag him into my room for a few minutes
before the wedding.

I glanced up and down the empty breezeway leading to the stairs.
"What are you doing here? Don't you have father-of-the-bride duties to
be fulfilling?"

He shrugged innocently. "Gwen wanted someone to check on the
bridesmaids, make sure they made it on time. They moved the ceremony
a bit farther down the beach, and she didn't want you to get lost."

Uh-huh. Sounded plausible. "How far?"

He grinned and stepped toward me. "Twenty, thirty feet. A very long
walk on the sand."

"Excruciating. I never would have found it on my own." Like a magnet
pulled me, I stepped closer. Our faces were only inches apart.

"You look beautiful," he whispered.

"Thank you," I whispered back. "We shouldn't be doing this."

"I know. But I can't seem to help myself."

"Me, neither." Leaning in, I kissed him lightly. Second time that morning. Something I never would have fathomed doing two days ago. All this time, I'd been ignoring my instincts, so sure that following my heart would lead to disaster.

Something about Mexico made me more willing to trust my gut. Or maybe I'd just found more confidence. I should send Yasmine from the Inner Diva class a thank-you card.

Whatever caused my change, Nathan must've liked it, because he kissed me back, hands resting on my waist. After a moment, he pulled away. "Don't get me too excited. I can't walk down the aisle with an erection."

Laughing, I brushed against him lightly before pulling back. "That would make quite the wedding photo. Really, why are you here?"

"Really, they sent me to check on the bridesmaids. I ran into Shannon on the walk over, so here I am, waiting for you." He offered me his arm. "I promise, I had every intention of respecting your wishes when you left this morning. We both need time to think."

Nothing to think about, really. I'd met the man of my dreams, fallen for him, had a drunken hookup—and would now spend the rest of my life suppressing my feelings to avoid upsetting my best friend. Not the best plan, but it was the only one I'd come up with.

I sighed wistfully. "I tried to feel Gwen out subtly over breakfast and she nearly went ballistic. I don't think we'll be braiding each other's hair and talking about this any time soon."

"What happened, happened," he said. "We're both adults. I normally don't advocate lying to my daughter, but our relationship is none of her business. We can ignore our feelings if that's what you want. But we've been dancing around each other for months now. It was inevitable that something would happen. We need to talk more later. But for now, I'm going to walk you to the wedding."

"Not so fast." I wiped a spot of lipstick off his mouth and tilted my head at him. "How's my makeup?"

"You might want to reapply when we get there."

"That bad? Hold on, I'll do it now."

"No, it's fine now. But I might not be able to resist kissing it off on the way over. It's a long walk."

I grinned and leaned in again. My cheek brushed his, and his breath caught. His lips parted, but I stopped, my mouth inches above his. "Don't you dare."

He laughed and reached for me, but I jumped back. "Okay, fine. After?"

Yes. Oh, hell yes. The wrongness only made me want him more. Even though I shouldn't. "Didn't you just say you could pretend nothing happened?"

"If that's what you want, but I'm not sure it is. You've kissed me twice this morning." He started toward the stairs, and I followed, catching up easily despite the heeled sandals.

He knew me too well. Pretending nothing happened wasn't what I wanted at all. I wanted to drag him back into my room, beg him to throw me up against the wall, and be a little late for the wedding. Or a lot late. He could see it in my eyes. I'd spent so long denying my attraction, now that I'd given in, I wanted to indulge as much as possible.

But I'd find a way to suppress my feelings. "We can talk after the wedding. I...honestly, I don't know. Is this some vacation fling? If so, shouldn't we wait until we get home to cut it off?"

He grinned at me. "What happens in Mexico stays in Mexico. We've got another night here before you leave."

"That sounds amazing. But what would Gwen say?"

"Gwen is getting married, then starting her honeymoon. She's not thinking about us."

"An excellent point," I said.

"Has it ever occurred to you that Gwen might be excited for us? Two people she loves, finding happiness together?"

I literally had not considered that possibility. Not when she'd made so many comments about how gross she found my interest. "Is that how she'll see it? Not a drunken, stupid fling that's going to make game nights awkward forever? Or a total betrayal?"

He remained silent as the two of us navigated the stairs down to the main level. The elevator would have been easier in my shoes and given us more privacy. Unfortunately, in grad school, the power once went out seconds after I'd left an elevator. It hadn't come back on for several hours. If I'd hesitated at all, I'd have been trapped. I no longer trusted the metal death boxes, no matter what was on my feet.

Knowing this, Nathan showed no hesitation before turning toward the stairs to walk the four flights down. One of the many things to love about him.

Er...like. Appreciate. Notice. *Not* love.

Other people were coming up, and even though we didn't know any of them, this conversation demanded waiting until no one else stood within earshot. At the end of the path waited a golf cart to transport us to the ceremony. Nathan put out a hand to help me in, but I paused.

"How much time do we have?"

"About half an hour. Why?"

"I'd rather walk."

"In those shoes?"

Bending down, I pulled them off. "I can put them on when we get there. But I'd like more time to finish our conversation."

"No problem." He handed the driver a five, thanked him in Spanish, and waved him on his way.

We walked down the tree-lined path toward the water. The beauty of the place overwhelmed me, from the tropical flowers in a variety of colors you'd never see in Boston to the wildlife running around among the bushes, to the tranquility of the path, to the man walking beside me. A beautiful, romantic walk that I intended to enjoy while I could.

The journey ended all too soon. Before I knew it, the beach came into view, followed by the pavilion and the cabana where Gwen was getting ready for the ceremony.

My friend waited in the bride's room upstairs. In her dress and makeup, she looked even more radiant than at breakfast. Her long red locks wound around her head in two pinned French braids, a more elegant version of her usual hairstyle. She wore a simple white gown, strapless and form-fitting. The fabric flared out around her feet, touching the sand. In a nod to a private joke between her and Cody, she carried a bundle of carrots rather than a traditional bouquet. She looked perfect.

Even when Lucas and I were at our best, I never glowed the way Gwen did. I air-kissed her cheek, careful not to leave lipstick on her face.

"There you are! Everything okay?"

Her question threw me off-guard. Why would she ask that? Did something seem weird about me walking with her dad? What did she know? My guilt was making me paranoid. It wasn't weird to ask your best friend how she was feeling. "Yeah, fine. Why?"

She shrugged. "You were late to breakfast. You took a long time answering texts this morning, and now you look…I don't know. Like something's bothering you."

I'm a terrible liar, so I deflected. I would never make it as a spy. How did anyone live like this? "You're not supposed to worry about me. It's your wedding day."

"Yes, and as the bride, I decree that my friends not hide their emotions to protect me."

God, I was a horrible friend. She thought I was lying to avoid ruining her big day. Which, okay, sort of, but it was mostly about how she'd hate me if she knew the truth. Still, my big (and amazing) lapse in judgment wasn't the only thing on my mind.

I racked my brain to come up with a good story, but Shannon spoke first. "Tyler kissed me last night."

My mouth dropped open. If it was a lie, it was perfect. But considering the way Shannon looked when I sat down at breakfast, I suspected she told the truth. Which meant I wanted the deets, probably even more than Gwen.

She immediately swung around to face Shannon, temporarily forgetting about me. "O.M.G. What did you do?"

Shannon's face turned beet red. "I pushed him away. It was so awkward."

"I'm sorry," I said. "I know you didn't want to hurt his feelings."

"It's so hard to explain. I like him as a friend, absolutely. But I don't understand what it's like to be attracted to someone without an emotional connection. We've been playing games together for the past year, but I still don't know him that well. I'm no more attracted to him than to Gwen's bouquet of carrots."

"What did he say?" I asked.

"He seemed to understand. But his ego was definitely bruised."

"It *is* a sexy bouquet," Gwen said, trying to break the tension. "But we get it. You don't have to explain yourself to us."

"And that is why I love you guys." Shannon extended her arms. We joined her in a group hug.

The wedding planner appeared at the door, signaling that everyone was ready to start. Shannon and I trailed down the stairs to make sure Cody couldn't see the bottom. Gwen waited at the landing until it was time to make her appearance. When we confirmed that her groom stood at the front of the aisle, we waved her forward and went to find our places.

Nathan stood near the door, sipping a drink with an umbrella in it. Oh, how I could use a drink. Shannon stopped to say hello, but I worried she'd notice how much talking to him flustered me and guess why. Stepping into my sandals, I padded down to the sand to talk to the other guests.

The wedding planner handed me my bouquet and reminded me that Tyler would walk down the aisle with me. Great. Less awkward for everyone if he didn't have to walk with Shannon.

Downstairs, Cody waited near the archway set up in front of the rows of chairs, chatting with his parents. As expected, Gwen's mother was nowhere to be seen. Too bad. I made a mental note to call Mamá when I got home and thank her for always being there for me. I couldn't fathom getting married without her in the audience.

The two groomsmen stood near the door, chatting. Each of them held a drink, so I wandered over to find out where they got them and whether I had time to score my own. It might be early for alcohol, but day drinking on vacation didn't count, right? Especially at a wedding. Something needed to calm my nerves before I snapped.

"Holly? You're here? Who's manning the store?" John's tone gave away the joke.

"Well, I would've guessed your wife, but she seems to have come with us. Hopefully, the games are okay on their own."

"It's so hard to find good help these days." He gave a mock sigh. "Tyler, you looking for a career change?"

He chuckled. "If you and Carla want to pay me an accountant's salary to man the register, let me know."

John's wife sat in the audience with the couple's two children. At the sound of her name, she turned and beamed at her husband, waving. My chest tightened at the tenderness on her face. All I wanted was for someone to look at me like that someday. Someone who wouldn't have to be a vacation secret, whom I could date in public and be with full-time.

Thankfully, the music started, forcing me to focus on why I'd come to Mexico in the first place. Cody stood at attention in his place, near an archway facing glittering white sands and the endless expanse of blue-green ocean. It looked like a postcard.

The guests turned to watch everyone walk in. Tyler offered me his arm. We moved slowly, in that wedding walk where it takes about twenty minutes to go five feet.

"How are you feeling?" he asked me as we started our snail-like movement.

"Okay, why?"

"You seemed to be having a great time last night."

Oh, no. Did he see something?

Trying not to show a reaction, I said, "Well, we are on vacation, after all. What better time to cut loose?"

"Touché. I've just never seen you drink that much. I wanted to make sure there isn't something bothering you."

This might have been the longest conversation Tyler and I ever had that wasn't about a game. I hadn't expected him to be so perceptive. At the same time, I couldn't go into all the things that bothered me. "Just trying to get out of my shell. Holly the Flirt is a lot more interesting than Holly the Stick in the Mud. I spent so long with my ex, and then getting over him. I'm spreading my wings a little."

He nodded. "I get it. Still, if you want to talk, I'm here."

Something in his tone made me wonder if *he* wanted to talk about things. Specifically, if he wanted to talk about the blue-eyed woman walking down the aisle behind us on John's arm. But there was no time to ask. We reached the end of the aisle and went to our places on opposite sides. A moment later, Shannon moved to stand behind me, and the music changed. Gwen appeared at the end of the aisle, beaming radiantly.

Typically at a wedding, the bride is the primary focal point. But I couldn't take my eyes off Nathan. He beamed as they walked, looking happier than I'd ever seen him. Since this was a beach wedding, he wore khaki pants and a dark blue shirt. Even though it wasn't a tux, formalwear couldn't possibly have made him look better. The ocean breeze tousled his hair, and all I wanted was to run my fingers through those dark locks. While kissing him.

I'd been to a lot of weddings, but never one as torturous as this one.

They chatted easily as they walked down the aisle. At one point, Gwen threw her head back and laughed, the first time my attention went to her instead of him. She looked stunning, even more so when she beamed at Cody. But despite my best efforts, my gaze went repeatedly to her left.

To my surprise, Nathan's eyes locked with mine. He smiled as if he read my thoughts. Maybe he did. Maybe he wanted to sink his fingers into my hair and rip my clothes off as badly as I wanted to remove his.

One night hadn't been nearly enough. I needed more time with him.

Just one more night. Tomorrow, I'd head home, and he was staying behind for a few days. With some distance between us, I could start thinking rationally again.

But first, I wanted to kiss those soft, sensual lips. I wanted to run my fingers over his chest, his arms, everywhere. I wanted to feel his lips in places I'd only dreamed about until last night. And I wanted it to happen *soon*.

Shannon poked me. "Hey, you're up."

What? I wasn't getting married. Then I realized that everyone was staring at me. Not just the congregation. The entire wedding had stopped. Gwen, Cody, the officiant.

"Did you forget the ring?" Gwen asked quietly.

"Oh! Yes! I mean, no." Everyone laughed as I fumbled with the base of my bouquet. As co–maids of honor, Shannon held Gwen's bouquet while I kept Cody's wedding ring. "I'm sorry, I'm just so happy for you."

"What a lovely sentiment," the officiant said. "Gwen, take this ring and repeat after me."

As I adjusted my own bouquet (a simple arrangement of native flowers, not carrots), my eyes met Nathan's. Without thinking, I turned toward him, and my face grew warm. His cheeks were flushed, his lips parted. He knew exactly why I was so distracted, exactly what thoughts kept me from paying attention to my duties. Unless I misread the look in his eyes, he was every bit as excited about tonight as I was.

The wedding and reception couldn't end fast enough.

The remaining vows, the kiss, the pronouncement all passed in a blur. I cheered with the rest of the crowd when Gwen and Cody walked back down the aisle, only a beat behind the others. On my way out, once again holding Tyler's arm, Shannon shot me a curious look, but I merely smiled in return. There wasn't anything to say. If she knew my plan, she'd talk me out of it. Even if I told her what had already happened, which I couldn't.

Not wanting to get talked out of a course of action guaranteed to shatter my heart, I skirted the edges of the reception, leaving Shannon to update John on the progress we'd made on *The Haunted Place*. He was still upset about having to quit our play-test group at the last minute, so she let him run a second campaign after she made some tweaks based on our feedback. They'd already played the first game.

Nathan mingled with Cody's family, getting to know the in-laws. Knowing my emotions were written all over my face, I avoided him too. I'd love to drag Nathan onto the dance floor and press my body against his in a socially acceptable manner, but this wasn't the time or the place to show how vividly I remembered every scene from *Dirty Dancing.* Instead I found Tyler, got us drinks, and sat down to listen to him pour his heart out about Shannon.

Poor guy. I felt for him. In a society obsessed with sex, people rarely talked about or acknowledged demisexuality. He had trouble wrapping his head around not feeling sexual attraction for strangers. I wished there was a way to make him feel better, but sharing my own problems seemed like a recipe for disaster. Instead, I let him talk.

About halfway through the reception, I went in search of a bathroom in the cabana where we'd gotten ready. The door to the downstairs bathroom was locked, so I went up the stairs, pretty sure there had been a second one where Gwen got dressed.

After doing my thing, I was about to return to the party when a breeze touched my cheeks. The door at the end of the hall swayed back and forth. I went to close it before realizing someone stood on the balcony, looking out over the beach.

My eyes couldn't make out much in the dim light, but something in the way he stood told me who it was. The same thing told me to turn and run. But I couldn't. Or didn't want to do. Same difference.

"Hey," I said softly, leaning on the railing beside Nathan. My hand brushed against his. "Beautiful ceremony."

"Yeah, it was." His voice was low, sending a thrill through me. "I couldn't take my eyes off you."

"Me neither," I admitted.

Below us, the reception remained in full swing. Gwen and Cody danced up a storm, surrounded by family and friends. The party showed no signs of slowing. I wondered if anyone would miss me if I vanished into the shadows and went back to my room. Taking Nathan with me. Now that the father-daughter dance was over, no one had reason to look for him.

Maybe I'd had too much to drink. Maybe I hadn't drunk enough, because I didn't have the courage to say the things I wanted. The possibilities made me shiver.

"Cold?" Nathan asked.

I wasn't, but I took the opportunity to nestle against him. He put his arm around me, enveloping me with his warmth. As I leaned against him, he put his face against my hair and breathed deeply, as if trying to imprint my scent. A low moan escaped me.

"Someone might see us." As protests went, it was weak. Especially since my traitorous body snuggled further into him as I spoke.

"They're backlit," he said. "No one would see a thing up here if they looked up."

"But what if they did?"

"What if they did?" He shifted, coming to stand fully behind me, nuzzling my neck.

A thrill went through me. I'd never been much for exhibitionism, but... my heart pounded at his suggestion. Or what I hoped he was suggesting. Rotating my hips, I pressed back against him, bringing our bodies flush. His breath caught, and one hand moved from the railing down my side, sending sparks of desire through me.

"We...shouldn't...be doing...this." Another half-hearted protest as his lips lingered on my neck. "Mmmm."

"I know. It's wrong." His voice suggested otherwise.

"Very wrong." I gasped as he moved his hand higher. "Don't stop."

"We only have one night. No sense in wasting the few hours we have left."

"Definitely not. We deserve to fully enjoy Mexico."

His lips found my ear. I couldn't breathe. I couldn't speak. All I could do was turn my head, an inch at a time, until my lips found his. It seemed to take eons. I moaned softly; he sighed into my mouth. "Do you have... anything?"

Great, Holly. I was twenty-eight years old, and I still couldn't say "condom" out loud. Thankfully, he knew what I meant. He nodded. One hand lifted the back of my skirt. "Keep watching the party."

I rocked back against him, hands gripping the railing. If the lights came on, if either of us made a sound at the wrong moment, we'd be caught. But for now, the music drowned out the soft noises that escaped me. I couldn't have stopped them if my life depended on it. When he moved against me, I didn't care if the whole world watched. All that mattered was this one day, because we might not get more.

Chapter 12

The Place you've stumbled into is no ordinary house. Be prepared.
Anything could happen next. Buckle up, hold onto your hats…it's going
to be a bumpy ride.

—*The Haunted Place* Player Guide

Two days later, I looked up from the register at Game On! to find Shannon
hovering near an endcap. Seeing her at the store wasn't unusual, but she
fidgeted and chewed her lower lip as if something bothered her. Quickly,
I finished ringing up my customer so I could go to her.

"Hey," I said. "What's wrong? Is Nana okay?"

"She's fine, thanks." At her words, the tension eased from my shoulders.
"I know about you and Nathan."

My mind raced for a believable half-truth. "You mean, you know I've
had a crush on him for ages and can't act on it because Gwen would freak?
I'm working on it, I swear."

"No. That's not what I mean at all. You know what I mean." She gave
me a long, piercing look before taking a deep breath. "Just like I know
that this crush isn't as one-sided as you pretend. I always suspected he had
some interest, but you were so sure nothing would happen. And I really
didn't think either of you would act on your feelings."

All the oxygen rushed from the room. My mouth fell open. A thousand
thoughts flashed across my mind, including the most obvious—*DENY IT,
HOLLY!*—but something in the way she spoke told me I wouldn't get very
far. Still, I tried to play it cool. "You know…?"

Tried and failed. Cool wasn't my strong suit.

"I see the wheels turning, and I know you're looking for a way out of this, so I'm going to save you some trouble. *I saw you and Nathan.* Together, in Mexico. After Gwen and Cody's wedding. Or more accurately, during the reception."

Oh, no. Just when I thought I couldn't be any more embarrassed. She'd seen us together? I prayed for zombies to appear and attack me, but unfortunately life isn't a board game.

A sound escaped me. It didn't so much resemble a word. "W-h-ow-y???"

Luckily, Shannon got what I meant. "I wanted to take pictures of everyone. I'd left my phone in the cabana before the ceremony, so I went to get it. Then I heard something. Don't worry, I didn't stay and watch. I left as soon as it became clear that the two of you were having…a private moment."

"Thanks," I mumbled. If my cheeks burned any more, I'd catch fire.

She sighed, smoothing the already perfect lines of her dress. "I hope you know what you're doing."

"I'm not doing anything," I blurted out. "I mean, I don't know. We said it would just be a vacation thing, something we'd put behind us and move on. If we can."

"Is that what you want?"

"No," I said automatically. "I mean, I don't think so. I don't know. It's going to be so awkward when he gets back, especially since we're roommates."

"What are you going to do?"

I shrugged. "I've got a date planned with Marc. He's still texting me, and I don't want to end things with him if Nathan and I don't like each other in Boston."

"Based on what I've seen over the years, that seems unlikely. But I get your point. And don't worry, I won't tell Gwen."

"Thank you," I said, feeling a thousand pounds lighter. "I'm sorry to put you in this position. Do you think anyone else saw us? Tyler?"

"He may have noticed you both went missing at the reception, but he'd never say anything. He's pretty chill."

"Yeah, I got that impression."

Something in her expression shifted. "Did he say anything about me?"

The change in subject surprised me, but I was glad to be talking about anything other than me and Nathan. "He didn't tell me about the kiss, if that's what you're wondering. Just made some comments about falling for the wrong person, told me he understood how it felt, and that he was around if I wanted to talk. We chatted a bit during the reception. Some friendly bonding."

"I feel so bad," she said. "I wish I could flip a switch and be attracted to him."

"But you can't. We both know you can't, and so does he. He'll move on. It's okay."

"Thanks." She flashed me a smile. "Anyway, back to the main topic here. Do you know what you're doing with Nathan?"

"Not even a little bit," I confessed. "I didn't plan for anything to happen. I've just…. I've had a crush on him for so long, and he was there, and I was there, and everyone was drinking. The first time, I thought I was dreaming."

"It happened *more than once?*" She exhaled slowly, then nodded. "Jesus. The guy at the resort. I should've known. I can't believe I didn't make that connection. Here I just thought you'd been sad after the wedding, thinking about Lucas, he comforted you, and it turned into a little kissing. It never occurred to me…What a dummy I am."

When she said "a little kissing," a huge wave of relief hit me. That's all she thought it was. The realization that my best friend hadn't seen me having sex on the balcony with my other best friend's father during said second best friend's wedding…a ten-thousand-pound weight lifted off my shoulders.

"You're not dumb. I lied. And I'm sorry I couldn't tell you the truth," I said.

"Yeah, I see why you think that. I'm not Gwen, though. I get it."

"You do?"

"Sure. You've had a crush on Nathan for ages. He looks similar to guys generally considered to be conventionally attractive. He's not that much older than us. My grandpa was twenty years older than Nana, and no one blinked an eye. Plus, it's not like you're a teenager. You're almost thirty. You're a grown woman. Fully capable of making your own decisions."

I hadn't realized how badly I wanted Shannon's approval until she hugged me. "Thank you."

"Don't thank me yet. I mean, I get it, but…Gwen won't."

The hope slowly growing in the pit of my stomach deflated. "No, she won't. I can never tell her."

"What if it works out? The two of you are going to sneak around forever?"

"I don't know," I said miserably. "It was just that one weekend. I haven't spoken to him since I got back. My plan was to avoid him, which I realize is a terrible idea, but it'll be too weird to see him every day. Which reminds me…Can I stay with you for a few days?"

"You're always welcome on my couch. If you think it'll help, you can absolutely stay."

"I have no idea what will make things better. Time and space can't hurt, though."

She shook her head. "I wish I knew what to tell you. You look so happy when you're around him. But…"

There was nothing left to say. That "but" hung in the air long after Shannon gave me a hug and left the store. It followed me as I assisted my remaining customers. It echoed each time my boots slapped the pavement on my way home, no matter how fast I walked. *But…but…but. But but but. Butbutbut.* I liked Nathan. He liked me. Gwen would never understand. We both loved Gwen; neither of us wanted to hurt her. We didn't want to hurt each other, either. Or ourselves.

No matter how many times I went around, even having all the pieces of the puzzle, I couldn't come up with any way to put them together so everyone would be happy.

* * * *

The next day, I'd scheduled a date with Marc after work. After hooking up with Nathan, I had mixed feelings. My first date with Marc went well enough, and I liked texting back and forth. He probably wouldn't love knowing that I spent the weekend with another man, but I didn't have to tell him; we weren't a couple. Maybe I just needed time to warm up to Marc. After all, I'd known Nathan for years before anything happened. It took time for me to trust him enough to open up and make myself vulnerable again. Last weekend didn't have to mean anything; it was what I needed to remind myself that not all guys were creeps like my ex.

Besides, I owed it to Marc to give him a chance. He'd sparked this whole "rebuilding my confidence" journey. He didn't insult me or send a dick pic within minutes of initiating contact. He wasn't my best friend's father or otherwise off-limits. On top of that, Marc seemed sweet. The idea that he made up gaming questions all this time while gathering up the courage to ask me out tugged at my heartstrings. He was also cute, interested in the same things as me, age-appropriate, and not likely to send any of my friends into a rage if we became a couple. All things I *should* want in a relationship.

Still debating the pros and cons, I got ready for our date. Marc refused to tell me where we were going, but said to wear comfortable clothes I could move in. Boston wasn't the place for mini-golf in the dead of winter, but maybe he wanted to take me bowling? Dancing? Either way, I took care with my makeup since my clothes were so casual.

When I emerged from the employee restroom, Marc waited near the front door. Like half the people in the area, he wore jeans peeking out from beneath a long black coat, black hat, and black gloves. He spotted me at the same moment I noticed him, and a smile split his face in two.

"Hey," he said, leaning forward to kiss me softly.

I smiled broadly. "Hey. It's good to see you again."

"You, too. You look nice."

"Thanks."

"How was Mexico?" he asked.

"Wonderful!" The word jumped out before I thought to censor myself. But it was true. Maybe I couldn't share the certain private details, but we could still chat about the rest of the trip. All the way to our destination, I told tales of the food, the beach, the scenery.

Before I knew it, Marc drew to a halt, putting one hand on my elbow to catch my attention. A gasp escaped me when I realized where we stood. A couple of years ago, a huge escape room warehouse opened up a few miles outside Boston. My friends and I came out when it first opened, but life got in the way and it had been a while since we'd been back. The games, or "quests" as they were called here, changed regularly. This would be a new experience.

"Oh my goodness! This is amazing," I said.

"There's more." Marc pointed to a sign on the door. *Closed for Private Event.*

"You rented out the entire facility?" Most quests took only a few minutes to either pass or fail but the more difficult ones could take hours to beat. Questers paid by the hour, so depending on how crowded it was and how long you stayed, most people finished anywhere from one to about half a dozen quests in a visit. But in an empty facility? I squealed and clapped at the thought.

"Not exactly," he said. "I'm friends with the owners. They're letting us use the place for exactly one hour tonight, but I owe them big."

"Your firstborn?"

"Something like that. You ready?"

"Is the pope Catholic?"

The door swung open to reveal Shannon standing inside, dressed not in her ordinary retro-style dresses but in a pair of yoga pants, a sports bra, and a tank top. After greeting her, I turned to Marc. "You...invited my friend on our date?"

"There's a three-person minimum for most quests," Marc reminded me. "Cody gave me Shannon's number."

"You know Cody?"

"All local gamers know Cody," Shannon pointed out.

That was true, although it made me wonder why I hadn't met Marc earlier. He smiled shyly. "Gwen was the one who suggested I visit Game On! while you were working."

"Of course she was."

"I hope you're not mad."

I considered that for a moment. Gwen's meddling didn't surprise me. Her heart was in the right place. Besides, she'd involved herself in my love life—and this relationship—for weeks. It didn't make any sense to get upset now.

"No, it's fine. It's nice to know she cares," I said.

"A lot of people care about you," Marc said. "You're very lucky."

"And so am I," Shannon cut in. "Because even though I feel like the world's most awkward third wheel, I'm glad to share this touching moment with you."

My face grew warm. Poor Shannon. "Sorry."

"I'm teasing," she said. "Just reminding you both I'm here. And we only have this place for an hour, so let's get started!"

Marc agreed, and I clapped my hands together in excitement. I couldn't wait to see how many rooms we beat. What a perfect, thoughtful date. Marc really was the right guy for me.

Chapter 13

While this game is cooperative, remember that each player has their own
secret goals. Determine carefully who you can trust. Ultimately, you're
on your own in there.
—*The Haunted Place* Player Guide

In the year and a half or so since Lucas and I broke up, I'd been
interviewed by police, the prosecutor, three additional lawyers, and one
local news station. I'd hired my own lawyer before reaching an immunity
agreement with the assistant US attorney. Which meant I'd been over and
over what happened. I could recite the events in my sleep.

The two of us met in high school. We started dating our sophomore
year after being paired up in a computer science project. We both loved
computers, and at fifteen, any mutual interest combined with attraction was
enough. For weeks, we made out in the computer lab after school before
we went on a real date. We stayed together through college and graduate
school. I majored in computer programming; he majored in business and
accounting. I loved him. We'd planned to get married. We started a venture
capital company together: I maintained the website and the systems, plus
did some customer support. He found investors and managed the financial
side. I trusted him to do his share of the work and never looked at the books.

Apparently, I should've paid attention to the numbers, because he also
laundered more than half a million dollars, including our entire shared
savings account and an inheritance from my grandparents. He turned
our business into a pyramid scheme, using funds from new "investors"
to pay dividends to the old ones. When the government found out, they
were less than pleased, to say the least. They weren't too happy with me,

and I wasn't too happy with Lucas. Even if I hadn't found out he'd been cheating on me around the same time, my decision came easily: I'd rolled over on him in a heartbeat. He'd betrayed my trust in more ways than one and no longer deserved my loyalty.

The prosecutor didn't have to say much more than "immunity" to get me to spill everything. Unfortunately, the terms of my plea agreement prohibited me from working in tech for a year and a half. My lawyer tried and tried, but they wouldn't budge, and I wasn't willing to risk going to jail. Thankfully, I liked working at the store, even though it didn't use my very expensive degree. In another few months, I'd be free to move on. It would be nice to stand on my own two feet again. I had already started scouring employment sites, reaching out to recruiters, and started practicing how to explain the eighteen-month gap on my résumé. Spiritual journey?

According to Terri, Lucas and his lawyer planned to conduct a fishing expedition, where they sought as much information as possible, in case any of it was useful. She suspected they hoped to blame me for everything and discredit me as a witness. Nothing could get me in trouble legally at this point, thanks to my immunity, but if the jury thought I'd masterminded everything, my ex might get off scot-free.

I had zero intention of letting that happen. The day of the deposition, my alarm went off at six o'clock in the morning. I'd been reviewing emails from Terri and texting her ever since. They had nothing. They couldn't faze me. This deposition was simply Lucas trying to exert control over me now that I'd wriggled out from under his thumb. Old Holly might have crumbled under the pressure, but Holly the Flirt and her newfound inner diva refused to let him win.

Shannon dropped me off at the prosecutor's office with a reminder to text her when I finished. It wouldn't make sense for her to hang around, and the facility she wanted to hire to produce *The Haunted Place* wasn't far away. Although she created the prototypes for the play-testing groups, it wasn't feasible to do the full production herself. She'd check out their space, meet with a few artists, talk about box design, and pick me up when I finished.

Once inside, I removed my coat and hung it on the rack near the door. The receptionist nodded at me and picked up the phone to call Terri. No one else waited to enter: Either Lucas and his lawyers were already here, or they hadn't shown up yet. With a deep breath, I smoothed the skirt of my black suit, surveying my appearance from head to toe. My four-inch heels weren't remotely practical for Boston in February, but Shannon had thoughtfully dropped me at the front door, so I only had to make it about three steps without face-planting. Lucas hated when I wore heels because he was only of average height, so today I wanted to tower over him. My ribbed tights made my legs look longer. The skirt hugged my hips, ending with a flare an inch above my knees. The matching tailored jacket lay smoothly, taunting me with its stupid fake pockets that couldn't hold anything. Beneath it, I wore a gray silk shirt, largely because Lucas hated me in muted colors. Whatevs. Deal with it.

The receptionist led me down the hall, where I found Terri, Lucas, a member of his legal team whose name I didn't know, a large conference table, a tray of coffee, and a video camera. My gaze skittered over Lucas, hopefully in a I-can't-be-bothered-to-acknowledge-you sort of way. I'd been worried how I would feel seeing him again, but a coldness settled into my bones. He'd once been larger than life, my whole world. Now, he looked so small, sitting between the lawyers. Paler than he used to be, with a slight sheen of sweat on his forehead. Getting arrested and moving into his parents' basement did not agree with him, a realization that made me glad I'd taken extra time with my appearance. Gazing down on him from my fuck-me heels—No, my Fuck-You-Lucas heels—only sweetened the moment.

Still, the intensity of his gaze unnerved me. I poured myself a cup of coffee, grateful my hand didn't shake.

"Still drinking it black?" Lucas asked with a knowing grin. My stomach twisted at his voice.

Ignoring him, I dumped four packets of sugar and a large dollop of cream into my cup, swirling it with a swizzle stick as I'd done a thousand times. When we dated, I always worried about gaining weight, so I drank black coffee even though it tasted like lighter fluid. Now I prepared it the way I liked.

"Please don't speak to Ms. McDonald directly," Terri directed him. "Holly, are you ready?"

With a nod, I took my seat. I hadn't uttered a word since entering the room. Eventually, I'd find my voice, but for a few minutes, I just wanted to drink my coffee and warm up.

"Great! Let's begin!" the lawyer said. "For the record, I'm Adam Covington III, attorney for the defendant. With me is my client, Lucas Miller. This is the third deposition of witness Holly McDonald, appearing without representation. Also here is Terri Chavez, attorney for the United States of America. Can you please state your names for the recording?"

Adam explained that I was answering questions under oath, I stated my understanding for the record, and we got started. They started out with basic questions: my name, age, current occupation. Nothing too daunting. I didn't know if they were trying to ease me in or just wanted a baseline to tell whether I was lying. Lucas should have told his lawyers: I never lied.

At least not before Nathan, and that didn't count. Not telling Gwen something that would hurt her wasn't the same as lying under oath.

Adam spoke, dragging my attention away from much more interesting things than this deposition. "Ms. McDonald, is it true that you were recently in Mexico?"

"Yes." Terri had long ago instructed me not to answer more than what they asked. Don't talk just to fill the silence.

"For what purpose?"

"Pleasure." A flash of irritation crossed the lawyer's face, and I suppressed a smirk. This was exactly what I wanted. *Drag me here to waste my time, I'm going to waste yours.*

"Can you be more specific, please? Why did you fly to Mexico?"

"To attend a friend's wedding."

"Was that an expensive trip?"

"Objection," Terri said. "What is expensive to you or me may not be expensive to Ms. McDonald."

"I'll rephrase," he said. "Ms. McDonald, what did the trip cost you?"

"Gwen bought my plane ticket using her miles. My father paid for the resort as my Christmas gift. I spent about fifty dollars on their wedding gift. The shuttle from the airport to the resort and back was provided by the hotel."

He consulted his notes. "Where did you get the money?"

I intentionally misunderstood. "For the shuttle? Like I said, it was included in the resort fee, covered by my father."

Lucas tapped his fingers against the table, which he did when annoyed but wanting to feign indifference. Also when he bluffed at poker. He probably didn't expect me to remember his tells. His lawyer shot him a look, and the tapping stopped. Lucas didn't say anything, but I felt a flush of pleasure knowing I'd gotten to him.

Adam said, "I meant, where did you get the money for the gift?"

"I have a job," I said. Rude? Maybe, but I didn't care. "Shannon and I went in together on a gaming cupboard for their apartment. We found it in an antique shop, and she fixed it up."

It went from there. Their reasons for asking most of the questions didn't make sense to me. Whatever they thought they were trying to prove, it didn't seem to work. I kept wondering if there was more, if I'd missed something. My plea agreement didn't stop me from leaving the country.

Plus, I'd talked to Terri before booking the flight. A couple of times, I glanced at the AUSA, but she appeared as mystified as I felt.

"Ms. McDonald, are you currently seeing anyone?"

The question surprised me. I flinched, a mental image of Nathan flashing before my vision. Except we really weren't seeing each other. We saw each other for about thirty hours, decided not to do it again, and had barely spoken since. There was also Marc, but we'd had two dates and a couple of fairly PG kisses. No reason to tell Lucas about either of them.

I struggled to keep my face as blank as a mask, but darkness clouded Lucas's eyes. He'd seen whatever he was looking for by having his lawyer ask that question. Suddenly, I understood. This entire day wasn't about the case at all. He just wanted to drag me in here as a way of getting dirt on me. Dirt I had no intention of giving, especially since answering "no" wasn't technically a lie. How annoying.

"Objection," Terri said. "A deposition is for finding *admissible* evidence. The witness's personal life has no bearing on the case or your defense."

"We believe it does," Adam answered smoothly.

"Tell it to the judge, then, because I'm instructing her not to answer. Get a court order."

I appreciated Terri's intervention, but the damage was done. Lucas knew there was someone else in my life, even if he didn't know the details. He wouldn't like that at all.

When I found out Lucas was cheating on me, I ended things immediately. Moved out that night, took all the things I cared about, and never looked back. He followed me to Shannon's place, where I stayed inside and refused to come to the door. I'd never forget the image of Nana coming out of her apartment in a bathrobe to read him the riot act for showing up outside a lady's house in the dead of the night. She told him that if he came back, she'd call the police. He must have believed her, because after that, he'd stuck to texting, calling, and emailing. I never replied to a single message. Not because I didn't have anything to say, but because my failure to engage would infuriate him more.

During the entire eleven years of our relationship, I took his advice, listened to his opinion, accepted his viewpoints. Nothing I could do after leaving him would upset him more than refusing to let him tell me to come back.

Except possibly dating someone else, if the look on his face gave any indication. Oh, well. Too late now. We were ancient history, and nothing would change that. I could only imagine how many other women he'd been with over the past two years—not to mention *while we were together*—so he had no right to judge me. He'd had his chance, and he threw it away.

About ten minutes later, the attorney wrapped up without asking anything relevant to the case. What a waste of time. I texted Shannon while Lucas and his lawyer filed out, remaining behind to talk to Terri—and to give them a big head start. Walking out with the two of them didn't appeal at all.

"Do you think they can pin anything on me?" I asked her after the door closed behind them.

She shook her head. "It seems that their entire defense involves hoping the jury's full of idiots. Wouldn't be the first time."

"Does that work?"

"I want to make a joke about the intelligence of the average American, but really, not often," she said. "Even the most unbiased jurors tend to be predisposed to feel sorry for the victims and to believe police officers when they testify. We've got plenty of evidence against him. Discrediting you shouldn't make any difference. Even if the jurors believe you were involved, he clearly engaged in extensive criminal activity. I'm not worried. If I thought they had anything, I might reconsider putting you on the stand."

"Okay, so I'm free to date?" I tried to sound casual, but, well, nothing about this situation felt casual.

"Do whatever you want. You're not on trial. You're not under investigation. Even if you were, your personal life is none of my business."

"Okay, thanks," I said. "I mean, I'm not really. A lot of internet first dates, mostly. It's just, you know, Lucas doesn't need to know about my social life anymore."

"Not unless you want him to." She glanced at her watch. "They're probably gone. Do you want me to walk out with you?"

"Nah. A friend's picking me up. Should be fine. Thanks."

I shrugged into my coat before taking the stairs down to the lobby. At the bottom, I skidded to a halt so fast, I almost broke a heel.

"We need to talk," Lucas said.

"No, we most certainly do not. What are you even doing here?"

He smirked. "You weren't on the elevator, so I figured you took the stairs to avoid me."

To avoid him. He didn't remember that I hadn't taken an elevator in years.

No way would I stop to talk to my ex. He'd twist everything I said, and for all I knew, he was secretly recording this conversation on his phone. Nothing said I had to talk to him. In fact, Terri would prefer her key witness didn't meet privately with the defendant—even against my will. I moved toward the door, half-expecting him not to move. He did, although it seemed more like a jump of surprise than any display of consideration. Het put one hand on my arm. "Wait. I want to talk to you."

Old Holly would have caved, willing to say or do anything to keep his approval. Even as recently as a couple of months ago, I'd have stopped. But as I slowly found my confidence, I no longer cared what he thought of me.

"No," I said firmly. "Let me go, or I'll call Terri and tell her to add a kidnapping charge."

"You wouldn't."

"You don't know me anymore. I've been through a lot, most of it your fault. You have no idea what I would or wouldn't do. Take your hand off me."

The color drained from his face, but he moved back. "You can't avoid me forever."

"Maybe not, but I can avoid you until you're in jail." Shoving the door open, I moved past him.

"You're going to regret this," he hissed. "Soon, you'll be begging me to take you back. You'll realize that no one else will ever care about you the way I do. You're better with me."

"Go fuck yourself," I replied, my voice firm.

"I'm the only one for you," he called as I walked away. "We belong together."

Keeping my head high, I kept walking, forcing myself not to show any reaction. But all the way to Shannon's car, I willed my legs not to shake.

Chapter 14

You'll fight different monsters to defeat each game and move on. Some
you'll need to outwit, hide objects from, or avoid. When in doubt, run.
—*The Haunted Place* Player Guide

The morning after our second date, Marc left on another business trip,
so we spent the next few days texting. Every time my phone beeped with
a new message, my pulse quickened. If something in me panged a little
at seeing Marc's name instead of Nathan's, I ignored it. Nathan wasn't
available. Marc was. I liked Marc. All I had to do was give him a chance.

For all I knew, Nathan was out picking up other women while I was
sitting at home, pining for him. Not that it mattered. We'd said we were
over, so he didn't owe me anything. On the other hand, if I wanted to keep
seeing Marc, I owed him my full attention. He deserved a woman who got
excited to see his name pop up on her screen.

Moving out of Nathan's place helped a bit. Seeing his stuff everywhere,
smelling his scent in the air reminded me constantly of the things we'd
done. Things I wanted to keep doing—but knew could never happen again.
And that was okay. We'd agreed to a one-time vacation thing, and now the
vacation was over. Our time together stayed in Mexico when I returned to
Boston, where I had a perfectly nice guy who wanted to see me.

Everything would be fine. I just needed time and distance to appreciate
that Marc was obviously the better choice. Much of my free time at work
went to chatting with him and reminding myself of all his positive qualities.
The rest went to trying to devise strategies for convincing Gwen that, no,
really, she *wanted* me to date her father. I'd never implement them, but I
couldn't help myself. None of my ideas seemed remotely workable. Although

if I could find a way for Nathan and me to save the world from zombies or Trump, I would absolutely go for it. That *might* win Gwen's support. Meanwhile, I spent my days at the store and my evenings pretending I didn't miss him. The week dragged.

Finally, finally, Gwen and Cody returned from their honeymoon. After staying to tour more of Mexico, Nathan landed in Boston later the same day. That night our group resumed vanquishing *The Haunted Place* of evil spirits.

Shannon arrived at the store ten minutes before closing, game in hand. She went to set up while I alternately hoped Nathan would be next so we got a few minutes alone, and that he would arrive last so we wouldn't.

A beep from my phone jolted me out of these thoughts.

Marc: *Good luck tonight! I have an early meeting, so I'll be asleep when you get home. Hope the game goes well.*

Me: *Thanks! Have a good night. TTYL.*

Marc: *You, too. :-**

What a sweet guy. Lucas never once wished me happy gaming. He'd just remind me not to wake him up when I came in at the end of the night.

As I put my phone away, the bell over the door jingled. Gwen and Cody entered, laughing at something one of them said while taking off their coats. A pang hit me. That's what I wanted. Love and laughter and unself-conscious kissing in public. Someone who challenged me, who I enjoyed spending time with—even little things like walking down the street together. Someone my friends would be excited to see me with. One day, that could be me and Marc. On the other hand, a future with Nathan would mean sneaking around, guilty looks, stressing out over every interaction with Gwen. No relationship could withstand that for long. We were doomed, so it was better not to try.

Refusing to dwell on those thoughts, I finished closing the store. Tyler and Nathan arrived right on time, carrying bags of sandwiches and a case of beer, respectively. They greeted me normally, and I forced myself to respond casually, insisting to myself that I didn't notice the way Nathan's black turtleneck fit his broad chest or the way his muscles rippled when he took off his coat.

It would be so easy to step closer, give him a kiss hello, run my hands over his chest. But the reason that couldn't happen stood less than twenty feet away. I couldn't give in to temptation. We had a game to play, friends to fool into thinking everything remained normal between us. We were casual gaming friends, roommates, and nothing more.

Tyler moved toward the back, and Nathan fell into step beside me. When he spoke, his voice was low. "Hey, so I went home to drop off my suitcase, and…I saw your key by the recliner. Then I realized your stuff is gone."

A whoosh of air escaped me. I really should have told him I was moving out, but I was too chicken. "Yeah. I thought we could use some distance. It's hard to be so close, and…you know."

"Yeah, I do. I get it." He raked one hand through his hair. I tried not to notice how sexy it looked when it fell back over his eyes. "That probably answers my question, but…how are you?"

Awful. Miserable. Confused. I couldn't think of a lie, so I plastered on a fake smile in case anyone happened to be looking at us. "I'll be okay, eventually. This feels weird."

"I agree."

"We can go back to normal, right?" Even as I said the words, I hated myself. We never should have crossed that line, because there was no erasing the touch and taste of him from my memory. No forgetting the sweetness of finally getting the one thing I wanted most.

"Do you really want to?" Nathan asked.

My heart leapt into my throat. No, I didn't. But…my feelings didn't matter here. It killed me to say the words we both needed to hear. "We have to, right? I mean…Gwen would never be okay with the two of us together. And I'm seeing Marc. I like Marc."

"Ah, yes. Sweet Marc. How is he?" He kept his eyes averted, denying me the ability to see how he really felt.

"He's great!" I smiled enthusiastically. "He's…sweet." *Good one. Why not just call him Marc-like?*

"Uh-huh. Glad to hear it." He stopped walking and reached out, rubbing the back of my hand with his thumb. Sparks shot up my arm. "Does he give you butterflies?"

I snatched my hand back. With a glance at the back room, I whispered, "That's none of your business. We can't be together."

"There's always a way, if you want it badly enough," he said. "If he doesn't give you butterflies, what the hell are you doing with him? Because butterflies are insignificant compared to the way I feel around you. You give me elephants."

My heart soared at his words. I wanted him so badly. I opened my mouth to say so when Gwen's voice filtered in from the other room. "Holly? Is everything okay out there?"

Gwen. The reason we couldn't be together. I glanced at the back room, then back to Nathan. The smile he'd been wearing since entering the store fell.

"Fine! I'll be there in just a sec," I called. In a lower voice, I said to Nathan, "We have to go in there."

His tone matched mine. "I know. But think about what I said. If you really like Marc, that's great. I'm happy for you. In time, I'll move on. But if any part of you wants to explore things between us, to give it a real shot—"

"I owe it to you to try?"

"No." His brow furrowed. "I was going to say, you owe it to yourself. You don't owe me anything, but you deserve to be with someone who makes you happy. Figure out who that is. You don't have to decide now."

Nathan made my heart sing, but things with him would be messy, complicated. Marc was safe, comfortable. My brain and my heart begged me to make different choices. I started to tell him I'd think about it when Gwen glided into the room, not noticing the tension between us. "Dad! You made it! I was worried your flight would be delayed because of the storm."

He turned to her easily, wrapping one arm around her shoulders. "Would I allow a silly thing like a blizzard to prevent me from reaching the people's beloved Queen Guinevere?"

She giggled, the way she did whenever he used his nickname for her. "Well, I'm glad you came here instead of going to work."

"My employees have been manning the shops without me for a week. I can wait until tomorrow to review their reports."

"Who are you and what have you done with my workaholic father?"

"Who knows? Maybe taking a week off for Mexico was good for me." At those final words, he peeked over Gwen's shoulder at me.

My face grew warm. On the one hand, those days were very, very good for me, too. On the other, there were so many reasons things could never work out. One of those reasons was texting me at that very moment. I'd never dated more than one person at a time, so I didn't know how to handle it. Nathan knew about Marc, of course. Marc knew nothing. If I told him that I'd slept with Nathan, he'd likely forgive me—but not if I kept secretly seeing them both. I needed to come clean unless I was prepared to make a decision before our next date.

Marc was a solid, dependable, safe choice. Nathan excited me. Thanks to Lucas, I'd had plenty of excitement in my life the past couple of years. Excitement was not what I needed right now. I needed comfort, caring.

But I'd never had anyone make me feel the way Nathan did.

Gwen laughed, bringing me back into the moment. No time to dwell on my relationship problems. My friends had come to play games with me, Tyler brought food, and my stomach reminded me that my lunch hour was early in the workday.

A detour into the staff room to grab some sodas and bottled water for people who didn't want beer gave myself a minute to compose myself. By the time I made it to the back room, Tyler had arranged the food and was studiously avoiding looking at Shannon. Seriously, the only way things could get more awkward would have been if we'd invited Lucas or Gwen's dickhead ex (who also happened to be the deadbeat father of Cody's nephew).

I plopped into my chair next to Tyler and handed Gwen a diet soda, determined to act normal. He cut the sandwiches and put them on plates, still not looking at Shannon. This unspoken tension would drive all of us out of our minds if we didn't find a way to dissipate it. At least Shannon would leave the room once the game started.

When Nathan sat beside me, I passed him a bottle of water with a smile, determined to make it no bigger or more vibrant than usual. After all, we'd been friends for years. I'd always been happy to see him. Nothing needed to change. If I let myself get all moony-eyed or gave in to the temptation to touch him, Gwen would zero in faster than a seagull spotting crumbs.

"Welcome back, lovebirds!" I said, thankful for an easy, non-awkward topic of conversation while we ate. "How was your week after the rest of us left?"

"Absolutely amazing," Gwen said, snagging half a sub from the middle of the table. "I can't wait for you to read about it on my blog."

Shannon stuck her tongue out at her. "Or, since we're all here, and you can't start playing until the food's gone, you could tell us about it now."

"Mexico is the best wedding spot," Cody said. "We didn't have to do anything. The resort picked the flowers, the food, the music…all we had to do was tell them that we wanted fast songs to dance to, and that Gwen's got a peanut allergy."

"Isn't that how weddings normally work for dudes?" Tyler asked. "The bride sets up everything the way she likes it, and the groom shows up when and where she tells him?"

"That's more or less how my wedding went," Nathan said. "Actually, now that I think about it, that's how my marriage went, too. Until she left."

His tone was light, but the seriousness of his words touched something in me. Nathan rarely talked about his ex-wife. Gwen never mentioned her mother, especially after running into her about a year and a half ago. She'd gotten her closure, finally, and that was enough. But it never occurred to me to wonder how Nathan felt about the woman he'd spent nearly a decade with, who walked out without a backward glance, to hear Gwen tell it. They shared a history and a daughter. That meant something, especially since he tried to make it work until the end.

"I'm no expert," I said carefully, "but I don't think that's a recipe for marital bliss."

"It's not," he said. "When I get married again, I'm looking for mutual interests, a great sense of humor, and a smoking hot bod."

"Dad! Gross!" Gwen threw a bit of bread at him, and he ducked, laughing.

"What? You're the one always telling me to get out there more, go on more dates."

Beside me, Tyler snickered. I shot him a glance, wondering again how much he suspected. He'd definitely caught me looking at Nathan once or twice during the wedding reception. On my other side, Nathan shifted beneath the table, bringing his leg up against my calf. It was a light touch, could have been an accident, but I pushed back, taking comfort from the warmth of even a small portion of his body up against mine.

I gave him elephants. My fingers itched to trace his thigh, but this wasn't the place. Someone would notice. I couldn't give in to temptation before I made a decision. With a cough, I shifted in my chair, moving my leg against the magnetic pull of Nathan's heat.

"I think what Gwen's saying is that, while she'd love for her father to meet someone and be happy and fall in love again, we don't need a diagram," Shannon said. "And really, that goes for everyone at the table."

"Agreed," I said. "Don't get too explicit with the honeymoon stories."

Cody snorted. "Right. Ready to play?"

We'd finished eating, so I cleared the trash off the table while Shannon set up the game. During our earlier sessions, we'd explored a fair amount of the board, and I couldn't wait to see what objectives we'd receive next.

It didn't take long to find out. An app on Cody's phone randomly chose me to go first. Our character pieces, called meeples, scattered across the board. The intent was to discover as much of the house as possible before the rules changed, which had worked out well during the previous games. By the second turn, each of us managed to move into a new area of the board. I went upstairs.

When Nathan also moved his piece upstairs, I raised an eyebrow at him, keeping my tone light. "Are you following me?"

"Would I do that? Why would the Jock possibly want to get the Flirt alone? Think I could get lucky?"

Gwen shrieked and covered her ears while Cody took his turn. She removed them slowly when he finished. "Are you two done yet?"

A dangerous question that I couldn't answer. "Does this mean my flirting's getting better?"

"A little," she said. "Don't quit your day job."

Shaking her head, Gwen picked up her meeple and sent it after Cody. The two of them would explore different portions of the main floor, so Tyler went to the basement.

On his second turn, the floor tile Tyler drew contained a note directing him to draw a card from the house deck and read it aloud. The house deck was a single-use set of cards, numbered, which we weren't allowed to peek at or even shuffle until the time came to read them. Each card furthered the story of the game, giving us new rules or objectives. Sometimes, when we drew one, bad things happened.

Tyler read aloud. "'A fissure erupts beneath you, filling the room with a noxious odor. The smell of evil permeates the room, burning your flesh wherever it touches you. Everyone scatters, racing for the nearest exit.' Dude, this does not sound good."

"Shannon, are you showering us with evil?" I called into the next room.

Her response revealed the smile in her voice. "Technically, it's coming from below you, so it's not a shower."

"So you created a bidet of evil and sent it to attack your friends?" Gwen asked.

"Pretty much. Keep playing."

"Someone's been streaming too much *Buffy*," Tyler muttered under his breath.

Shannon must have been listening from the doorway, because her response came instantly. "Not everyone can afford cable, Tyler."

He turned red but didn't respond. Instead, he turned his attention back to the card. "'All players in the room where the fissure opened must move to the nearest adjacent room. Players may choose which exit to use, but pick carefully: This room cannot be crossed again until the fissure is closed. Don't isolate yourself from the rest of the house. Open Packet G.'"

Cody went into the box and pulled out a small cardboard container, then waved a red sticker. "I'm assuming this is the fissure? There are a bunch more. We may be screwed."

"No problem," Tyler said, moving his meeple from the dungeon to the nearby cheese room. "We don't have to go in there again."

"We do if we want to beat the level." Cody pulled a card out of the box and waved it. "We've got a new objective. Want to guess what?"

Nathan asked, "Close the fissure?"

"You got it. And any others that open. There are like thirty stickers."

The next card directed us to roll the dice, once per player, and place additional fissures by comparing the results to a chart on the card. We each took a turn. On my first roll, a fissure opened up on the second floor, cutting off access to one wing. Nathan miraculously rolled double sixes, so he didn't have to place anything. Cody wound up placing another fissure in the basement, and Gwen's went on the ground floor. As we played, certain events might trigger other fissures, and if too many sprouted, the house would collapse around us.

At that point, we'd have to pay a heavy point penalty to continue the game, which no one wanted, so defeating this level became crucial. Even though we were only play-testing, we still wanted to do as well as possible.

The Flirt didn't have any special abilities to help with this level, so I watched Nathan out of the corner of my eye while everyone else studied the board. I knew I shouldn't, but I couldn't resist. The air crackled between us.

Then my phone beeped again. Another text from Marc. This time, he sent me a picture. A popular board game, set up for one player, lay spread across a hotel table. *You're not the only one who can play games tonight. Wish you were here.*

Despite myself, I smiled. Gwen perked up. "Who you texting over there?"

My face grew warm. "Oh, it's, um…nothing."

"It's Marc," Nathan said flatly. "Isn't it?"

I nodded, refusing to meet his eyes. Until about twenty minutes ago, I hadn't believed I needed to choose between the two of them. Nor had I started figuring out who to pick. But I put my phone away without responding, turning back to the game.

To close the fissures, we needed specific objects hidden on cards in the item deck. After a character upgrade, Gwen possessed the ability to look at the top three cards before choosing one, which helped enormously. Cody's character had also been upgraded following the second game, allowing him to jump across entire rooms. That skill allowed him to hopscotch around, searching for items while avoiding rooms with fissures.

With careful strategy, we maneuvered the board. Nathan initially suggested splitting up, which seemed like a sound idea, but after all the minor fissures closed, we discovered that everyone had to be in the basement at the same time to close the original gap and complete our final objective.

"How do we do that, exactly, when most of us can't cross the rooms between here and there?"

"Magic," Gwen said with a smile.

"Did you get a new special ability you forgot to mention?" Tyler asked.

"Nope," she said. "But Shannon said there's a magic elevator that travels to any room in the house. We need to find it."

"And stay close together so we can get in it before the fissure spreads," Cody said.

Less than an hour after Tyler discovered the first fissure, we'd found all the items we needed and converged in the dungeon to close it. As the one who caused the original opening, Tyler had to arrive after everyone else. Once entering, no one could leave until we completed the steps outlined in the rule book.

He got to the room where everyone waited, played his cards, rolled his dice. Then Cody, Gwen, and I followed suit. Nathan went last, drawing a card from the deck after rolling.

He read it aloud. "'With the echoing screams of a thousand corpses, the smell recedes through the flooring from whence it came. A figure arises from the depths, reaching toward you. Your group surges backward, trying to escape its grasp. Most of you make it! Unfortunately, the Jock is a bit slow on the uptake.' Uh-oh, that's me, isn't it?"

"Did the fissure just kill you? Can we die in this game?" Cody asked.

My heart pounded. I didn't want him to leave. I cherished these game sessions with him, especially now that I was sleeping at Shannon's. Life didn't give me any other excuses to see him unless I wanted to buy a car and make it break down. "What? No!"

"Hold on. Maybe I'm not dead," Nathan said. He went back to the card. "'Cold, gray fingers close around the Jock's throat. The others move forward, grasping to keep him rooted on this plane. Unfortunately, you are no match for the ghostly being. With a strong pull, the Jock is hauled into the pit in the floor. The others must let go to avoid being sucked in, as well.'"

"Okay, yeah, I'm dead."

Chapter 15

Most of the cards in this game are intended to be read aloud. Packet contents are shared with the group. You can't win if you don't communicate.
—*The Haunted Place* Player Guide

A gasp of dismay escaped me at Nathan's words. This couldn't be happening. Sure, it was only a game, but he couldn't *die*. I wanted Nathan sitting beside me when we finished. Or at least until we figured out our relationship. Or until I hit my head and woke up with no memory of our weekend together.

"Shannon!" Gwen yelled through the doorway. "You didn't tell us people could die in this game!"

"Save it for your feedback survey," she called back. "Read the next card."

I plucked another card from the top of the deck, figuring that since Nathan already announced his own demise, someone else should deliver the rest of the bad news. "Oh, it's okay! You're only mostly dead."

The card informed us that we'd successfully reached the end of the level. Apparently, losing one of our characters was considered a win in this game. For the next session, we had a new objective: Save the Jock. If we succeeded, he would rejoin the game, possibly with some enhanced character traits (or so we hoped).

At the end of each game, we updated a log on the back of the Player Guide so we could remember what happened and where to pick up for the next session. We also got to choose from a list of game upgrades, which could give our characters powerful new traits, add additional dice to the pool, or make it easier to move around the board, among other things. Before packing up, we took a moment to discuss the options.

"We've got a bunch of new upgrades," Cody said. "What's the plan for next week?"

"Well, personally, I vote you save me," Nathan said.

"Seconded." Gwen chimed in before I could say anything.

"Hold on a sec..." Cody picked up the rule book and flipped through it, turning to a page near the beginning. "Okay, look. You can't actually die. I mean, your character can, but the players aren't out. We should get new characters, and you'll pick one of those if we don't save you. Or you could be the character we haven't used yet."

"Pick the character who's invincible," Tyler suggested.

"Thanks," Nathan said dryly. "I'll keep that in mind."

We packed up quickly. It wasn't late, but our games averaged about two hours, including setup and choosing end-of-game upgrades. The forecast called for heavy snow starting around eleven, so everyone wanted to get home early.

A noise drew my attention to the doorway, heart in my throat. Not Nathan, as I'd been desperately pretending not to hope, but Gwen.

"Hey."

"Hey." She closed the door behind her, leaning casually against it. "Can we talk for a minute?"

All the air went out of the room. *She knew.* I couldn't begin to figure out how or why, but what else could she want to talk about? All of my senses urged me to run. Unfortunately, Gwen stood between me and the door. Shoving her out of the way and bolting wouldn't make things less awkward. Especially not with our years of history. I owed her this conversation.

Hoping I sounded cool, I said, "Sure. What's up?"

"I'm worried about you," she said.

Maybe this wasn't about Nathan after all. With no idea what she meant, I cautiously said, "I'm okay."

"Are you? You've been weird and distant ever since the morning of my wedding. I know you said you were okay with me getting married before you—"

"Oh, it's nothing like that," I said. "I'm so sorry. I am one hundred percent over the moon for you and Cody. I don't care that you got married before me. I wouldn't care if Shannon got married before me, or anyone else. If I'd gotten married, I'd be getting a divorce on top of probation and not being able to work in IT and everything else. You and Shannon saved me by catching Lucas cheating."

She let out a breath. "Then what is it? I know something's up, and I kept hoping you'd talk to me about it, but I can't wait forever. I miss you."

A wave of guilt hit me. "I miss you, too. I guess I thought you and Cody would want some alone time, since you're married now."

"Okay, I get that, but…you've been weird during the games, too. The last couple of sessions, you're barely looking at my dad. Did he threaten Marc or any of the other guys you're dating? He used to do that to me, but you know he was joking."

"No, nothing like that," I said slowly. "He hasn't talked to any of my dates. I always meet them in public. No one's come home with me."

"Ah, okay." She sat at the table, which left me free to go through the door. Of course, leaving now would have been more awkward than staying. "So what's wrong?"

I couldn't tell her the truth, that I was head over heels infatuated with her father and we couldn't be together, but maybe I could get some roundabout advice. She was, after all, still one of my best friends, and I hated feeling like I had to lie or avoid her. "How did you know you could trust Cody?"

Realization dawned across her face. "To be fair, I really didn't. I thought he was cheating on me."

"True, but you also listened when he explained and gave him another chance."

"My gut told me Cody was worth it, so I took the risk," she said. "Is that the problem? You think Marc might cheat on you like Lucas."

Close enough. "Cheat on me, steal from me, lie to me, get me arrested…"

"I get it. But you know, that doesn't happen often. You're talking about one very specific situation with one guy who was absolutely the worst."

"I know that *now*," I said. "But I loved him. I wanted to spend the rest of my life with him. I had no idea how awful he could be. You knew he was the worst. You hated Lucas from day one."

"You were *fifteen* when you met him," Gwen pointed out. "I was twenty-three. Maybe you wouldn't have liked him, either, if you'd met him at twenty-three. Or maybe you wouldn't have liked me at fifteen. I was all emo in high school because I didn't have a mother. People change."

"True, but then. Say I go for it with Na…with Marc." For a horrible second, I worried she'd notice my slip of the tongue, but then she had no reason to suspect we talked about anyone other than who I claimed. "What if he changes? What if I do?"

"What if Cody or I change? People grow up. If you're lucky, you grow together. If you're not lucky, you grow apart. But you were always such a champion for love. I hate seeing how Lucas has left you so guarded, especially after all this time."

"I don't trust myself anymore. I was so very, very wrong about the person I knew best. How can I know when to trust someone new?"

She came around the table and gave me a hug. "You can't. I didn't know I could trust Cody. But I took a chance on him because he was worth it. There are good guys out there, guys who don't cheat. Guys like Cody, Tyler, my dad. You'll find one of them."

It was the perfect opening to tell her the truth, but I couldn't. We were having such a nice moment, and I didn't want to ruin it. Instead, I changed the subject. "I saw Lucas last week."

She grimaced. "At the deposition? How did it go?"

"The deposition went fine. He cornered me after." I summarized what he said in the stairwell. By the time I finished, she was on her feet, eyes flashing, pacing back and forth.

"That little…Oh, if I could just get my hands on…How dare he?! He's lucky he's going to jail soon." She stopped and looked at me. "I'm ready to cut a bitch on your behalf. Why are you smiling?"

"I've missed you," I said. "And I appreciate your outrage on my behalf."

"I never liked that guy," she said. "But look, you don't *want* someone who loves you the way he did. I kept my mouth shut during your relationship, but face it, Hol, he was terrible. He told you what to eat, what clothes to buy, how much makeup to wear, everything. He stole from you and cheated on you. Worse, he made you think you didn't deserve better. That something was wrong with your instincts. The last thing you should *ever* want is another guy who loves you the way Lucas did."

I'd never thought about it like that. Of course not, because my ex got inside my head like no one else. "You're right. Thanks."

"Don't just say I'm right. Do something. Call Marc. Ask him to meet you. Tell him you really like him and why you've been holding back. Think about all the things you told me when I was pushing Cody away, and take your own advice. Life's too short to be afraid to go after what you want."

My genuine smile of thanks wavered at the pang of guilt that hit me in the gut. If only Gwen knew she was helping me fix a relationship with the last person she'd ever want me to go out with. Because she was right. Life was too short not to go after what I wanted—and I wanted Nathan. It was time to put my fears aside and see if we could work things out.

"Thanks. I love you."

"I love you, too," she said. "Next time, don't wait for me to find you. You need help with anything, text me. Getting married doesn't mean I forgot my friends."

"You're right. I'm sorry."

I let my concerns for Gwen's reaction overwhelm everything else. Sure, she might react badly to me dating her father. She probably would, at least until she got over the initial shock. She'd also be hurt that we hadn't told her. But I couldn't live my life for other people. My relationship with Lucas taught me that. Once Gwen left, I'd go to Nathan and tell him how I felt.

"You're forgiven. Now get over here and give me a hug."

Gwen, Cody, and Tyler left a few minutes later. I didn't hear Nathan, so I didn't know if he'd gone home, but I texted him a request to talk as soon as the door shut behind Gwen's retreating form. He sent back a thumbs-up, which told me nothing.

Two minutes later, I found him waiting by the front door. Shannon was nowhere in sight.

"So…" The ability to form complete sentences suddenly abandoned me. The Flirt had left the building when the game ended.

"So." He put his phone away. "What's up?"

My fingers twisted around each other in much the same way my insides twisted with the enormity of what I was about to do. What if he'd changed his mind? But I had to take the plunge. I'd never be happy if I didn't learn to trust my instincts again, and my gut wanted Nathan. "I miss you."

He broke out into a huge smile that told me immediately I'd made the right decision. "I'm relieved to hear it."

"What about my job search? If I wind up getting an offer in Providence…"

"It's not that far. We'll work it out," he said.

"You mean it? Because I talked to a recruiter. I'm looking in Boston, but open to other places. I don't know what's going to happen."

"That's okay. All I know is how I feel when I'm with you. What we have is too good to walk away without exploring it. We both know it."

My heart thrilled at his words. My fingers itched to reach up, trace the line of his jaw, put my lips on his. "I've missed you so much. I spent the last week worried that you didn't feel the same way about me."

"But now you know I do," he said. "Let's go home."

"You mean it? It's not too fast to go from living in the same house to 'living together'?"

"I want you near me. I want you to fall asleep on my shoulder waiting for takeout while we watch *The Office*. I want you to be the last person I talk to at night and the first person I see when I wake up in the morning. I want to explore what's happening between us."

"Me too. I should never have moved out. At the deposition last week, all the ways Lucas hurt me came rushing back. It's hard to trust my own judgment when I was so wrong about him for so long. I got scared, and I freaked out."

"What happened?"

"He started asking questions about my love life, getting personal." I took a deep breath. "He said I belong with him, that I'm at my best when we're together, and that no one else will ever care about me the way he did."

Nathan's expression tightened. "That's complete bullshit. You know it."

"That's exactly what Gwen told me."

"She's a smart woman. You can do a million times better than that jerk."

"It's one thing to know it, and another to *feel* it," I whispered.

He moved toward me, putting his arms around me. I savored the feel, not caring where Shannon was or if she saw us. Knowing her, she'd locked herself in the bathroom with her phone when she saw us talking.

"I know the past couple of years have been rough on you," he said. "They'd have broken someone lesser. But you've bounced back. You've got a job, you're getting out more, you're moving on. You're learning who you are apart from that relationship. That's all healthy. Lucas saw the strong, amazing woman you've become, and he wanted to tear you down, bring you to his level. He couldn't stand how much better than him you are."

Without a moment's hesitation, I leaned forward and kissed him. My arms circled his neck, and I didn't ever want to let go. "I'm sorry. I'm a dope for letting him get to me."

"You're not. We all go through hard times. Just remember that hard times are easier when you ask for help."

"You're right. Thank you."

He leaned down, kissing me again with such tenderness that my toes tingled. "Does that mean you'll come home with me?"

"No one will wonder?"

With a laugh, he nodded toward the bathroom. "Well, Shannon might if she comes out and we're gone."

"I'll tell her before we clear out. But she's not the one I'm worried about."

"You've been living with me for over a year now. I never told anyone you left. Did you?"

"No," I said. "It would have raised questions I didn't know how to answer. And Shannon wouldn't have mentioned it. We didn't even see anyone until tonight."

"See? It's perfect. We get time alone to see how things go. I want you to spend the night with me, but if it's too soon or you're not comfortable, it's okay. You don't have to. But I hate the idea of only seeing you once a week, having to pretend I'm not dying to pull you into my arms."

Pulling me into his arms might not be necessary. If he kept looking at me like that, I'd lunge at him.

Behind me, the bathroom door slammed, reminding me that we weren't alone. A moment later, Shannon cleared her throat loudly. She held the game, gazing as intently at the still blank cover of the box as if the secrets to the meaning of life were written on it. "You ready, Hol?"

With a big grin, I shook my head. "Thanks, Shannon, but I've decided to go home."

Chapter 16

Don't lose track of the forest for the trees. Keep your eyes on the prize.
—*The Haunted Place* Player Guide

My heart sang as Nathan and I walked toward the T together. My feet beat out a happy rhythm on the pavement.

"Is that you?" Nathan asked.

I stopped walking, but the song continued. In my excitement, I hadn't even realized that the sound came from my phone. "Sorry. Hold on a sec."

With one glance at the display, my heart sank. How could I follow Nathan home—and move back in with him—without a single thought for Marc? Sweet Marc, who brought me dice as a gift on our second date and rented out an entire escape room warehouse to give me the perfect date. Marc, who at that very moment was calling me. Who I honestly liked and didn't want to hurt.

"You go on ahead," I said to Nathan. "I have to take this."

His face fell. "It's the other guy, isn't it?"

Not knowing what to say, I gazed at him helplessly. "I can't just ghost him…"

"No, but do you have to answer your phone right this second, when we're talking about us? When we're on our way home together?"

My ringtone trailed off, rendering his question moot.

"No, of course I don't," I said. "I'm sorry. I've never been in this position."

"Do you like me?"

I nodded.

"Do you like him?"

I nodded again.

"Who do you want to be with?"

My phone beeped with a text from Marc. *Hey, beautiful. Sorry to miss you. You're probably already on the T and I have an early meeting, so I'll talk to you tomorrow.*

The sweetness of the message sent a pang right through me. My heart lodged in my throat. "I don't know. I don't want to hurt anyone."

He sighed and pulled me toward him, his arms offering comfort rather than passion. "I'm afraid that's inevitable. But it's not your fault, it's bad timing. We're grown men. Whatever you decide, we'll get over it. Take your time."

"Thanks." My voice trembled with the effort of holding in all these mixed emotions. "Can I still come home?"

"Of course you can. But if you want to sleep in your old room until you figure things out, I understand."

With a sniffle, I wrapped my arms around his waist. "Thank you. I'm sorry I'm such a mess."

"You're not a mess. You're you, which means you care about other people. Never apologize for that." He pulled back and kissed my forehead. "Go ahead and call Marc back if you want. I'll wait for you outside Harvard Square so you don't have to ride the train alone."

"Not to rock the boat, but why are you being so accommodating here? You're not upset that I'm about to call some other guy?"

He shook his head. "Getting angry would only push you away. When you pick me, I want you to be confident you're making the right decision."

* * * *

The next few days passed in a blur. Months ago, I'd volunteered to do inventory at the store overnight for some extra money. Several days in a row found me crawling into bed, exhausted, sometime after four o'clock in the morning.

Which meant that by our next gaming session, I was tense and anxious. I'd barely spoken to Nathan or Marc, and I still didn't want to hurt either of them. Cody, Gwen, and Nathan showed up at the store together, sending a pang through me. If I chose Marc, my friends and I could be chatting and laughing and making plans for double dates. On the other hand, a future with Nathan meant sneaking around, lying to my friends, and hoping the amazing sex relieved some of the guilt.

"Hey!" I said, determined not to let my feelings show. "Shannon's running late. I asked her to let me pick up the game on my way here, but she's guarding that thing like it's the Holy Grail."

"No problem," Gwen said. "We're early. That gives us time to order dinner while we wait."

"And I brought dessert." Nathan held up a bag. "You've got a microwave in the staff room, right?"

"We do. If Gwen and Cody can order pizza without us, I'll show you."

"I'm practically famous for ordering pizza," Cody said. "This place even knows my voice."

Since Gwen knew what I liked, I led Nathan to the back, my heart pounding at the thought of being alone with him. This was ridiculous. Yes, we had amazing chemistry. We'd had a great time in Mexico, but I'd barely seen him since moving back into his house. I missed him horribly, both as my friend and as someone with the potential to be more.

I shut the door behind me, savoring the few minutes of privacy. The room was narrow, with a fridge at one end, a long counter containing a sink and a microwave, and a tiny table in the far corner. Nathan moved ahead of me to the counter, emptying the bag.

Heart in my throat, I watched him remove a cake mix from the bag. "You want to bake a full-sized cake in the microwave? Not, like, those little mug cakes?"

"Trust me," he said.

My expression conveyed my skepticism. "It's just that I don't want to set the staff room on fire two months before my probation ends."

He laughed. "I have a pan that lets you bake anything in the microwave. It's in the bag. I've done this before."

I wasn't convinced, but we didn't have an oven. I liked cake, and if this worked, I'd get cake. "If we accidentally burn the store down and I lose my job, you have to hire me at the shop until I can work with computers again."

"Deal." He expertly ripped open the box and poured the contents into the pan, which I was relieved to see appeared to be silicone, not metal. "Got a spoon?"

"Oh, yeah. Sorry. In the drawer." I was so bad at this. I wanted time alone with him, and now that I'd gotten it, I couldn't speak about anything other than cake. Damn Lucas for shaking my confidence.

Even my conversation with Gwen didn't fully chase the voice of his ghost from the back of my head. I didn't deserve this. Like everyone else, I had a right to be happy. It was time to trust in myself, to trust Nathan not to screw me over like my ex. After all, I'd known him for years and nothing even hinted that he possessed the ability to hurt me.

Wasn't I supposed to be playing a role? The Flirt wouldn't stand back, tongue-tied, when the man she wanted stood less than three feet away. I stepped forward, putting one hand on his arm. The muscles rippled beneath my fingertips. "I'll get it for you."

"Thanks." His voice went husky at the contact.

Opening the drawer, I quickly turned toward him, holding up the item. Ignoring it, his eyes locked on mine. My tongue darted out to moisten my lips, and his gaze followed.

"I've missed you," I whispered.

"Me too. When you moved home, I couldn't believe my good luck. But I've barely talked to you all week, so I worried you changed your mind. Decided to be with Marc instead."

"I've been working late. I haven't made a decision." But the way my heart pounded told me that it had already chosen for me. "Maybe you could help convince me?"

"I'd like that." A laugh from the main room interrupted the descent of his lips toward mine. His eyes darted to the closed door. "They could come in any second."

I stepped closer, closing the minuscule gap. "Door's locked."

He groaned softly, putting his hands on my hips and crushing me against him. My lips parted beneath his, and I met him as if I'd been lost in the desert and he were my oasis. I thrilled at the feel of him against me, bringing my hands up to run my fingers through his hair. By the time the spoon clattered to the floor, I'd forgotten where we were.

In the store. Making microwave cake. To feed our friends, including Gwen and Cody. Who stood on the other side of that door.

"I'm sorry," he said. "We should make this before someone comes looking for us."

"How long does it take to bake?"

He looked at the directions. "Five and a half minutes. Why?"

With a smile, I whipped off my sweater and leaned back against the table. The Flirt had finally taken over. "Because I know an excellent way to fill the time. I need you."

"You're not worried they might hear us."

"That's an old microwave. It's *loud*," I said. "Besides, Shannon will be here any second. They'll be busy setting up and won't even notice we're gone. If you hurry."

"What if she comes in?"

"She won't, even if the door wasn't locked. She knows how I feel about you. She guessed a long time ago. Even before I admitted it to myself." Not wanting to spoil the mood, I didn't mention that she'd seen us together. It didn't matter.

Seconds later, the microwave door slammed shut. A few button presses and Nathan crossed the room in one step, pulling me against him. Our clothes evaporated. And by the time the timer went off, I was thanking Jesus that my bosses had invested in a sturdy table for the break room.

* * * *

While Nathan and I cleaned up and prepared to join the others, my phone went off in my pocket. A sinking feeling filled my stomach as I realized that I needed to tell Marc that we were over. It was time to face the facts: I wanted Nathan. Marc was a perfectly nice guy, and I hoped he found happiness, but it wasn't going to be with me.

I understood what I needed to do. The fling wasn't staying in Mexico. Our feelings were too strong. This wasn't just sex for either of us. Yes, Gwen would object. Yes, that presented a real logistical problem, and I hated the idea of hurting my friend. But Nathan and I had to come up with a way to get past that. We could be happy together. The only thing keeping us apart was our fear of how someone else would react. We were grown adults, and we couldn't let Gwen control us—especially when she didn't even know she was doing it.

I'd spent my entire adulthood trying to be what someone else wanted. Wearing the clothes Lucas liked, styling my hair the way Lucas liked, eating the foods he suggested, maintaining my weight lower than I wanted. I went to the grad school near him, despite being accepted to other great schools. At almost thirty years old, I couldn't think of anything I'd done solely because it made me happy. Except for the time spent with Nathan.

He caught the look on my face and tilted his head. "Marc?"

I nodded. "I need to break up with him."

"Does that mean you pick me?" A smile snuck onto his face, almost as if he was afraid to let it show.

Leaning over, I planted a soft kiss on his lips. Even the slight contact sent a shiver down my spine. "Yes. Absolutely, I choose you. There was never any contest."

"I can't tell you how happy I am to hear that."

"That doesn't mean it's going to be easy. Even after I talk to Marc…"

"We need to talk to Gwen. I know," he said. "And we will. When the time is right."

It was on the tip of my tongue to retort that I'd wait to tell Marc when the time was right, but I knew what he meant. My phone beeped again, so I pulled it out. Immediately, I felt like a total jerk.

Marc: *We still on for tomorrow night?*

Right. Marc and I had planned another date. I wanted to face him about as much as I wanted to get a root canal, but he deserved to know the truth. The least I could do was let him down in person.

Marc: *I'm planning something special. Can't wait to see you.*

I couldn't break up with him in the middle of a special, surprise date. With shaking fingers, I typed out a response. *I'm so sorry, I have to close the store tomorrow night. Can we meet for a quick dinner around 6?* It wasn't true, but I wasn't about to tell him the truth in a text.

When I put my phone away, Nathan's eyes pierced my soul. He didn't say anything.

"We have a date tomorrow," I said.

"Cancelling it?"

"Switching it to something low-key. I want to talk to him in person. This is hard."

"That's what she said." Part of me worried that he would get upset at my going out with Marc one last time, but the joke put me at ease.

"C'mon," I said. "We've got a game to beat."

We left the cake to cool and met the others in the back room, trying not to grin like idiots. When I walked by Shannon, she met my eyes with a knowing look. I suppressed a smile, avoiding looking at Gwen or Cody. Instead, I greeted Tyler. Everything would be much easier if I picked Marc. Or if Nathan and I didn't have to hide.

Although I didn't miss Lucas in the slightest, in my weaker moments, sometimes I longed for the ease of our relationship. No drama, no questions. He told me he liked me, we started holding hands between classes. We only applied to colleges near each other, both getting accepted to Boston-area schools. We moved from California to Massachusetts together. Ten years after that first kiss, we were engaged. Easy. Until the lying and the cheating and the thieving started, anyway. Not to mention that he only liked me as long as I did everything he said.

Maybe an easy relationship wasn't as great as it sounded on paper.

My eyes went to Nathan, leaning back in the chair beside my usual seat, his long legs stretched lazily under the table as he munched on a buffalo wing. I grabbed a slice of meat lovers' pizza from the box and sat beside him.

Over the course of the past few games, we'd managed to uncover a fair amount of the house, stickers covering the surface. Some rooms had caved in or gotten blocked off, but thanks to a couple of secret passages, the magic elevator from the last session, and dumbwaiters, we moved with relative ease throughout the house. The game got more difficult with each progressive play, but just enough to keep it interesting. A legacy game that could be beaten easily wouldn't hold anyone's interest. Reviewers would crucify it, and the poor game would be sunk within a week of its release.

Before opening the deck of cards that told the story and gave instructions, Cody reminded us that the Jock had died at the end of the last game. Either Nathan needed to come in as a new character, or we'd spend the evening trying to save him.

"Does that mean I should go frost the cake while I wait for everyone else to decide my fate?" He glanced at me, and my face turned red. If he went back to the kitchen, I'd happily chuck my character into the fissure behind his and follow him for round two. This time with frosting.

Tyler looked up from the Player Guide. "It says players can sit out a game or two of the progression, but I don't see what happens if you die."

Cody held up the top card of the game deck. "You're still part of the team. We've got a separate, smaller board for this level only. We need to search the room for specific items to save you, but there are ways for you to help."

"But feel free to go get us cake, anyway," Gwen said.

If she only knew what she was suggesting.

Shannon said, "I can frost the cake. It'll give me something to do other than fret over whether this level works. It was one of the hardest to design."

Digging into a packet referenced by the cards, Nathan found and unfolded the special game board we needed for this level, setting it in the middle of the table. Cody continued reading the cards to himself. Meanwhile, Tyler pulled extra pieces out of the box, while I gathered the trash from dinner and refilled drinks.

On my way back to the table, something drew my attention to Gwen and Cody. They sat on the far side of the table, fingers dangling entwined between them. Cody leaned and whispered in Gwen's ear, and she blushed before responding. A pang hit me at the reminder of how I once thought Lucas and I had what they did. How badly I wanted someone who looked at me the way Cody looked at Gwen. But Gwen was right. I didn't need someone who "loved" me like Lucas did. I could do better.

The time I'd spent with Nathan was great. I enjoyed every second of it. My body thrilled at the slightest touch, and part of me even loved getting away with something forbidden. But we didn't have a relationship, not yet. He couldn't hold my hand in public. We couldn't even *go* in public together as a couple.

"Everything okay?" As if he read my thoughts, Nathan settled into the chair beside me and offered me a bottled water.

"Yeah, fine." My voice caught in my throat, betraying the lie. I didn't want him to think I was trying to pressure him into something more, but at the same time, I needed to know if we might have a future. "It's nice to see them so happy. I wonder if that'll happen for me."

"You're not happy now?" He kept his tone light, both of us very aware that other people sat in this room and could hear us.

"Well, I mean, I have *great* friends. My job is fun, although I can't wait to get back into programming."

"I think what Holly's trying to say is, there's no substitute for finding that one person you know will love you and be there for you, no matter what." Tyler's words did nothing to ease my suspicion that he guessed what was going on between me and Nathan. His sharp gaze missed nothing. Unfortunately, there was no way to ask.

"I still think Marc can be that person," Gwen said. "Just give him time."

"Yeah. We didn't happen overnight," Cody said.

They were right, of course. It took them months to get together. Shannon and I watched Gwen struggle with her feelings, with getting over her own issues and allowing herself to be happy. Their story hadn't been cut-and-dried, either.

"We're all here for you, Holly," Nathan said.

"Thanks," I said. "We don't need to talk about this now. Let's save Nathan."

"Yeah, one thing at a time," Gwen said. "Holly's been out with Marc what, three times? They still need to get to know each other. After that, we can worry about finding your happily-ever-afters—both of you."

"I'm doing fine on my own," Nathan said, finally dragging his gaze away from me. If Gwen noticed the way he looked at me, she kept it to herself.

"Oh yeah? Is there something you want to share with the rest of the class?" she asked.

He shook his head. "Not yet."

Gwen grinned at him. "For now, I'll take it. But I want details later."

Oh no, you don't.

"When I'm ready to share, you'll be the first to know," he said.

"And that'll have to be good enough for now because it's game time," Cody said. "Are we ready to play?"

This level came with a timer, so once we started, the time for small talk ended. We had one hour to save the Jock, or Nathan would be required to choose a new character for the remaining games, losing all of his upgrades and special abilities. No one wanted that. Or he could leave the game, which would be worse in many ways but saved us from playing with a relatively not useful character.

The game board contained a picture of a study, complete with desk, armchair, pictures on the wall, a bearskin rug, and fireplace. A random number printed on the doorknob directed us to draw a card from a special deck used for this game only. From there, we were off and running. Nathan didn't have a character piece to move this round, but he was allowed to participate. When we found a word search as part of the puzzle, he gladly went to work. Gwen and Cody pieced together parts of a map to find hidden clues.

And with ten seconds to spare, I drew a card that gave us the key. The key opened a safe hidden behind a painting. Inside, we found a spell. Tyler read the words, drew another card and—with one second on the clock, Nathan was saved! What a relief.

At the end of the night, Nathan and I walked out together. Gwen stopped to dig for more details on the "mystery woman" he'd hinted at earlier. Nathan appeared to be enjoying himself as he steadfastly refused to give any details.

"What about you?" Gwen asked me. "Have you seen anyone? A strange woman in the kitchen? Sneaking out early in the morning?"

How I managed to keep a straight face, I'd never know. "I can honestly say I haven't seen any strange women sneaking in or out of your dad's bedroom."

"And she won't," Nathan said.

"Keep your eyes peeled," Gwen said. "I want to know every little detail."

She absolutely didn't, but I couldn't say that. This whole conversation made me want to shower. I hated lying to anyone, but especially to Gwen, and especially about this. Thankfully, Cody saved me.

"Don't listen to her," he said. "Next thing you know, she'll have you drilling a hole in the bedroom wall. Gwen's just excited at the thought of seeing her dad happy."

"Absolutely, I am," she said.

Nathan smiled at her. "The moment I have information worthy of Queen Guinevere's notice, I vow that I shalt make it known."

She rolled her eyes. "You don't think I need to know anything. Holly, keep me posted."

"Okay," I managed to choke out.

We said our good-byes, and the two of them turned toward Cody's apartment while Nathan and I headed for the T stop. The moment they moved out of sight, he drew me into his arms.

"That was awkward," I said.

"I know," he said. "And I'm sorry for putting you in that position. I wasn't thinking."

"I know, and it's fine. Just…what a night. At least you're not dead anymore."

"That's definitely a good thing." He laughed, but sobered up when our eyes met. "I'm glad you picked me."

"It wasn't even really a contest. I just hope Gwen can be okay with us."

"She will be," he said. "She has to. It's the only way we can be together."

Chapter 17

Try everything. Even things that don't make any sense.
—*The Haunted Place* Player Guide

The next night, I asked Marc to meet me at the restaurant for our date instead of picking me up at Game On!. I didn't want to prolong the evening more than necessary, and making small talk as we walked to the nearby coffee shop felt too awkward.

When he arrived, Marc leaned over to kiss me hello. I turned my face so his lips landed on my cheek. The utter lack of sensation told me I'd made the right decision. Still, a pang stabbed me as his face fell. "Did I do something wrong?"

For a long moment, I studied him before I replied. Marc was a nice guy. We had an amazing time doing escape rooms. That had been the most thoughtful date anyone ever planned for me. The conversation flowed easily, and he made me laugh. He could be a good friend. And despite the fact that he was cute…he wasn't the one I wanted.

We could be good together. We could hit it off and probably date for a while. Years, maybe. We could get married and play games together and get along reasonably well. Maybe the two of us would be happy. He wouldn't try to control me the way Lucas had. Marc didn't bat an eye when I ordered a cheeseburger instead of a salad. He didn't give backhanded compliments. I really liked him. Unfortunately, he wasn't Nathan.

The thought of throwing myself into a relationship that didn't excite me made me want to build a blanket fort, make a giant bowl of chocolate chip cookie dough, and settle in to watch every episode of *The O.C.* or *The Office.* I deserved better, and so did Marc.

In answer to his question, I said, "No, you didn't do anything wrong. You're a really nice guy."

The kiss of death, and we both knew it. I took a deep breath to say more, and his face fell. "You don't have to explain."

"I'm so sorry. I've had a great time these past few weeks. I really like you. There's probably an alternate universe out there where we fall in love and get married and live happily ever after with two-point-five kids and a white picket fence."

"What about this one?"

"In this one...I'm sorry to say, I've got feelings for someone else. I didn't think it would ever amount to anything, but now it has. As much as I like you, I need to pursue it."

He nodded, running one hand through his hair. "Well, thanks for your honesty."

"I feel terrible."

"Don't be ridiculous. You can't help how you feel. But if things don't work out, would you hang on to my number?"

I didn't want to give him false hope. I also didn't want to slam the door on a sweet guy I enjoyed spending time with. After a long moment, I nodded. "Can we still be friends?"

He hugged me before turning to go. He hadn't even managed to sit down and order dinner. And while I felt bad for hurting him, I couldn't wait to go home and fall into Nathan's arms.

* * * *

The next morning, I woke without an alarm, despite the lack of sunlight peeking through the curtains. Although the room remained as dark as the middle of the night, the display on my phone read almost six o'clock. I lay there for several minutes, wondering if I should get up, snuggle into Nathan to wake him, go back to sleep, or...do nothing. Since he was warm and the outside air was cool, I went with the first option. Nathan lay so peacefully, lashes inky against his skin. Like most native Bostonians, he was pretty pale this time of year. He slept on his stomach, one arm slung casually across my torso, holding me close. I had zero interest in moving.

When the alarm went off at six as usual, he yawned and pressed snooze, which I'd expected based on the number of times I used to hear his phone chime through the wall.

This morning, however, he didn't roll over and go back to sleep. Instead, he turned to me, blinking to clear his vision. "Good morning, beautiful."

"Good morning yourself." I moved closer, snuggling against him, reveling in the feel of his skin against mine. A girl could definitely get used to this. He turned toward me, and I thrilled to see the effect I had on him. "Do you have to go to work right away, or do you have some time?"

"Well, I do own the business," he said. "There must be some perks."

Before we could talk about exploring those perks further, his phone beeped. My own device buzzed on the nightstand a moment later.

"Severe weather alert," I said. "More than a foot of snow coming. Good thing today's my day off."

"Oh yeah," he said. "I closed the shops after checking the forecast last night. My employees don't need to travel in this—or worse, get stuck. Sorry I forgot to turn off the alarm."

"I was already awake," I said. "But now that you're up, what should we do?"

His wicked smile told me that his mind had already taken the same path as mine. A full day free, together? No reason to get out of bed. We snuggled back under the covers and stayed there for several glorious hours, taking full advantage of our time together.

When we finally ventured out of bed, I made *tres leches* pancakes using the Star Wars molds Gwen bought Nathan for Christmas a few years ago and a recipe Mamá made for special occasions. Half an hour later, Nathan and I found ourselves back on the couch, happily ensconced in blankets, drinking Mexican hot cocoa while watching a geeky movie marathon. Outside, big, fluffy flakes fell into white piles.

By lunchtime the snow stopped, so Nathan went outside to shovel the driveway while I made grilled cheese sandwiches and tomato soup for lunch. Not fancy, but delicious.

"This is perfect," Nathan said after taking his first bite. "Thank you."

"Any time. Or at least any time we find ourselves with a rare day off together." I smiled at him. These little domestic moments excited me, knowing we could act like a couple in the cocoon of this house and not worry about getting "caught."

We could hang out in public, of course, and we would, but Boston was ultimately a pretty small town for a "big city." I'd never be able to hold Nathan's hand in public or lean over to kiss him, because I'd be too afraid we might run into Gwen or Cody. Or someone might see us and mention it to them, like one of Nathan's many well-meaning and very nosy neighbors who'd known Gwen since she was eight. We planned to tell her about us eventually, but we didn't want her to hear it from someone else.

"You bring up an interesting point," he said. "We almost never spend time together during the day. What do you want to do?"

I wiggled my eyebrows at him suggestively.

He laughed. "I just shoveled a foot of snow off the driveway. Give me half an hour."

"Well, in that case, do you want to play a game?"

"Always. What are you thinking?"

I thought for a minute. "Well, we could play strip poker..."

"Except you know my tells and I'd be sitting here naked in no time, with you fully clothed," he said.

"That's not so bad."

"Or we could play strip something else."

"What do you have in mind?"

Instead of answering, he pushed back from the table. Leaving the dishes for now, I followed him to the game closet in the living room. We surveyed the options together until he leaned over and pulled his favorite deck-building game from the pile.

His selection made me grin: He'd picked up the first game we ever played together, when I joined Gwen for Thanksgiving dinner during our first year of graduate school. It had quickly become one of my favorites. The twinkle in his eyes told me he remembered our first game as well as I did.

I raised an eyebrow at him. "I'm intrigued, but I'm not sure how this is going to work."

"We play. For each difference in points at the end of the game, loser removes one article of clothing. Three to five games. By then, we should both be done with the game and ready to move on to, er, more interesting things."

"You're on."

Back in the kitchen, Nathan cleaned up the lunch dishes while I set up. Both of us moved at lightning speed. Less than ten minutes later, we faced off over several rows of cards.

After shuffling my starting deck, I drew a hand that gave me four coins to spend. I purchased an attack card, hoping I'd be able to get Nathan out of most of his layers in only a game or two. He followed suit, and the two of us settled into the game, drawing cards, making purchases, and shuffling at lightning speed. I'd played this game hundreds of times, but a new urgency filled the air. The faster we got to the end of the game, the sooner we'd be back in bed. The swiftness with which Nathan played each hand told me he felt the same way.

With conversation and trash talk, the game ordinarily took anywhere from twenty to thirty minutes for two players, but barely fifteen passed before Nathan triggered game end. We counted our points eagerly. My pulse raced. This was by far the hottest game I'd ever played.

"Thirty," I announced triumphantly. "Strip."

"Not so fast," he said, lying down his cards. "I've got thirty points, too."

We stared at each other. No one had mentioned what would happen if we tied. According to the directions, the player who took fewer turns would win in this scenario, but we'd each played the same number of hands.

With a shrug, I reached for the hem of my sweater and tugged it over my head. "In a tie, we should each lose something."

His lips curved upward in that slow, sensual way that made me want to forget the game and climb into his lap. "Works for me."

I leaned over and gave him a long, lingering kiss. His hands came up to cup my face, and a thrill went through me. My pulse sped up as my hands reached under his T-shirt, exploring his chest as if I imprinted the memory forever. When I leaned out of my chair, straining toward him, he laughed and grabbed my hands.

"Not yet," he said. "We're playing a game, remember?"

I pouted. "I can think of some other games we could play instead. One involving special dice I picked up in the novelty section at work."

"All good things in time," he said. "The anticipation adds to it."

He was right, of course. Already he had me squirming in my seat, and he'd only removed his sweater. The entire afternoon stretched before us. If I got my way, after another game or two, we'd move to the bedroom and refuse to come out until morning. Still, I playfully huffed at him while righting myself in my chair.

"You're cute when you're pouting."

"You're cute when you're pretending to resist me," I said.

"Not resisting. Delaying. Trust me, it'll be worth it." The way his eyes lingered on my chest told me those words weren't an empty promise.

I licked my lips, thrilling in the way his gaze traveled upward. When our eyes met, his pupils dilated. This game was new to me, but in the end, we'd both win. If making me wait turned him on, I'd sit here until someone finally invented flying cars.

"You were worth the wait once," I said. "I suppose we can play another game."

"Until one of us is naked."

"Or both of us."

We separated the cards and set up for a second game. At the end, I wore only a long T-shirt that barely covered my panties. In the third game, Nathan lost his shoes and shirt. After each scoring break, our kisses grew longer, more heated.

His hands moved to my waist, then started to move lower. I leaned into him with a soft sigh, praying he would end the charade of playing a game and throw me onto the floor. Or the table, the counter, up against the wall. It didn't matter. My entire body burned for him. Here, there, anywhere.

These thoughts consumed me to the point that I almost didn't notice when Nathan's hands stopped moving, his lips stilled. Thinking it was time to start the next game, I reluctantly forced my breathing to slow. Then he pulled back so fast I nearly toppled off my chair.

"Oh, my God." Gwen's voice rang clearly through the kitchen doorway from the front hall. "What are you doing?"

Chapter 18

Savor the little victories, as the game is designed to hand you many defeats.

—*The Haunted Place* Player Guide

Gwen's words hung in the air like a fireball hurtling toward its mark. I didn't want to face her, but I didn't have a choice. Tugging my shirt down further to cover my panties, I forced my gaze to move toward the kitchen doorway, wishing I still wore pants. Gwen stood there, mouth open, making a noise I couldn't even identify. My heart twisted.

At the sight of her, Nathan sprang to his feet, chair clattering to the floor behind him. I rose more slowly, not sure whether standing or sitting would be better. My mouth moved soundlessly as I fought for anything resembling an explanation. I didn't have any idea what to say.

Nathan moved in front of me, like a human shield. I appreciated his initial instinct to protect me, but at the same time, I was tired of hiding from my best friend. I sidestepped, enough to see her still standing in the entrance, but now covering her eyes.

"Nice to see you, Queen Guinevere," Nathan said, with an exaggerated bow. "How may I be of service?"

She lowered her hands slowly. Her gaze traveled from him to me, back to him, to his bare chest, back to my face, which must have been beet red at that point. "Don't deflect. You two. You. How could you? Holly? I thought you were my friend."

"I am your friend," I said. "I never wanted to hurt you or upset you. I'm…"

When my voice ran out, Nathan stepped up. "Holly and I have been seeing each other for a few weeks."

"No," she said. "No way. This is not happening."

"Sweetie, I know this is kind of a shock, especially finding out like this. I'm sorry," he said.

"I'm sorry, too," I interjected quickly.

Nathan continued as if I hadn't spoken. "You've been on me for years to start dating again. Why not take out one of the other moms on the street, you'd ask. Or you'd point out women while we were at the movies, on the T, whatever. Hell, you spent weeks trying to get me to sign up for online dating—even after you saw what kind of creeps use those sites."

"This isn't about me," she snapped. "I did that because I love you, and I want you to be happy."

"I *am* happy," he said. "I mean we. We're happy. It's early, but things are going well."

Part of me wanted to let them hash it out, but I also couldn't stand there with the two of them talking about my relationship like I couldn't hear them. "You've been pushing me, too. Telling me to get out of my shell, flirt, find someone new. Well, I took your advice, and I finally met someone I want to be with."

"I meant you should date someone *age-appropriate*," she snapped, crossing her arms over her chest. "Seriously, what were you thinking? Do you have anything in common?"

"I'm really sorry," I said. "It just happened. We were going to tell you. We just hadn't figured out how."

"And we have everything in common," Nathan pointed out. "Just like you and I love superhero movies and board games and video games and hanging out with friends and going to the beach...Holly likes all that, too. It's why the two of you are such good friends."

Gwen said, "A *friend* wouldn't do this to me."

Something in her tone pissed me off. My spine straightened. "This isn't about you. It was never about you. I've had a crush on Nathan for years, and you've always known it."

"I thought it was a joke!"

"On some level, so did I," I admitted. Nathan shot me a look, but I ignored him. "I mean, the attraction was there, and I loved spending time with him, but I assumed he'd never look at me twice. Then he did, and everything changed. I had to take a chance."

"What about our entire conversation where you were wondering what to do with Marc?" Realization slowly crossed her face. "You made that whole problem up. Another lie."

"I didn't lie, just vagued up who I was talking about." Her hostility hurt. Even though I'd known she'd be upset, I hadn't been fully prepared for the force of her anger. "You're the one who said I deserve to be with someone who makes me happy."

"I never would have encouraged you if you'd told me the truth." Pain filled her eyes, reminding me that Gwen was the wronged party here, even though she'd put me on the defensive.

"I know, and I'm sorry," I said. "I shouldn't have lied, but it felt so good to talk to you. And everything you said was right. I did deserve better than Lucas. I mean, I do. I never dreamed a relationship could feel like this."

"Oh, please? A relationship? That's what you call using my father to act out your own daddy issues? Your father abandoned you, so you steal mine?"

Her words sparked a fury within me. How dare she imply that I just wanted a replacement for my own father? Our relationship might not be the ideal father/daughter model like hers, but Dad and I got along fine when we saw each other. This wasn't about him or Gwen or anyone other than me and the way I felt. But I was too angry to even get into that. "If that's what you think, the door's behind you."

"You can't kick me out of my own house! Why don't you leave?"

"Hey, hey," Nathan said. "Calm down. Gwen, Holly's been living here for over a year. She pays rent, which means she has every right to be here. Unlike you, who I might add, moved out. If we can't discuss this rationally, you should go. That crack about her father was completely uncalled for."

She shook her braids defiantly and crossed her arms over her chest, but didn't respond.

Nathan said, "Listen. I gave up dating for years to raise you properly. I gave you a good, loving home. I've never regretted that. But I also never expected to fall for someone again. Now I have. I'm not going to walk away to make you happy. I've sacrificed enough. I'm head over heels for this woman, and I think it could turn into something amazing."

His words sent butterflies spiraling through my stomach. I stepped forward, squeezing his hand. "You know I feel the same way, right?"

He nodded and kissed the tip of my nose. "I know. But thank you for telling me."

Gwen groaned from the doorway. "It's not that this isn't adorable. Oh wait, it's not. Seriously, guys. This is the most terrible idea either of you has ever had. It's a guaranteed disaster."

"Then it's *our* disaster, our decision to make," I said. "Not yours. I hoped you'd be happy for us, like we were happy when you fell in love with Cody."

"We get that you're upset," Nathan said. "It must be a big shock, especially to find out this way. But we hope you'll eventually be happy for us."

She shook her head. "Don't bet on it. And don't come crying to me when it blows up, either of you."

There was nothing left to say. She was hurt, obviously, and we'd expected that. We also didn't expect her to get over it immediately. That was one reason we'd wanted to break the news to her gently at the right time. Neither of us wanted this. But we couldn't change what happened.

All I could do was apologize, which I did. After the shock she'd experienced, showing her how happy we could be together wouldn't help the situation. She wasn't ready to see it.

"Gwen, I really am sorry," I said. "I'm going to my room to give you two some time to talk things out."

"Oh, *your* room?" she asked. "Are you talking about *my* room? The bedroom I gave you, because we're friends and you didn't have anywhere else to go?"

Or maybe I should stay and fight it out. I tossed my hair back and met her glare with my own. "Nope. I meant the room I slept in last night. Where I intend to sleep tonight, and every night from now on. The master bedroom."

Gwen made a strangled sound, and Nathan shot me a you're-not-helping look. At that point I didn't care. Yes, we all knew Gwen possessed a wicked hot temper. You couldn't live with someone for three years and play games with them and be their friend and not notice. But I didn't have to let her insult me.

It hurt that she would be so mean about me finding someone after all this time. Even though I'd known she wouldn't like it, deep down, I'd still hoped she'd be all hugs and smiles when she found out.

Maybe she would congratulate us later, but now she stood in full battle mode. Eyes flashing, head high, jaw clenched. The pain etched on her face drained my own anger. Suddenly, I couldn't fight anymore. All my energy trailed away. Carefully not looking at my friend, I scooped my pants and sweater off the floor and turned to walk away.

Gwen's voice followed me down the hall. "I can't believe I ever considered you a friend. I never want to see you again."

The waterworks started as soon as the bedroom door shut behind me. I couldn't choose between my best friend and what could be the best relationship I would ever have. If she was going to force the choice, she would wind up out in the cold.

But I worried what would happen if Nathan came to the opposite conclusion. After all, I would never ask him to pick me over his daughter.

Even if I wanted to displace her, which had never been my intent, I wouldn't want to be with a man who put someone else ahead of his only child.

Nathan's voice traveled through the door. "You're being ridiculous."

My spine stiffened, but then I realized he hadn't followed me. He still stood in the living room, talking to Gwen. Their voices carried down the hall to my ears.

She replied. "Me? What about you, chasing after a girl half your age?"

"She's not half my age. She's a grown woman, and we care about each other," he said. "Look, I've always treated you like an adult. But you're acting like a child. You've told me over and over that you want me to find someone. Now I have, and you're mad—why? Because I didn't tell you?"

"Because she's supposed to be my friend. Friends don't screw friends' dads."

"She is your friend. And if you are really *Holly's* friend, you would be happy for us."

"Come on. You've got to stop seeing her."

"No."

"What?" Gwen's voice grew higher, as if she couldn't believe her ears.

Part of me felt bad for listening. This was a private conversation between them; I shouldn't be eavesdropping. On the other hand, they knew it was an old house with thin walls, the conversation was about me, and the only way to avoid hearing it was to walk back through the living room and out the front door. Unless I wanted to go stand in the bathroom with the shower running. I didn't.

"I'm not going to break up with her, Gwen," Nathan said. "I'm not going to apologize to you for following my heart. I've put you first my whole life. Now you're married and on your own. It's time to live for me. Of all people, I would've thought you'd be excited for me."

"I don't know what to say."

"You could congratulate me on finding someone after all this time."

"That's not going to happen." Her voice cracked, reminding me that my friend was in pain, too. Pain I'd caused.

"Then you should go," he said. "This is Holly's home, and she doesn't deserve to be belittled, insulted, or to feel like she has to hide in a bedroom."

"You're throwing me out?"

"Only until you're able to apologize," he said. "I know you're upset, and I'm sorry. I'm not surprised. We didn't want you to find out like this. We can talk after you calm down."

Gwen's footsteps reverberated through the house. A moment later, the house shuddered with the force of her exit.

I moved to the window to watch her stomp down the driveway, headed toward the T stop. Near the sidewalk she paused, just for a beat, as if hoping one of us would follow her. My heart told me to go out there, tell her how sorry I was. But as upset as we both were, I'd probably only make things worse. Before I made a decision, she moved farther down the sidewalk, out of sight.

A moment later, the bedroom door opened. "I imagine you heard."

I nodded. "You didn't have to do that for me."

"I didn't do it for you," he said. "I did it for me. Gwen's a big girl; she'll get over it. But I can't let my daughter dictate who I date. I meant what I said: I'm falling for you, hard and fast. I want to see where this goes."

Turning, I found Nathan a few inches behind me. I fell into his arms, resting my head on his shoulder. "Me too. More than anything. But I never wanted to destroy your relationship with her."

"You didn't. She'll come around."

"What if she doesn't?"

For a long moment, my question hung in the air. Nathan buried his face in my hair and inhaled deeply. I clung to him, half afraid to hear what he said next. When he finally spoke, his voice cracked. "She has to. I can't lose either of you."

Chapter 19

Although *The Haunted Place* is designed to be played with the same four
to six people, because it's cooperative, it's fine if someone sits out a round
or two. Just try not to kill them. You'll miss them when they're gone.
—*The Haunted Place* Player Guide

The next day, I threw myself into the job search in earnest. For more
than a year, my life had spiraled out of control. Starting to date again
was one way of taking it back. I felt good about myself for the first time
in ages. It was time to focus on the next step, which meant resolving my
career. I loved Game On!, but minimum-wage cashier was supposed to
be a temporary position.

Most companies would take at least a couple of months to interview
potential candidates, make a decision, and conduct background checks,
so it didn't hurt to explore my options now. I started with the recruiter
who'd gotten me interviews a lifetime ago, before the situation with Lucas
prevented me from taking a job in computers.

To my immense relief, Rob not only remembered me but seemed glad
to hear from me. "Holly McDonald! Are you ready to let me find the
perfect job for you?"

"Maybe," I said. "I won't be able to start for a couple of months."

"That's a shame. I've got a company hiring a programmer, but they
need someone ASAP."

"Does April count?"

He laughed. "No. Then again, I'm aware of someone else going out on
maternity leave in the spring. If you'd be open to a temporary position,
we can talk."

"Keep me posted? I'd prefer something permanent, but I'm not closing any doors right now."

"I'll keep you in mind," he said. "If you're not looking for a job now, what can I do for you?"

"Just sending out feelers. Reconnecting. Wondering if you've heard of any other openings?"

"Are you open to relocating?"

My mind went instantly to Nathan, but we'd been dating only a couple of weeks. It was way too soon to know if we had long-term potential. It didn't make sense to limit myself because of him. "I'd happily consider Providence, even though that might require relocating. I'm not sure about the commute, but I can think about it. Worcester, Central Mass is fine. I'd rather avoid anything farther west or New Hampshire, but if you stumble across a perfect fit, let me know."

"Will do. A lot of these companies allow telecommuting at least a couple of days a week, if that helps."

"It might. Thanks."

"But that's not what I'm talking about," he said. "There's a company in New York that needs new programmers in the next couple of months. And the Providence company that offered before is opening a new branch in Phoenix, if that interests you."

The suggestion tempted me. Maybe a fresh start was exactly what I needed. New York or Phoenix presented new opportunities. The chance to get far, far away from Lucas's influence for good. But then a pang hit me: Nathan. Providence was one thing. The Boston commuter trains went there. No big deal. Could I really move across the country, closing the door on our relationship?

At the same time, could I put my career on hold again because of a man? Not the same situation as Lucas, sure, but I'd still be letting someone else affect my decisions. We'd hadn't been dating long enough for me to put Nathan ahead of my own need to earn a living.

I couldn't answer those questions, but Rob waited for me to say something. Nothing ventured, nothing gained. It wasn't like I had to accept any job he found me. I could explore my options until I found the best fit. What if Nathan broke up with me before Rob found me anything?

"Absolutely! I'll forward you an updated résumé."

* * * *

The first Tuesday after The Incident, as I called it, Nathan and Tyler showed up at Game On! right before closing as usual. No surprise there. Nathan brought Chinese food, as promised. Gwen was nowhere to be seen, which we knew would happen. Her quick temper usually cooled down equally as fast, but Nathan and I expected her to take a couple of weeks to get used to the idea of us as a couple. Even when she accepted our relationship, she wouldn't want to see us together right away. Still, the table would seem empty without her. Shannon arrived ten minutes later, game in hand. With Cody.

I hadn't expected him to show. The fact that Gwen didn't stand within about three feet of him didn't surprise me, for all that it made him look naked. He held a box from the cupcake place in one hand, which I interpreted as a peace offering.

"Thanks for coming," I said, as we all walked toward the back to get set up.

He nodded. "It's a game, right? I'm always here for games. Especially knowing Shannon's on a time crunch to get this tested and produced so her backers get their copies."

"Thanks. I'm glad to see you."

"I'm not here to talk about what happened. I'm Team Gwen, one hundred percent."

"As you should be," Nathan said.

"I don't know why she's so pissed," Tyler said. "It was obvious you two had something going on."

I blinked at him. "Really?"

"Yeah. The glances, the footsie under the table, the little touches. Maybe Cody and Gwen missed it because they're so wrapped up in each other, but I noticed weeks ago."

Nathan's face flushed, but he laughed. "I guess we're not as subtle as we thought."

Tyler shrugged. "She's probably embarrassed she didn't see it. Especially since she knows you both so well. Can we play, or should we sit around and gossip?"

"Food and gossip," I said, opening the bags Nathan had set on the table. "We're not getting grease on the game."

"Fair enough."

Despite my comment, I wasn't up for gossiping about my best friend or my newish relationship, so I was relieved when the conversation went first to the food (good, cheap, a little greasy), then to the game.

"Is anyone else concerned that we're starting this next level with no objectives?" Cody asked. "I mean, the game's fun, but at the moment, we have nothing to do but wander around the house aimlessly."

"It's never aimless," Shannon said. "You'll get your first objective when you read the Game 6 cards. The game will tell you what to do."

"Somehow, that's not reassuring," Nathan said. "So far, the game has sent zombies to attack us, trapped us in a room slowly filling with water, opened fissures in the ground, killed me…What else?"

"It's called *The Haunted Place*, not *Candy Land.*" Shannon smirked. "What did you expect?"

"Ghosts? But for all that the game can be demoralizing, it's awesome. Even better than *Betrayal Legacy.* I'm really enjoying it," I said.

"Good." She stood, brushing off her hands and collecting the empty dishes. "Because you're on your own."

Cody set up the board while Nathan found the card with the introduction to Game 6 and began to read. "Here it is: 'Your objective is to find the bell tower. This room must be located on the top floor of the house."

"Upstairs? Woo-hoo!" So far, we kept getting drawn to incidents on the ground floor or in the basement. Most of the downstairs layout had unfolded, so the thought of exploring a place previously unexamined made my mouth water.

Nathan continued reading. "Open Box 7 and remove the top floor room tiles. Shuffle the stack and draw a random tile. Decide as a group where to place it."

The rules required us to match at least one doorway with an existing room and to leave at least one unblocked exit per floor. That way, each floor could expand with new tiles until we ran out. As a result, some stuff wound up in odd places. The staircase to the upstairs landing was located in the pantry—which sat not off the kitchen as one would expect, but adjacent to the conservatory. Then again, considering we had a cemetery located upstairs, maybe it didn't matter. We weren't building a house made of logic here. At least we loved the game.

"Combine the remaining tiles with the others." Nathan handed me a stack of cards. I shuffled quickly, trying not to let my gaze linger on Gwen's empty seat.

Was this how it was going to be? My best friend avoiding me. Skipping the rest of our game sessions? Would Shannon pick sides? What about Gwen's relationship with Nathan? They were the closest father/daughter I'd ever met, acting more like friends or brother/sister than parent/child. They got along better than the Gilmore Girls. Even her reaction to my jokes about dating him was like I'd suggested hitting on a brother. It was part of why Nathan never seemed older than me: She treated him like one of us. I couldn't imagine talking to either of my parents the way Gwen talked to her father, but it worked for them. Or at least, it used to.

Nathan's hand closed over mine, bringing my attention back to the table. "I think the cards are shuffled well enough."

"Sorry, I got distracted."

His eyes followed mine to the empty seat. "Don't worry. She'll come around."

"I certainly hope so." Leaning over, I kissed him briefly.

Cody cleared his throat loudly. "None of that. We're in the neutral zone. All games. No Gwen talk, no kissing."

Part of me itched to point out that he and Gwen used to make out at the table between turns, but Tyler beat me to it. "Seriously, dude? *Now* you put a moratorium on kissing at the table? After I sat through five games with you and your girl attached at the lip?"

His face turned red. "That's different. We're newlyweds."

"And they're newly...hooking up or whatever. Sorry," he said to me and Nathan before turning back to Cody. "Look, I get it. Gwen's not cool with this. But you're Switzerland. No commentary, positive or negative. That's the only way we're gonna finish this game, and I, for one, want to play. No non-game drama at the table. Got it?"

"Got it. Sorry," he mumbled.

Nathan went back into the box to pull out our character cards and tokens. I slipped into my role as the Flirt, batting my eyes and turning to Tyler. "Thank you, kind sir. I've always depended on the kindness of strangers."

"You're welcome, Scarlett." His lips twitched.

"Blanche DuBois," Nathan corrected. "*A Streetcar Named Desire.*"

"Ding ding ding," I said. "And the winner goes first. Because it's as random as any other way of picking."

No one argued, so Nathan started by moving his meeple toward the staircase. It took a few rounds to get upstairs, partially because different characters moved at different speeds. From the upper landing, Nathan, Cody, the piece representing Gwen's empty seat, and Tyler fanned out in each direction. Since the game didn't allow for diagonal movement, I followed Nathan and pulled a card.

"The bell tower. We found it!" I placed the sticker on the board and read a note on the backing. "Turn to page 112."

Nathan picked up the book and began to read. "*As you enter the room, a loud clanging fills the air. You drop to the ground, hands clutching your ears. It's so loud, you've never heard anything like it. A swarm of bats flies out of the bell, coming straight at you. They attack!"*

"Did the game just kill me for fulfilling our first objective?" I raised my voice. "Shannon!"

"No comment!" came the reply. It sounded a bit muffled, like she was trying not to laugh.

"Thanks for the heads-up, *best friend*."

"I love you, too," she shouted back. "Keep reading!"

"The bats feast on your unconscious form, then move on to the next room, devouring anyone they find there." Nathan looked up "If it's any consolation, I'm dead, too. Again. 'Players located in these two rooms have been turned into vampires! Tear up your character cards. These characters are no longer part of the game.'"

"This is crap," I grumbled.

"You should've been the Virgin," Tyler said. "The Virgin always makes it to the end."

"I'm coming to bite you first," I replied. "And I'm not tearing up my card."

"You have to, it's in the rules," Cody said. "Besides, we're using index cards. This isn't a final copy of the game."

"But doesn't Shannon need other people to play-test this?"

"I can make more index cards," she called from the adjacent room.

Everything in me rebelled at the idea of destroying part of a game. Games were sacred. When I lost a part to *Feasts of Odin*, I cried, and that game came with about a thousand pieces. No one would ever miss a coin.

I lifted the card with a shaking hand. "Not sure I can."

"Here, we'll do it together," Nathan said. "Count of three."

Cody counted to three slowly, then laughed when I continued to hold the card without making any effort to tear it up.

Nathan put one hand over mine, sending warmth up my arm. He held my eyes and counted again, this time ripping the card with his other hand as he spoke. I twitched when he finished, but took a couple of deep breaths.

"You okay?" he asked.

"Not sure. Are we both out of the game?"

He turned back to the directions. "Open Packet H."

Cody dug in the box for a second, then held out an envelope. "You're both getting new character cards. The Flirt and the Jock are dead—which is what you get for sneaking off to the bell tower to have sex in the middle of a crisis—but now the game changes."

"Hey! You don't know we were having sex," I said.

Tyler gave me a skeptical look. "We've all seen horror movies."

Losing my character hurt, not just because of my general unwillingness to destroy game pieces, but also because I *liked* that character. I'd built up her sensitivity and stamina. Up until about a minute ago, I'd had the most sensitivity, putting me in place to hit my secret goal at the end.

"We've got the Butler and the Cook," Cody said. "We've found the original inhabitants of this house, hiding in a closet."

"Well, you're certainly not the Cook," I said to Nathan with a laugh as I handed him the Butler card. "The Takeout King, maybe."

The Cook started with reduced stamina, but high intelligence and speed. My new character came with poison and garlic, which delighted Cody to no end. My new secret goal was to end the game with the most stamina. Apparently, I wanted to put everyone else in a food coma.

Since we didn't have a kitchen yet, I started in the pantry, which meant I could go right upstairs and start fighting vampires. As the Butler, Nathan's piece went back to the front door, so he needed to navigate the entire house again.

We had three new objectives: make a wooden stake, find holy water, and defeat the vampires—all without getting killed. Anyone who got eaten could choose from the unused characters at the beginning of the game, but we only had one left. Unless the next packet we opened gave us more character cards, we could only afford one more death. The game included an "Emergency" box to be opened if necessary, but no one wanted to find out what it contained. If this game was anything like the other legacy games we'd played, opening the emergency box would carry a steep point penalty at the end.

The game gave us two new object cards: one a stake, the other holy water. We shuffled them into the top half of the item card deck. Cody insisted it felt like cheating not to shuffle them in with all the other cards, but it *was* in the rules, and we didn't have that many upstairs rooms to explore. Since the only way to find an object was to place a new room sticker, we might never find objects that wound up on the bottom of the deck.

As awkward as it felt to move Gwen's character without her and make decisions that affected her, the game progressed smoothly. No fighting, no bickering. I shrugged out of my role as the Flirt, instead adopting a terrible French accent as the Cook.

An hour later, Tyler stabbed the last vampire, narrowly escaping death with one hit point left. Thankfully, hit points reset at the end of each game. I'd lost a bit of strength, but gained a stamina point, and used my garlic to kill the other vampire. Gwen's empty chair found the holy water, which she kept for future missions. If she came back. Meanwhile, Cody fell through a laundry chute into the basement, and Nathan found most of the rest of the rooms on the top floor. The Butler turned out to be an extremely useful character, since his knowledge of the house let him discover two room tiles per turn, instead of one.

Our next game most likely would involve a rescue mission, at which point having so many rooms of the house already on the board would help. In the game Shannon had based her creation on, players could lose if the house was too small when the end game started.

If only Gwen had been there to share with us, it would've been a perfect evening. I tried not to let her absence get to me, but I knew Nathan felt it, too. The tone was far more muted than in prior games, even when we won.

Nathan and I walked back to the T in silence, lost in our own thoughts. Neither of us spoke until we sat down on the train.

"Good game, huh?" he asked.

"Yeah, it was fun." I didn't mention the elephant in the room—or in this case, the elephant that *should* have been in the room.

He took my chin in one hand and tilted my head back to look at him. "Listen to me, Holly. Gwen will come back to the game. She's too competitive to walk away."

"It's a cooperative game," I pointed out.

"She still wants to win. It's got to be killing her that we played without her."

He had a point. When Gwen and Cody first started hooking up, she took a chance at sabotaging their entire relationship to make him lose a game. It wasn't even about her winning; she just wanted him to come in last. Shannon and I always thought it was a miracle that he'd still wanted to date her after that. But he got that game behavior stayed at the table. Clearly, Gwen had found the perfect guy for her.

And now, so had I. My heart warmed every time I looked at Nathan. When he was near me, the world seemed brighter. But more than that—he understood me in a way that Lucas never had. Lucas worked all the time, spending so many hours at the office he'd come up with nosebleeds and have to sleep for half a day. The way he wore himself out working was one reason I'd never suspected he cheated on me. He didn't hang out with my friends; we didn't play games together. In retrospect, I don't know why I stayed with him as long as I did.

On the other hand, Nathan and I liked the same things, we got along, he laughed at my jokes. Even the stupid ones. He knew how scared I was that we'd made a huge mistake, that Gwen would never forgive me. She'd have to forgive *him* eventually. After all, he was her dad. She'd never cut him out of her life completely, especially when she didn't have a relationship with her mother.

But she didn't have to forgive me. If things didn't work out, I lifted right out of her life. In another few months, my probation would be done, and I'd be allowed to resume working in computers. As much as I loved Game On!, I also loved using my degree and being able to pay the student loans I'd been forced to defer. It would be time to move on. She knew that, and she could easily avoid the store until I left. If I got a job in Providence, I'd spend little time in Cambridge except on the weekends, giving me no reason to run into her. Or worse, if I moved to Phoenix or New York, I'd never see her again.

My heart broke at the thought. Wanting to reach out, to open communication, I pulled out my phone. Before I could decide what to say, a Facebook notification popped up. Tyler had tagged us all in a picture of the game. Well, most of us: me, Nathan, Cody, and Shannon. Gwen's name was there, but for some reason, he didn't link to her. Weird.

The photo listed three comments, but only two loaded.

Beside me, Nathan chuckled, also on his phone.

"What?"

"Nothing. Just Gwen's comment on Tyler's post."

"Gwen commented?"

"Yeah, see?" Turning his phone, he held it out. And there I saw, clear as day, Gwen's comment, nestled between Cody's and Shannon's. I looked back at my phone. Nothing.

My best friend had blocked me.

Chapter 20

Like life, this game is full of surprises.
—*The Haunted Place* Player Guide

Learning that Gwen had blocked me on social media hurt. Over the next few weeks, I racked my brain for anything to say or do that might make a difference, but I kept coming up blank. Nathan still thought she'd come around on her own, and talking to him about it didn't help. Since I didn't want to argue with him, too, we avoided the subject. The whole debacle strained our relationship. I wasn't sure how to fix things, other than making up with Gwen. Which seemed impossible.

We played a few more sessions of *The Haunted Place*, but it felt wrong without her. Cody and Tyler were fine, and Nathan was great, but the empty seat constantly reminded me of the hole in my heart. I kept going to work, going home. The end of my probation loomed, so in my spare time, I applied for every programming-related job within about forty miles. I did a couple of phone interviews, but the gap in my employment record hurt, especially once an interviewer looked up the name of my previous employer—my company with Lucas. The internet is forever, and so are indictments.

I couldn't leave the work history off because then I looked like I hadn't worked in four years. I couldn't disclose it, either, not if I wanted a prayer of getting hired. My best bet seemed to be to hope that Rob would find me something. Thankfully, his history with Lucas put him on my side.

At night, I went home to Nathan. Things were good, but something felt off. Not with him—with me. I couldn't allow myself to be happy while

Gwen was so upset with me. We spent too many nights vegging on the couch, watching *The Office*, because I felt so sluggish and down.

I wanted to put Operation: Gain Gwen's Forgiveness into effect right away, but the universe made other plans. After weeks of stress and sleepless nights and interacting with the public during the germiest time of year, the Plague hit me. While Gwen might appreciate me groveling at her feet, the gesture would lose some of its effectiveness if I lay prone on the ground because fever prevented me from standing up.

Not wanting Nathan to get sick, too, I moved back into my old bed for a couple of days. On Day 5, I was scheduled to close the store, so I slept until noon and woke up feeling much better. Carla and John probably wouldn't mind if I took another day to get back to a hundred percent, but when I called in, one of them had to work late, which meant less time with their kids. I hated to take that away from them.

Besides, I couldn't afford to take many days off in a row. Massachusetts law required employers to give employees forty hours of paid sick leave a year, but we earned it over time, starting in January. It was only March, and I'd used everything from last year.

Tucking copious amounts of ginger ale into my bag, I set off while Nathan went to run some errands. He would've told me to take it easy an extra day, to lie down and watch Netflix while eating chicken soup until the nausea faded for a full twenty-four hours. He didn't have my student loan debt. Loans I took out expecting to use my inheritance to repay them once I turned twenty-five, back when I had one.

Sure, my bills were low since Nathan refused to charge me market rent or my fair share of utilities, but I made up for it by keeping his fridge stocked and cooking when we were both home. Besides, I needed to rebuild my savings after Lucas took everything. That required going to work.

Carla greeted me with a smile when I entered. "Welcome back! How are you feeling?"

"Gross," I said. "But I'm here. I'll make it."

"Something nasty's going around. Take care of yourself."

"It's fine," I said. "I'm mostly better. I'm not stuffy or sneezy or anything. Just tired and achy. And my stomach has decided to reject all food. I'm living on tea and crackers."

She laughed. "I remember those days. And I don't miss them. You sure I can't tempt you with some solid food? I'm ordering Chinese."

My mouth watered, but my stomach revolted. "No thanks. I'm going to make tea, then I should be ready to clock in."

In the break room, I set the kettle to boil, then sat down at the table to wait. Next thing I knew, Carla was shaking my shoulders. My head rested on the cool surface, although I didn't remember putting it there. "Holly? Honey? Maybe you should go home."

"No, I'm fine," I said. "I don't know why I'm so tired. I'm sorry. I just need to get up and start moving."

"You fell asleep. It's been forty-five minutes since you sat down." She studied me closely. "I'm here for another hour. It's slow. I was going to review the stock orders for next month, but you should rest a bit longer. I got you some soup."

I started to protest, but she waved me off.

"I know you said you didn't want it, but you need to keep your strength up. Especially if you refuse to go home, which honestly, you should."

"I'm out of sick leave," I said. "Can't afford to go."

"I should make you."

"Please don't. I really need the money."

She sighed. "I'll stay with you as long as I can. Maybe if it's slow, we'll close early. Can you have some friends come in, start a game so they're here if you need anything? And maybe give you a ride home? You don't look like you're in any condition to take the T."

Shannon was always up for a game if she wasn't working on her own projects, and I said so. Nathan would be furious at me for coming in, but he would have no problem sitting here and keeping an eye on me. He could invite Tyler or some of their poker buddies.

"I'll be fine. Usually I feel better in the evenings. Maybe even well enough to eat later. Thanks, though."

Carla set the container of soup in front of me, and I thanked her weakly. I opened the lid and leaned forward, inhaling the glorious steam and the mixture of spices. My stomach churned. I jerked backward, away from the table. Broth sloshed everywhere, but I barely registered it. One hand over my mouth, I made it to the sink seconds before the meager contents of my stomach poured out.

Leaning against the sink, I kept my eyes closed, wishing I could open them and find myself at home in bed, dreaming. The odds that Carla hadn't noticed me puking in the break room sink in front of her seemed slim. What a nightmare. I couldn't remember the last time I'd thrown up.

To her credit, Carla didn't say anything. The fridge door rattled, then the next thing I knew, something cool pressed against the back of my neck. Frozen peas, kept in the freezer for emergencies.

"I'm so sorry, Carla," I said. "I don't know what to say."

"Here, come sit with me." She led me back to the table, then glanced out into the main room before sitting down beside me. "How long have you been feeling bad? Tired, achy?"

I thought for a minute. "I've been down the past few weeks. Mostly because Gwen isn't talking to me. But I'm working on a plan to fix that. I've only felt *this* bad for a few days."

She nodded, rubbing her chin with one hand. "I was the same way. Tired, down, then sick all the time. For weeks."

"Ugh, seriously?" I didn't remember her being sick recently. "I'm not going to get better for weeks?"

"If my suspicions are correct, this condition is going to last for about eight more months." At my confused look, she leaned forward and placed her elbows on the table. "Forgive me for asking, but have you missed any periods?"

My ears roared. The impact of her words slammed into my already aching belly, and I wanted to start heaving again. Unfortunately, there was nothing left. It had been…many weeks. Since before Mexico. I hadn't even noticed.

"Oh my God, Carla." It hurt to form the words. "Are you saying I might be pregnant?"

She nodded. "I think so. You're tired, achy, and short-tempered. You said you've been nauseated for days, but you don't have a fever or any other cold and flu symptoms. Plus, you just threw up."

"This can't be morning sickness. It's the middle of the afternoon!"

"I'm sorry to say, that term isn't entirely accurate. During my first pregnancy, I was nauseated most of the day and evening."

The room swam before my eyes. Not knowing what to say, I sat there being assaulted by different emotions: fear, excitement, concern over what Nathan might say, frustration over how I could be so stupid…then back to fear. A long time passed before I could reply. "Oh, no. What do I do now?"

"Now you take a test. In case it's something else."

Willing to grasp at any straw, I smiled at her and nodded. "Thanks. I'll pick one up after work."

Maybe she didn't believe me, because she studied me for a moment before responding. "Do you want me to go to the drugstore for you before I leave?"

A wave of relief quelled some of the nausea. "Yes, please. I can't sit here and wonder until the end of my shift."

She patted my arm. "Drink some water. I'll be back in ten minutes."

After she left, I went over our interaction in my mind. It could be something else. Nathan and I had been careful. Sure, everyone *said* condoms weren't a hundred percent effective, but no one actually believed it. Leaks, breaks, and failures were one of those things that happened to other people.

Carla returned a few minutes later, test in hand. I hadn't moved a muscle, just sat staring into space while I contemplated what this meant. I'd been planning to finish my probation, get a better job, get my own place, become self-sufficient for the first time in my life. And now, I might have to be responsible for someone else. I'd never get a new job while pregnant.

After thanking her, I took the test into the staff restroom and tried not to have a panic attack. In less than five minutes, my entire life could change. Everything I'd wanted, everything I planned, out the window.

When I was younger, I'd wanted kids. I hated being an only child, because that left me no one else to take care of. I'd been excited when my dad told me his wife was having a baby, until she turned into the stepmonster. It killed me when my attempts to foster a relationship with my half sister got thwarted. Still, I loved playing with Tessa's son. I'd always assumed one day I'd fall in love, get married, and have my own kids.

But I'd also never planned to fall for someone so much older than me, and I realized with a start that I didn't have the first clue whether Nathan wanted more kids. Who could blame him if he didn't? He'd given up his adolescence to raise Gwen. Skipped the keg parties and going to college and pledging a frat to get a job and change diapers. Now that she'd moved out on her own, was I going to ask him to do it all again? It didn't seem fair.

These thoughts all went through my head in the space of a few seconds. According to the directions, it could take up to three minutes to get results. In actuality, the display flashed before I finished washing my hands. One word: PREGNANT.

Chapter 21

Don't despair. Things change quickly. Something might look hopeless,
but you can still turn it around.
—*The Haunted Place* Player Guide

Man, this sucked. Where did I file a complaint? Whoever spread the
myth of "pregnant glow" had lied. I felt like death, all the time. When I
wasn't trying not to puke, I was exhausted and needed to sleep. *All the
time.* Not just in the mornings. Which sucked doubly, because oh, wait, *I
couldn't even drink coffee.* To top it all off, I hadn't mustered up the courage
to tell anyone yet, including Nathan, so I pretended to be knocked out with
a really bad flu. At his insistence, I even went to the doctor, although not
the type of doctor he thought.

Until they did the ultrasound, I allowed myself to believe the test had
been a mistake. I could be stricken with a tumor maybe, or a tapeworm.
Or even a bout of the flu, like I told everyone. Even knowing that it's
virtually impossible for an over-the-counter pregnancy test to return a
false positive, I still hoped right up until I walked into my doctor's office.
But then I heard that little heartbeat, and things got real. I pictured Nathan
holding a tiny baby in his arms, the three of us as a family, and my vision
blurred. With all my heart, I wanted that future for the two of us. If only
there was an easy way to tell him.

Pregnancy explained my symptoms, but knowing the cause didn't make
me feel better. My body rejected all food that tasted good: no pizza, candy,
cookies, ice cream, cake, cupcakes, brownies, pie, Nutella, cookie butter,
chocolate chip cookie dough, French fries…I couldn't eat anything.

Only crackers and water didn't make me puke. Oh, and Taco Bell, for some weird reason. That should've made me concerned, but whatever. Regardless of the time of day, I consumed tacos. Mamá would have been horrified if she knew I ate these instead of making my own. But I hadn't mustered up the courage to tell her yet, and wouldn't until after I talked to Nathan.

After about a week, he started to get concerned. I either needed to tell him, move out, or come up with a very good lie about my condition. The longer I kept it a secret, the more likely he'd figure it out on his own. Or break up with me for having a complete personality change. It's tough to hide feeling horrible all the time. I spent most of my free time lying on the couch, moaning and wondering why anyone ever had more than one kid, outside of multiple births.

Too bad men couldn't give birth They'd have made the process as seamless—and pain free—as using the Starbucks app.

The only relative bright spot was that we got a temporary reprieve from the weekly gaming sessions. While we'd been playing *The Haunted Place*, Shannon had set up a few other groups of play-testers, all at various stages of the game. John's group bypassed ours, and they found a major flaw in the tenth game, a game stopper. As a result, she asked all of us to put things on pause following game nine, so we could try the fix once she'd finished working through it.

The delay didn't bother me. I liked the game, but I wanted to play after Shannon completed it, not when major bugs would ruin the experience. More than anything, I wanted Gwen to rejoin us for the final table. The longer we waited, the more likely she would decide to forgive me. Also, less time spent playing games meant that Tyler, Cody, and Nathan wouldn't start wondering about my sudden aversion to takeout. I could only offer to bring Taco Bell so many times before they wondered if I'd been invaded by a body snatcher. That number was probably once.

But before I talked to Nathan, I needed to see Lucas. Not to tell him about the baby, obviously. In a lot of ways, I never got closure with my ex. To move forward with Nathan, I wanted to confront my past. For some reason, it seemed like it would be easier to tell people about the baby after I said a final good-bye to Lucas. Close one door before opening the next.

Terri would have thrown a fit if she knew what I planned, but better to ask forgiveness than permission. She'd told me at one point that Lucas had moved back in with his parents after posting bail, so I waited for him outside their Back Bay home.

He'd cut his hair since the deposition, probably wanting something more clean cut than dreadlocks for his court appearances. Honestly, removing them made a huge improvement. He seemed paler, too. Without an influx of stolen money, tanning beds probably became cost-prohibitive.

When he saw me leaning against the low wall separating the front yard from the street, he smiled widely. "Missed me, did you? Want another ride on the Lucas train?"

I repressed a shudder. As much as I wanted to point out that I'd be more likely to have sex with anyone else in the world, offending Lucas wouldn't open this conversation on a productive note. "No, but thanks for asking."

"Oh. Then why are you here?"

Until I started to speak, I didn't know what I planned to say. "I guess I wanted to know...Why? You're a smart guy, you got a good degree from an excellent school. We had our future mapped out, and we could've been happy. We *were* happy, or at least I was. Why throw it all away? What possessed you? Why would you cheat on me, steal from our friends and family, betray everyone's trust like that?"

"What do you want me to say, Hol?" He looked down at his hands. "Obviously, I messed up. I lost you, I lost our home, my car...and I'm facing a lot of jail time. Decades. I hope you're not looking for life advice from me."

Of course I wasn't. But if I understood what led him to his actions, it could help me find closure. That's what I needed to move on with my life and let myself enjoy Nathan and the baby. With or without Gwen's acceptance.

I smiled sadly, still unable to fathom how the sweet boy who'd once helped me with my chemistry homework wound up facing multiple felony charges. "No. I'm wondering where we went wrong. Were we doomed from the start because we were so young?"

"Maybe. It started a few months before we graduated. I was doing research, trying to figure out how to get our business off the ground. You were so smart, so good at the programming stuff, and I was worried about letting you down."

My first inclination was to call him a liar. Lucas never struck me as someone with self-confidence issues. But as I'd learned, the best way to feel confident is to fake it. His perceived inadequacies explained a lot about why he'd started controlling me. Not that it excused his behavior. "Why didn't I know about any of this?"

"I never told you." He chuckled. "Maybe if I had, things would have been different. Outside, I seemed so cool, I had it all together. Inside, I was panicking. Then one night, this guy at the library told me he had something that could help me stay awake, help me work better. I said okay, and he handed me a packet of white powder."

"Drugs? You did all of this for drugs?" At first I didn't want to believe it. But then I thought about the clues. Working long hours, then crashing. Random nosebleeds. The way he became so aggressive when Shannon and Gwen confronted him about cheating on me. All things I had explained away at the time.

The more I thought about it, the more fury replaced my confusion. He threw everything away to get high?

He shook his head. "Same old sad story, huh? I only got clean once they arrested me. My head is finally clear. I realize I ruined everything. And I'm sorry."

"So you took my inheritance and put it up your nose?" Frustration made the words come out louder than intended. On the sidewalk, a well-dressed woman walking her dog while talking on her cell phone shot me a dirty look. I lowered my voice. "That's the answer?"

"Look, I'm sorry," he said. "I know it was wrong. I don't expect you to forgive me."

"You think?"

All the times I'd pictured this conversation, never had I expected an explanation that had nothing to do with me. Part of me thought he would say I didn't deserve to be happy. Or that I wasn't good enough for him.

Maybe that was what I was waiting to hear. That I deserved to lose Gwen. I deserved to lose my career. I didn't deserve Nathan. But none of that was remotely true. Everything that went wrong was because of Lucas. He didn't think about me because of his own selfishness. I'd wasted more than enough time on him.

"For what it's worth, if I could go back and do it again, I wouldn't," he said.

I believed him. Not because he hurt me, because he took money our friends couldn't afford to lose, or because he felt contrite for scamming so many people. He didn't regret any of those things. No, I believed that if he could go back and do it again he wouldn't because he got caught. It amazed me that I'd been so blind to Lucas's flaws during our relationship. But at least this conversation had opened my eyes.

I nodded. "Thanks."

"Is there anything else I can say or do?"

"Can you give me my money back?" Instead of answering, he shifted his gaze to the ground. There was nothing left to say. "Good-bye, Lucas."

Before he could reply, I turned and left. As I walked away, I hoped with all my heart that we never saw each other again outside the courtroom.

During our relationship, Lucas had controlled everything. I wore the clothes he liked, I used a lot of makeup because he said it made me look more polished, I filled the roles he gave me. The man Lucas wanted to be would never have lowered himself to marry a woman who worked behind the counter in a game store. He never even joined us for game nights before Gwen met Cody, back when we could've used a fourth for most games.

Since our breakup, I felt more like myself than ever. I wore clothes I liked, ate what I wanted, went where I wanted, and did what I pleased. I spoke my mind. At some point, maybe I'd become as selfish as Lucas. The first night with Nathan had been a fluke, fueled by jokes about turning into the Flirt, the giddy feeling that accompanies weddings, a longtime secret crush, and too much alcohol. It could've ended there, and no one ever would've known. But it felt good, so I didn't even try to stop myself. I made a couple of half-hearted attempts to transfer my feelings to Marc, but that was it. Was hurting Gwen—and Marc—for my own pleasure any better than what Lucas did?

Sure, I didn't take anyone's money, but I definitely put my own interests ahead of people I cared about.

Instead of going home, I got off the T in Harvard Square, headed to the store. It was still cold, but after weeks of temperatures in the single digits, thirty-five degrees felt like a tropical paradise. The snow melted in the sun, so students filled the once-grassy areas, some tossing a ball back and forth, others studying or chatting. Here and there, a couple sat on a bench, her head in his lap or leaning against each other, fingers entwined. Lucas and I used to do that. Were all these couples doomed, too?

A realization hit me. With Nathan, I'd found what those students had. When the two of us were together, the rest of the world fell away. Boring things seemed more interesting. Cold days felt warmer. Everything looked happier and brighter. Not because of him, but because of the way I felt when we were together. With Lucas, I'd never felt like "enough." With Nathan, I became the most cherished person in the world. He didn't care where I worked or how much makeup I wore.

That's why I took a chance on him. The human need to be loved overpowered everything else. I'd betrayed Gwen's trust because I found something worth the risk of upsetting her. Because the hope of being loved and having a relationship like hers and Cody's let me believe that everything would work out. I deserved to be happy, and until that morning in Mexico, I hadn't been. I'd thought my friend would eventually be happy for me, in the way that friends should be, once she saw how well Nathan and I fit together.

The faster I walked, the more my thoughts finally came together. I went up one street and down the next, fueled by a burst of realization. Lucas was selfish, weak, and scared. He could have avoided everything by talking to me about his fears, but instead, he put his needs first. The need to be the richest, the smartest, the most successful. Then the need for drugs. He destroyed our life, and while he regretted the probability of going to jail, he didn't have any remorse for hurting me. We were nothing alike. He didn't deserve my forgiveness, but letting go of my animosity would make me feel better.

On the other hand, I deserved Gwen's forgiveness. She needed to understand that I hadn't done this to hurt her, that I wanted Nathan to be happy every bit as much as she did. He wasn't going to get hurt, not on my watch. I wasn't trying to replace her or come between them, but I made him happy in a way she couldn't. In a way she *shouldn't.*

I'd spent enough time waiting for her to come around. As soon as I told Nathan about the baby, I was going to get my best friend back.

Chapter 22

Always be aware of how your actions affect the other players.
—*The Haunted Place* Player Guide

That night, the time came to share my news. I couldn't put it off any longer. Nathan needed to know about the baby so we could plan our next steps. Hopefully, he'd be as excited as I was, but I couldn't count on that. This was his second unplanned pregnancy in thirty years, and he might not be prepared. We'd only been dating about six weeks. If he wanted to throw me out, I needed to know. If he got excited, knowing he wanted the baby would make me feel much better. As would having someone to support me.

After seeing so many funny pregnancy announcements online, part of me wanted to set up something exciting and video it. At the same time, he'd be suspicious if he walked in to see me filming. And I didn't feel well enough to engineer much. Showering, putting on clean clothes, and cooking dinner sapped my energy. I nearly fell asleep on the couch waiting for him to come home and eat.

When his car pulled into the driveway, I lowered the lights and lit the candles on the table. Then I waited.

A moment later, the front lock clanked open, and footsteps filled the front hall. "Honey, I'm home!"

"Hey!" In my nervousness, the words came out more like a croak. I sipped my water, wishing more than anything that it was wine. Then I tried again. "In here."

He stopped in the doorway, letting out a low whistle. "You look amazing."

"Thanks." The way his gaze lingered on my breasts made me glad I'd taken the extra effort to look nice. But that look was going to very quickly lead us away from productive conversation.

"There's something I need to tell you."

His smile dropped. "Is everything okay?"

"Yeah, absolutely!" I'd planned to lead up to this, but maybe faster was better. Like ripping off a Band-Aid. I didn't want to unnecessarily worry him. With a deep breath, I pasted a smile on my face. This was, after all, amazing news, even if I was terrified to tell him. "I'm pregnant."

"You're...having a baby?"

I nodded.

"My baby?"

I nodded again, this time a little exasperated at the question. Who else's baby could it be? Before we got together, I hadn't had sex in well over a year.

A massive smile split his face in two. With a whoop, he raced across the room and swept me into his arms, spinning me in a circle that would have been exhilarating if it didn't also make me want to puke. "Holly, that's amazing!"

Relief flooded me at his words. "You're not mad?"

"Why would I be mad?"

"Well, we didn't plan this."

He kissed me briefly, tenderly. "I don't care. I love you."

My heart swelled. We'd never said it before, but I'd been sure of my feelings for a long time. Now I knew he felt the same. Everything would be okay. "I love you, too."

"Let's get married."

His words sent a shock wave through me. In all the time I'd spent thinking about how he would react to the baby, a proposal had never crossed my mind. Not after his first marriage ended in such disaster. I pulled away, disentangling myself from his arms. I loved him, absolutely. I wanted to be with him. But to get married because of a broken condom?

I weighed what I wanted to say. Here Nathan was offering me exactly what I wanted: him, forever. A public declaration of our relationship. And yet, while my heart should be singing with joy, it felt like I'd dropped into an icy bath. I didn't want him like this. How could I ever trust that he wanted me for me and not for the baby?

Before I could stop myself, a single word slipped out. "No."

In a heartbeat, he went from looking like he'd won the lottery to like someone kicked his puppy. My heart lurched. I hadn't wanted to say it like that.

"I'm sorry. That's not what I meant," I said.

"Did you mean to say yes?"

"No." This was going well. I took a deep breath. "I love you. I want to be with you. When I was growing up, I dreamed about someday falling in love, getting married, and having a baby."

"Why do I feel like you're about to say 'but'?"

"In my fantasies, I was marrying the man of my dreams *because he loved me and wanted to marry me.* Not because he 'had to.'"

"Who says I *have* to marry you?" he demanded, hands on his hips. "Did I say that?"

"I know that's why you married Gwen's mom—"

His face shuttered closed as he interrupted me. "So you think you know everything about me? You think I don't know what I want, that I'm repeating the same dumb mistake I made at fifteen?"

My heart clenched. When he said it like that, it sounded bad. At the same time, yes, that was exactly what I thought. He had offered to marry me because it seemed like the right thing to do, not because he wanted to spend the rest of his life with me. Especially when the proposal came spur of the moment, with no ring, after finding out about the baby. He didn't plan this. The words came out because of the baby. Exactly like with Gwen's mom.

When I didn't answer, his shoulders dropped. "Okay, I see how it is. Thank you for protecting me from myself."

"I'm not saying we can't be together. I want to raise this child with you. I just don't want to rush into marriage." What I didn't say was, *I don't want you or our baby to resent me for trapping you, the way Gwen resents her mother.*

"I know it seems fast, but we've known each other for years. We've been living together since before we started dating, and we make a great team. You've seen me at my worst, nursing me through a broken leg. I've seen you dealing with everything Lucas threw at you. When you're around, I'm happy. And I make you happy, too."

"You do, and those are great reasons to continue dating, even continue living together. I want to be with you. I just don't think marriage is a good idea right now."

"What could be better? I love you, you love me, we're having a baby. Marriage is the next logical step."

"Come on, you never would have proposed if I wasn't pregnant. Right? We were perfectly happy the way things were." He didn't answer, but the truth of my words was written across his face. I continued, "Getting married because of a baby is a terrible idea."

As soon as the sentence left my mouth, I wanted to take it back. I meant us, not Nathan and Gwen's mom. And yet...some of the same principles applied. They hadn't been dating long when they found out about their baby. They wouldn't have gotten married otherwise. It turned out to be a huge mistake. Gwen's mom made him miserable. She took more than ten years from him. I couldn't ruin his life like that.

"You don't get it." He shook his head sadly. "Maybe none of this is a good idea. Maybe this whole thing was a mistake."

My heart shattered. In all the time we'd been together, I'd always been an equal, even though he was older and more successful. But he thought getting involved with me was a mistake. Suddenly, I felt like some dumb kid. "I'm going to Shannon's."

He didn't answer, calling my bluff without words. I didn't want to leave, not again. I wanted to stay and fight for us, to hear him say we could still be together. We didn't need to get married right now. But his silence spoke volumes. I didn't know what to do, other than keep up the pretense of wanting to go.

Like a sleepwalker, I went to my room and pulled out my bags, waiting for him to appear, to say anything. I gathered my stuff from his room as if lead filled my veins. When I finally had everything packed, Nathan still stood in the living room, arms folded across his chest, mouth set firmly in a hard line across his features. He hadn't moved an inch.

He remained there as I took my stuff down the hall. As I left my key on the table beside the door. As I walked out of the house. All the way to the T, I listened for footsteps, praying he'd stop me. He never did.

My phone rang before the train reached my destination. My heart skipped a beat before I realized it was my regular ringtone, not *The Office* theme song long-ago assigned to Nathan. With a deep breath, I lifted the phone to my ear. "Hello?"

"Hi, Holly? It's Rob."

Despite the fact that my whole world was crashing in on me, I still needed a job, so I forced myself to sound cheerful. "Hey! How are you?"

"Great! I've found a couple of jobs that might interest you. Are you still open to relocation?"

Without Nathan, Gwen, or a job, very little tied me to the Boston area. It was an expensive place to raise a child. Sure, I'd have to come up with a way to share custody, but one thing at a time. First, I needed income. "Yes, absolutely. Although I'd prefer to stick with companies that will offer me a package to offset moving expenses."

"No problem. I've already talked to two places about you, and both want to set up an initial phone interview. One in Phoenix, one in Albany."

"Sounds great!" At least Albany wasn't far. We scheduled phone calls for both companies. Then I said, "But do me a favor and see what you can find nearby?"

"Still on it."

After I thanked him, we said good-bye and disconnected.

The pending interviews should have made me feel better, but dread swamped me. Moving to another state would close the door on me and Nathan forever. Not that I had a choice. Even if we worked things out, I couldn't continue to mooch off his generosity while working at the game store, making barely above minimum wage. My current pay wouldn't cover day care in the Boston area, and I couldn't expect Nathan to pay for everything. I needed to stand on my own two feet, and that meant finding a job wherever possible. If we didn't work things out, Boston no longer held the same appeal for me.

When I got to Shannon's, I pushed the bell and stared at the ground, praying she answered and not her roommate. I hadn't thought to text ahead. Not that it mattered. With nowhere else to go, I'd wait as long as needed.

The door opened. "Oh, no. What happened?"

I stepped into Shannon's open arms and finally allowed myself to dissolve into tears.

* * * *

After my argument with Nathan, I gave myself the weekend to mope. People came back from worse fights, but I didn't know what the answer was. I couldn't let him rush into another marriage because something slipped by the quality-control people at the condom factory. If he didn't see that I'd refused because I loved him, I didn't know what to do. And if his stance was all or nothing—well, marriage couldn't resolve that. So I took two days to binge-watch TV and accept that we might not be able to work things out before I rejoined the land of the living. He didn't text me; I didn't text him.

The phone interviews both went well, and each company requested a second, in-person interview. I made plans to drive to Albany to meet with the head honchos the following week. Then the Phoenix company offered to fly me out. Things were starting to look up.

Too bad my professional life didn't start to improve until my personal life descended into chaos. With my relationship with Nathan up in the air—probably over, if I got either of these jobs—and a baby on the way, I needed the support of my friends more than ever. We'd gotten each other through grad school, helped Gwen resolve her issues with her mother. They helped me when Lucas got arrested, and we both helped Shannon when Nana got sick. Now I needed them both.

With that in mind, I rededicated myself to getting my best friend back. Gwen tended to heat up fast, but she'd never held a grudge this long. Her sustained anger felt like a reaction to what she saw as an extended betrayal. I understood, but hoped to fix things.

Since she'd blocked me on Facebook and Twitter, it seemed unlikely she'd answer the phone when I called. I sent a couple of texts, but there was no way to know if they'd gone through. If she'd blocked my number, I could spend the rest of my life sending texts into the abyss, waiting for a response that never came.

I could text her from Shannon's phone, but I didn't want to put our friend in the middle. Instead, I checked Gwen's blog daily to see when she'd be in Boston. Meanwhile, I kept going to work and practicing in my head what to say.

Finally, I got my chance. I had an early shift at the store, and according to *Gallivanting Gwen*, my friend would be in Boston for a few days before flying to warmer locations until spring arrived. As soon as work ended, I steeled myself for a confrontation and examined my secret weapon: a box of Shannon's Nana's award-winning cupcakes, brought from home.

Friendships usually couldn't be fixed with a five-dollar bribe, but a quality baked good often put Gwen in a good mood. Nana's red velvet cupcakes were her favorite.

Normally, they were my favorite, too. Unfortunately, all foods still nauseated me. I couldn't even look at baked goods. The only way to transport them without getting sick involved putting the box in several bags to block the sickly sugary smell. My stomach churned, anyway. Hopefully, I'd manage to hand the package to Gwen without incident.

A long time passed after I knocked on her door. I wondered if covering the peephole would make them more or less likely to open up. At the same time, if she would leave me standing on the front porch in the still-not-much-above-freezing cold, it was time to give up.

New moms didn't have a ton of free time, right? I didn't need friends. I'd find a new job, probably in another state, and the baby would take up my time. The door blurred as I thought about the loneliness of that life.

At least I'd get to see Nathan when I brought the baby for visits. I didn't doubt for a second he'd want to be involved.

In the back of my mind, I realized that other options existed. Being a single parent wasn't my only choice. We hadn't been trying to have a baby, this wasn't planned, and raising a baby on my own would be tough. But at the same time, as miserable as I felt, I didn't even consider not keeping the baby. It was a part of me, a part of Nathan, a reminder of our time together. When I wasn't panicking about the future, having a baby felt right. I already loved the little nugget inside me.

This wasn't the time to let my hormones take over. I needed to think positively. Pasting a huge smile on my face, I lifted the box of cupcakes where anyone looking through the peephole would see it and rang the bell. Maybe they hadn't heard my knock.

By the time the door swung open, a chill had settled into my bones. Gwen stood there, staring at me with her arms crossed. She said nothing.

"Hey," I said.

She didn't reply.

I lifted the box. "I come bearing baked goods. Please give me a few minutes."

She turned and walked away, leaving the door open. I followed before she changed her mind. Removing my coat seemed overly optimistic, but I left my boots in the rack near the door before padding into the living room behind her.

"I'm sorry," I said.

"You're sorry you slept with my dad, or you're sorry things didn't work out?"

Of course he'd told her about our fight. A pang hit my stomach at the realization: If he told her we broke up, he must really believe it was over. He wouldn't have mentioned an argument if he wanted to work things out. I wondered if he told her why we'd fought, but didn't ask.

"I'm sorry I hurt you," I said. "It kills me to know I may have destroyed what would have been a lifelong friendship."

"You're not sorry you did it?"

Sorry for falling in love? Sorry for being with someone who made me feel good about myself, even though it didn't last? Sorry for the baby growing inside of me? Absolutely not. "No. I loved him."

"Good. Because Dad's a wonderful guy, and I'm not about to stand here and listen to you talk bad about him."

"Never." Things seemed to be going okay, so I held the box out again. "Cupcake? Nana made them."

She quirked an eyebrow at me. "This doesn't make everything okay. And I'm not sharing."

"That's fine."

She pulled layer after layer off the box, snorting at how well-packaged it was. "You couldn't have added a few more bags?"

"Just keeping the rain out." A partial truth.

Finally reaching her goal, she broke the tape and lifted the box to her face. The scents of chocolate and vanilla comingled in the air. My stomach rebelled, and I took a small step backward under the pretense of adjusting my coat.

Gwen removed a cake from the box, examining it. She licked her lips, and I forced my gaze away. Everything about food made me sick. What a terrible idea. I should've brought her a new game instead, or a funny T-shirt.

"It hurt when you went behind my back," she finally said. "If you'd told me up-front that you had real feelings for him, I would have had time to deal with it. Things might have been different. But as long as I let myself believe it was a joke, I didn't have to consider how I would feel if you two got together."

I nodded, still trying to repress the growing nausea from the scent of the baked goods. "If I'd known something was going to happen, I would have come to you first. We didn't plan it. And after we got together, I didn't want to ruin your wedding day. I figured it was a one-time thing, no reason to upset you. Once we decided to make it work, I should have put the relationship on hold until we had a conversation."

"Yes. But it's more than that," she said. "He's one of the most important people in my life. For so long, we only had each other. That creates a tight bond. There's nothing I want more than for him to be happy. I hated to think you were using him to get over Lucas, of all people."

My lips twitched. Gwen never liked Lucas. I hadn't thought about it that way, but I could see how she might be doubly offended to think I'd hurt her dad because of my ex. "It was nothing like that. There's something between us. Or there was. It's probably over."

She met my gaze, held it for a long time. "He's miserable."

"Me too."

"Good. It's your fault."

I didn't point out that it took two to tango. And it didn't matter, because she was right. I could've tried harder to stay away. I could've done something to cool my feelings before they got out of control. I hadn't wanted to. I'd wanted him to love me.

My eyes filled with tears, and I blinked them away. Too late. Gwen's face softened the tiniest bit. "I'm sorry, Hol. I know things have been rough."

Sniffling, I nodded. "They really have. But I swear, I wasn't using him. I wanted things to work out. But sometimes two people aren't meant to be together."

There was so much more I wanted to tell her. If she knew about the baby, she'd overcome her remaining hesitations about our friendship. But I didn't want her back that way.

"Here." She shoved the box at me, putting it right under my nose. "Maybe I can share, after all."

The sugar smells kicked me in the gut. So much wonderful sweetness that I'd have loved under ordinary circumstances. Not now. I couldn't handle it. With one hand over my mouth, I turned away, praying my lunch would stay in place. But it was too late. I barely managed to get away from the cupcakes before I puked all over the carpet.

Gwen stared at me, eyes wide. Oh, no. I couldn't. Panic filled me. Not knowing what else to do, I bolted for the front door. Pausing only to pick up my boots, I streaked down the front steps, leaving a horrified Gwen behind me still holding the open box.

Chapter 23

Never lose hope. The deck may seem stacked against you. But the darkest
hour is right before the dawn.
—*The Haunted Place* Player Guide

Crashing on Shannon's couch when Lucas and I first broke up hadn't
been a big deal, but after the weeks spent in Nathan's soft, luxurious bed,
the novelty of sleeping with springs poking my back wore off quickly.
Wanting to puke all the time didn't help. After only a couple of days, I
realized that I needed to find a permanent solution. For one thing, her
roommate had taken to glaring at me when she thought I wasn't looking.

I'd always gotten along with Ellen, but she'd made it clear I'd worn
out my welcome. Luckily, a few days after I arrived, she went home for
spring break. That gave me a couple of weeks to scan roommate listings
and apartment ads in peace.

Quickly, I came to two conclusions: One, I couldn't move in with a
stranger, unless they were renting out two rooms instead of one. Signing
a one-year roommate agreement while pregnant didn't make any sense.
I'd have to move again when the baby was born, assuming I could find
someone to even give me a lease for just a few months. The vast majority
of Boston residents renting out a room in an apartment were students.
The rentals fell into one of two categories: sublets from June-August for
students who'd gone home for summer break or one-year leases starting
in September. Neither of those worked for me, since it was April.

Second, I couldn't afford a two-bedroom place with my income from
Game On!, unless I wanted to move about forty miles outside of the city
(and possibly not even then). Moving away couldn't be ruled out completely,

especially when I had interviews lined up in other states. At the same time, I wasn't about to work at a game store for barely over minimum wage with a two-hour commute on each end. Not while paying to leave a child in day care. Nathan would help out—or I assumed he would—but I didn't know how to talk to him. I'd been avoiding his calls. I needed to find myself, to stand on my own, and not grab on to anyone who drifted along. I couldn't be with Nathan because it was expected or the "right thing to do" or easy, the way being with Lucas was easy. He needed to want me for me, not because we were having a baby.

Maybe things would get easier after the baby was born, but I doubted it. I needed to get my own life figured out and not rely on him to bail me out. I wasn't his ex-wife, and I didn't want to need his help. Living with Nathan and letting him take care of us was the easy solution, but it was time to stand on my two feet for a change. I'd been treading water since the breakup, working at Game On! because I needed income, with no plans for my future. I bounced around, accepting what was offered. It was past time to think for myself and decide what I wanted.

Traveling for my interviews gave me plenty of time to think, but I didn't feel any clearer about what to do. Both companies seemed interested. Both would pay me to move. One had on-site day care, the other allowed me to telecommute. Neither would allow me to be near Nathan. My heart panged at the thought, but we weren't together at that point, anyway. As much as it would hurt to move away and close that door, it hurt more to be so near him and not see him. I missed our gaming sessions, our late nights binging *The Office*. We used to Netflix and Chill long before that phrase took on new meaning. Now even watching TV reminded me of my loneliness.

A fresh start would help. After the baby was born and I had time to heal, we could visit. Albany was much closer to Boston, but Phoenix had a good airport and better weather.

The day after I returned from my interview in Phoenix, I was sitting at the kitchen table, scouring Craigslist on my tablet and trying not to panic when the doorbell rang. Probably UPS, so I ignored it. Most of the drivers knew to ring once, open the outside door, and leave packages in the inside hallway. The entryway only led upstairs to Shannon's apartment or downstairs to Nana's, so anything left was safe from theft and the elements.

A moment later, the bell rang again. Grumbling, I dragged myself away from an apartment listing that detailed at great length a roommate's expected responsibilities. (Weekly grout scrubbing? If not for HGTV, I wouldn't even know what grout was. Why would anyone scrub it? Weekly?) It might be time to start looking at the listings in other areas, just in case.

Pasting a smile on my face, I reached the door as the bell rang a third time. UPS was never this persistent. If the person on the other side of the door started encouraging me to accept Jesus Christ as my Lord and Savior, they were about to get an earful they'd never forget.

The door swung open, and my heart stopped. On the porch, clutching an umbrella and wearing an impatient expression, stood Gwen. The last person I'd expected to seek me out. Not quite believing she was there, but not wanting to shatter the illusion if she wasn't, I simply stared.

"Nice to see you, too," she said. "Are you going to invite me in?"

Still unable to speak, I nodded, stepping back to allow her to pass. She leaned her umbrella against the wall, hung her dripping jacket from one of the hooks Nana had installed about forty years ago, and headed up the stairs toward Shannon's apartment.

It took almost a full minute for me to get over my surprise enough to close the front door and follow her. When I got back to the kitchen, she stood at the counter, tapping her fingers against the tile.

Finally, I found my voice. "Hey."

"Look, I know I've been a real asshole," she said. I responded in some kind of blinking Morse code, which she took as encouragement to continue. "For a long time before I met Cody, Dad was my whole world. He was my best friend—still is, as much as I love you and Shannon and Cody."

I nodded. I knew all this. But since she was apologizing, I didn't want to break the spell. Instead of saying anything, I sat at the table, looking up at her.

"And, of course, I always knew you had a crush on him. You didn't exactly hide it."

At that, I smiled. "At first, it really was a joke. I never dreamed of acting on it."

"What changed?"

"I changed," I said. "Part of it was the game. Tapping in to my inner flirt helped me come out of my shell, be more confident. That Inner Diva class helped, too."

She grumbled. "Great. I created a monster."

"You helped me a lot." With a chuckle, I said, "But it was more than that. Being on my own, out from under Lucas's thumb, helped me find my own sense of self. But even as I started feeling better about myself, I knew how you felt about the two of us. I never would've gone for it."

"You're saying he started it?"

"It was mutual," I said. "But I wouldn't have found the courage to act on my feelings if I hadn't gotten so drunk. There we were, in this beautiful foreign country, this romantic setting…with a lot of alcohol. Nathan and I happened to run into each other after the rehearsal dinner."

"Please don't give me any more details."

"Cross my heart. It was so much easier to bury my feelings when I thought he'd never reciprocate. Once I knew he liked me, too, things spiraled. I really am sorry for hurting you. Something inside me wouldn't let me give up without trying."

"I know the feeling," she said. "Remember when I met Cody?"

"I remember that you *hated* him." Now that the conversation seemed on relatively okay ground, I got up to refill my cup with tea. "Do you want a diet soda?"

"No thanks." She shifted her weight. "I know how hot it can be to go for someone forbidden. And I know that once you start, it's easy to get carried away. But seriously, Hol. *He's my dad.*"

"I know," I said simply. "He's also a forty-three-year-old man. Young, vibrant, funny, caring, and someone who deserves to be in love."

She shook her head. "So it wasn't just a fling? Something you did because you knew you weren't supposed to?"

Her words cut through my heart like a knife. "We've known each other for almost five years. Do you really think I went after him to hurt you?"

"Of course not. I'm sorry." Her voice cracked on the words. "And yet, here we are. I'm the bitch, you're…back living at Shannon's, no offense, but looking like absolute hell. Dad's more miserable than when Mom left."

"Really?" Perhaps I sounded too hopeful, but I couldn't help myself. I craved news of Nathan, and hearing that he missed me made everything seem a little bit better.

"Yeah. That's why I'm here. He looks worse than you. Stopped shaving, stopped showering. Sits in his recliner, playing old video games. He hasn't been to the shop in a week."

"You're kidding."

"I wish. I spent years trying to get the man to take a vacation. Barely got him to Mexico for the wedding. But now…he looks destroyed." Her voice softened. "It took spending the day with him yesterday to realize how much he cares about you. How horrible I am for trying to keep the two of you apart."

"You're not horrible," I said. "You were hurt. We betrayed your trust. And we lied to you about it, for weeks. When I think about the way you found out…"

She shuddered, but she was smiling. "Please don't remind me. I might need therapy."

"Sorry. Again."

"I know. Me too." She opened her arms, and we hugged.

I don't know how long we stood there, too happy at this development to ever want to move again. When we pulled away, her shirt was wet from where my face pressed against it.

"Friends again?"

"Best friends," I said.

"Great!" She pulled out a chair and sat. "And I know you said this before, but please tell me that your breakup didn't have anything to do with me. I can't stand thinking I'm the reason that two of my favorite people are so miserable."

In a way, she was the reason, but not like she thought. I didn't want to tell her, to make her feel worse. At the same time, I was done keeping secrets from my best friend. This secret would reveal itself soon enough, anyway.

"It wasn't you." I took a deep breath, willing my voice not to crack. "We broke up because...I'm pregnant."

Her mouth fell open. An excruciating moment passed before she remembered how to speak. "Oh my God. Seriously?"

I nodded.

"I thought you were on birth control."

"When the business went under, my insurance changed. I could've gotten a new prescription from MassHealth, but at that point, I didn't see myself ever having sex again. Taking the pill every day reminded me of being alone, so I thought I'd be happier without it. Figured I'd get a new prescription if and when I started seeing someone. And then, well...things happened unexpectedly."

She put her hands on her face. "I don't know what to say. Wow. I'm going to be a big sister?"

"Looks like."

"And...Dad broke up with you? Because of the baby."

This time, my voice cracked. "He proposed."

"Oh, no." The joy drained from her face. She got it immediately. "So this is because of me."

"Not directly."

"You broke up with him because you didn't want him to give up the things he wanted to raise another unexpected kid. Like he did when he was in high school. How is that not about me?"

She knew me too well. She knew both of us too well.

"That wasn't your fault. You didn't ask to be born." I sighed. "I love him. I want to be with him. But I want to be with him because he wants to be with me, not because he thinks he has to."

"Well, if it helps at all, he loves you, too."

"I know. But we can't be together, not like this."

"Seriously, Hol, listen to me," she said. "I'm the first person to admit my parents were wrong for each other. When Beverly left, did it bother him? Of course. But not because they shared some epic love. Because he blamed himself, because he had the idea of the perfect nuclear family."

"I get that. But I'm not going to be her replacement."

"That's the point. You're *not a replacement*. He's in love with you. He wasn't in love with her when they got married. They grew some affection over time, but she never made him happy."

For a moment, I felt the tiniest bit of hope in my stomach. Or possibly the baby was objecting to the eggs I ate earlier. "He told you that?"

"He didn't have to. I know him, remember? Sure, I was only ten when she left, but even I could tell how miserable he was." She leaned forward. "Listen, because I'm only going to say this once. This isn't easy for me."

"I know, and I appreciate you being here."

"I'm trying to get over my issues. And I will, eventually. But you two need to get over your issues, too. If you want to be together, it doesn't matter what I think."

"What if he wants to be with me for the wrong reasons?"

"Trust me, he doesn't."

"That's not the only thing," I said with a bit of hesitation. "I'm still trying to find a job—and there's nothing near Boston. I may have to move."

"Then you have to decide what's more important." She checked the time on her phone. "Okay, I'm driving to New Hampshire for the afternoon, and I don't want to fight traffic. I've gotta go. But seriously, talk to him, especially before you take a job out of state. Don't let your pride ruin a good thing. I almost did that with Cody."

"I'm glad it worked out for you," I said. "Not everyone gets the fairy tale."

"Maybe not. But you will, once you get out of your own way and realize you deserve to be happy. He wouldn't have proposed if he didn't love you. Not again."

She gave me another hug and was gone, like my fairy god-stepdaughter. For a long time, I sat and thought about her words. I loved Nathan. I'd believed he loved me, too. But we'd never talked about forever before this happened. In all the years I'd known him, he'd never indicated any interest in getting married again.

Was Gwen right? Would he want to be with me without a baby?

I wanted to believe her. I also, for the first time in my life, wanted to stand on my own rather than relying on other people to prop me up. If Nathan and I were meant to be together, we'd figure it out. But I couldn't marry him because of the baby. I couldn't move back in with him and let him take care of me.

Outside, a car door slammed. An engine roared, taking Gwen back to her glamorous life on the road. I sat down at the table, picked up my tablet, and went back to searching the job and apartment ads. The baby would have a good home, one I provided for him or her.

* * * *

Three days later, I sat at work, afraid to contemplate the email sitting in my in-box. The Albany company wanted me to work for them, and they'd pay for a move. I could start whenever I wanted. Their facility included on-site day care. I should have been ecstatic. But Gwen's words from the other day stuck with me. Taking a job in Albany meant severing things with Nathan forever. Did I want to take a job out of state without talking to him? After seeing how excited he was about the baby, how could I think about moving away? Albany was only a three-hour drive, but still. On the other hand, I needed income. Just because Nathan would pay support didn't mean I could live off of him.

As these thoughts spiraled around in my head, my phone rang. Technically, I wasn't supposed to use it while on the clock, but John and Carla didn't mind, as long as there weren't any customers. I shifted so I could see the front door if it opened, lowered my voice, and answered.

"Holly? It's Terri." She sounded pissed.

Uh-oh. I'd never told her about my trip to visit Lucas, partially because I knew she'd be upset, and partially because the proposal and breakup and everything had driven it from my mind. But her voice told me she'd found out. She clearly didn't like what I'd done, even though I'd checked my plea agreement before I went. Talking to Lucas didn't violate any of the terms.

Keeping my voice casual, I said, "Hey, T. How are you?"

"Oh, I'm doing quite well, actually." She paused and cleared her throat. "Have you, by any chance, been communicating with your ex? Gone to see him or asked his lawyer to give him a message?"

Yup. She knew. My mouth went dry. "Um…I'm sorry."

She sighed. "Ordinarily, I'd be giving you a long lecture right about now. But lucky for you, whatever you said, it worked a miracle. Instead of forcing a lengthy and expensive trial, Lucas accepted a plea bargain."

"What?!" From the beginning, we'd expected this case to go to trial. My ex had steadfastly refused to reveal where any of the money was, refused to cooperate with authorities, and declined to even consider a deal. He'd always planned to go to trial and throw me under the bus in hopes of winning sympathy points with the jurors. The fact that his defense was a total jerk move unfortunately didn't make it illegal, according to Terri.

"My thoughts exactly," she said. "But he's had a change of heart. Maybe the realization that he could spend most of the rest of his youth in jail finally got to him. He was facing ten to fifteen years on multiple counts, and I told him I'd ask the judge to make each term consecutive."

"A change of heart is good, right? What's the deal?"

"He offered to plead to the money laundering charges, as long as we make the sentences concurrent. We'd drop intent to defraud. Twelve years, with good behavior, he could be out in eight."

"Wow." A lot could change in eight years. On the one hand, it didn't seem like enough to make up for what he'd taken. On the other hand, he'd done me a huge favor by showing his true colors now, instead of when we were fifty. "So that's it? The case is over?"

"Not exactly. I told him we'd only accept the deal if he gave us the remaining money. And it turns out, there's a *lot* left. He stashed it overseas, presumably to help fund his lifestyle once he fled the U.S., but he never got the chance to spend any of it."

My ears perked up. "How much?"

"Not all of it, I'm afraid. But almost two-thirds. The attorney general will distribute the money among all the victims, but even so, you're going to get back close to two hundred thousand dollars."

Oh my. I couldn't breathe. I'd kissed that money good-bye over a year ago. I'd come to terms with the fact that I wouldn't be able to buy a home in the Boston area ever, that I probably wouldn't be a business owner, but... this changed everything. Doors suddenly opened all around me. "That's amazing! Thank you so much."

"Don't count your chickens yet. It'll take a few months to get it. But I wanted you to know it was coming," she said. "There's one more thing."

"It gets better?"

"He insisted we release you from probation now, since your testimony is no longer necessary. It'll take a few weeks. You're not off the hook until he's sentenced. But it'll be sooner than expected."

Wow. In my wildest fantasies, I'd never imagined this could happen. "Not to look a gift horse, but…why?"

"His lawyer said he realized how much his actions affected you. He wanted to make things right. Personally, I wouldn't question it."

A squeal of joy escaped me. "Wow. That's amazing. Thank you! I can't believe it!"

The end of my probation would free me up to start the Albany job as soon as I could find a place and move. Having that money opened up so many possibilities. For the first time in a long time, instead of fumbling along and doing whatever came up, I could control my destiny.

Things weren't perfect. I still needed a job—I wasn't dense enough to think that a couple hundred thousand dollars would last forever, especially with a baby on the way. But not being desperate for work gave me leverage I hadn't expected. After thanking Terri profusely, I called the HR department in Albany to discuss the generous offer they'd made me.

Chapter 24

Congratulations on making it this far! By now, you probably have a plan for attacking the final level. Unfortunately, the best-laid plans tend to go awry.

—*The Haunted Place* Player Guide

After my second call, I picked up the phone again, this time to talk to Shannon. She and the rest of our friends would be arriving at the store to play the final episode of *The Haunted Place* in about six hours. She usually came straight from work, but I hoped she'd have time to help me with something first.

Then I called the rest of the players, except Nathan. Everyone offered me encouragement. I spent the rest of my shift pacing back and forth and practicing what to say. Knowing I wouldn't *need* Nathan to support me, to take care of me and the baby, gave me the freedom to accept that I wanted him in my life. This wasn't about floundering along, taking whatever came up, like with Lucas, or Game On!, or going out with Marc because he came into the store and seemed interested. This was about what I wanted.

Shortly after Shannon got to the store, Tyler, Gwen, and Cody arrived. Even after my afternoon talk with Gwen, a massive weight lifted off my shoulders at the sight of her. She deserved to be here for the final game. So did Nathan, although he hadn't arrived yet. It hadn't occurred to me that he might skip it because of me.

I didn't want to ask, but Gwen saw me looking around and picked up on my unspoken question. "He's running late, but said to go ahead and eat dinner. He'll be here soon."

Excellent. If necessary, I would have gone to his house after the game, but I wanted to talk to him as soon as possible.

Finally, he appeared in the doorway. All the oxygen left the room. Gwen said he was miserable without me, but he looked fantastic in a green, long-sleeved Henley shirt and jeans. It took all my restraint to avoid throwing myself at him where he stood in the doorway.

Instead, I waited for him to take his usual seat next to me. "Hey. You look good."

He smiled at me. "So do you. How are you feeling?"

"Much better." I hoped the look I gave him conveyed that I wasn't only talking about my physical wellness.

"And how's the baby?" He squeezed my hand under the table, so maybe he got what I wanted to convey. But maybe he just wanted to make sure I stayed healthy for the baby's sake.

"Still making me nauseated a lot of the time, but otherwise strong and healthy. We can talk more after the game?"

He nodded. "Absolutely. I want to be here for you."

I wanted him there for me, too. And not just when I felt like puking.

At the conclusion of the last game, the house began disintegrating around us. Now our primary objective was to escape before it killed us all—but that was easier said than done. For one thing, we needed to find a key to the front door. For another, at the end of each round, a random die roll potentially would require us to cross off random rooms on the board, rendering them unusable and impossible to pass. Moving around became more difficult on every turn.

Still, we managed to plod along. If we beat this level, we'd win the entire game. We'd get a point total that, if we were playing the finished version of the game, could be used to go online and compare our score with other players around the world. Our characters possessed the skills and tools we needed. The only thing left was working together and executing a plan.

Finally, we made it into the home stretch. Tyler rolled the dice to avoid a collapsing ceiling, making it down to the main level. Behind him, the roof caved in, leaving the stairway impassible. Thanks to the elevator being taken permanently out of service in the last game, anyone on the top floor would have been trapped and out of the game.

The rest of us were on the two lower floors, although that was a mixed blessing. If we didn't all get out within the next five or six turns, we'd lose. I had to hand it to Shannon. She'd done a great job of making the game escalate each time we played, until we found ourselves with the tools and knowledge needed to pass the finale.

We couldn't move each other's pawns, but we could share items. Although I neared the exit and escape, I moved deeper into the house to give Tyler a potion so he'd move faster. If I'd taken my chance to escape, I'd survive, but the other players might not—and I'd have no means of helping them from the outside.

Once done with my delivery, my remaining movements took me back to the foyer. Nathan rolled the dice, which gave him an oxygen tank to move through the poisonous gas in the basement, up the stairs. He met me in the foyer. Cody and Gwen stood on the far side of the main floor. They hopscotched through the vanishing and blocked rooms, entering the foyer just as the second-to-last room collapsed. There was only one clear path through the house. Tyler rolled the dice to see which room would go next.

The ballroom. It wasn't on the path. The door remained clear.

I let out a whoop. He danced his character through the house, joining the rest of the group just as the basement gases reached the stairs and started to seep into the main hallway where we all stood. With no time to spare, we'd won!

"That's it! We did it! Everyone escapes the house!"

We cheered and high-fived and jumped up and down like we'd won a trip to Disney World. At one point, Nathan swept me up into a hug. Caught up in the excitement, I threw my arms around him. Then we both realized what we'd done and stiffened. He pulled back awkwardly, avoiding my eyes. After the way I'd treated him, I deserved that, but pain lanced my gut.

"Guys!" Cody held up his hand for attention. "This is awesome, but we still have to read the end-of-the-game story."

Right. This moment was as important to me as the rest of the game.

Gwen picked up the book and began to read. "Congratulations! You have successfully defeated *The Haunted Place*. Now you may claim your reward. Hand Box Q to the youngest player."

"Technically, the baby is the youngest player," I said, hands on my belly.

"We love the baby, but he or she didn't contribute to our victory," Gwen pointed out. "Cody?"

He pulled out the box and held it up while Gwen continued reading. "Open the box and pull out the contents. If the Butler is still in the game, hand the item to the Butler and read the enclosed slip of paper. If the Butler accepts, game over. If he or she declines, the player to your right draws another slip."

A confused look crossed Nathan's face. The rest of us suppressed smiles. It hadn't taken any time to convince Shannon to make some minor modifications to the game end scenario to help me re-create one of Nathan's and my favorite scenes from television. Everyone else had agreed readily to the plan when I'd asked them after I got off the phone with Terri.

Cody pulled a small item out of the box and handed it to Nathan. Men didn't wear engagement rings, so I'd put several, multi-sided dice of varying sizes into the container. Cody also withdrew a slip of paper. Holding it in front of him, he held out the die and read slowly. "Nathan, will you marry me?"

He shot me a sidelong glance. I struggled to keep my face neutral, when I wanted to beam at him and give the game up now. Gwen nudged me under the table with her foot, and I bit my lip.

Nathan looked back at Cody. "Thanks, but no."

Cody passed the box to Gwen, who also drew a die with a slip and read the text. She offered the ten-sided die. "Dad, will you marry me?"

He chuckled. "Thank you, my darling Queen Guinevere, but even in medieval times, marrying one's own daughter was frowned upon."

"Well, that's a relief." She passed the box.

Tyler skipped the die and read his slip. "Nathan, will you marry me?"

"No thank you."

"Figures."

I took the box and set it on the table. There was one item left in the box. Pulling it out, I turned toward Nathan and pushed back from the table. Although he appeared to be enjoying this scene, and he knew exactly what I was doing, part of me worried about humiliating myself in front of all my friends. I'd be crushed if he turned me down. Still, life without risk wouldn't be very interesting.

"I spent a lot of time thinking about where to find a two-sided die, something to represent that we're two sides of the same coin. But then I realized, we're more than that now. We're a family. You, me, the baby. Gwen. Cody. So I got you this instead." I handed him a five-sided die. "I know we've had some ups and downs, but will you please take a chance on me? I've found a job in Albany, and they've agreed to let me telecommute all but a few days per month. I'm not going anywhere. I want to be with you. For as long as you'll have me."

As I spoke, his smile widened until it split his face in two. He took my hand in both of his, cradling my fingers and the die. "Before I answer, there's something I want to say."

My heart stopped. Oh, no. He wasn't just going to turn me down, he was going to make a big speech first. I'd ruined everything. Then, just as I started to panic, he leaned over and kissed me softly. The warmth of his lips eased the growing dread inside me and gave me the strength to smile up at him. "Go ahead."

"Well, the thing is, you're kind of stepping on what I'd planned, privately, for after the game."

A thrill went through me. "Oh, yeah?"

"Yeah. I love you. When you told me we were having a baby, it was one of the happiest moments of my life. But that's not why I asked you to marry me. I was planning to propose eventually, but after the whole thing with Gwen, it seemed better to wait."

"Sorry," Gwen said. "For the record, I am totally cool with my BFF becoming my stepmom. And I know I shouldn't have been such an asshole before."

I grinned at her, but my heart still beat a mile a minute.

Nathan shushed her, then pulled a box from his pocket and knelt next to me. "You are the last person I want to see when I go to sleep at night, and the first person I want to see each morning. There's no one I'd rather game with. You're the person I want by my side whether I'm shooting bad guys, exploring haunted houses, crashing our plane in the desert, or saving the world from deadly viruses."

My lips twitched at the way he'd worked several of my favorite games into his proposal. How very thoughtful and even more perfectly us than my proposal.

"I never should have let you walk away from me. I've cursed myself a thousand times for not saying this a month ago. I've wanted to be with you from the beginning. It's not about the baby. It's about you and me, and the way I feel when we're together. I understand why you said no but I swear—I'm not repeating my past mistakes. This isn't a do-over. This is about finding the one person who makes me feel like the luckiest man in the world. I want to spend the rest of my life making you happy." He pulled a ring from the box and held it out to me. A gorgeous, custom-made, incredibly geeky ring.

The center stone was a ruby shaped as a heart, surrounded by tiny diamonds. A pattern on the ruby and the sides of the ring mirrored the heart container in *Legends of Zelda*. It was absolutely the most perfect engagement ring I'd ever seen in my life.

"Holly, will you marry me?"

Even knowing what was coming, I gasped. My heart swelled.

"I asked you first," I said.

"Technically, that's not true. I asked you weeks ago."

"Well in that case…Yes!" I gasped, throwing myself into his arms. He caught me and wiped the happy tears streaming down my face before capturing my lips in a heart-stopping kiss. The world fell away, and I didn't know how much time passed before I pulled back. "I'm so sorry I left. I love you, and I never want to be with anyone else."

"It's okay. As long as you promise never to leave me again, I forgive you."

"I promise."

"That's all that matters. And I promise not to let you go. I do have one condition, though."

"Anything. Name it."

His lips twitched as he turned back to the group. "Can we read the real game end story?"

~*~

Acknowledgments

I can't believe this is my fifth book. For various reasons, it was one of the more difficult to write. I owe a huge debt of gratitude to everyone who gave me emotional support, a mental break, or held the baby so I could write or edit (or sleep).

First, thank you to my husband, Andrew. I absolutely could never have done this without you. We're the best team I've ever been on. Thank you to everyone at Kensington, including Wendy, Norma, Lauren, Alex, and Samantha. Thank you to my agent, Michelle, for your endless patience and willingness to help.

Thank you to everyone who read early drafts for me. Elizabeth, Farah, Kara, Kelley, Laura, Marty, Michelle, and anyone I can't remember at the moment between pregnancy brain and new mama brain. Please know I appreciate you.

Special thanks to Rob Daviau. If you hadn't invented the legacy game, Holly and Nathan would have a very different story. Even though my game is fictional, your games inspired me.

And a huge thanks to you, my readers. None of this would be possible without you.

I hope you enjoyed Holly and Nathan's story. If you did, please consider leaving an honest review with Amazon, Apple, Barnes & Noble, Goodreads, Kobo, or your favorite retailer.

Read on for a preview of
Laura Heffernan's next Gamer Girls romance
MAKE YOUR MOVE
Available in fall 2019 from Lyrical Press

Chapter 1

It costs nothing to be kind to someone in need.

—Nana

Boston was a hotbed for crime lords and tax evaders. According to my mother, at least. She droned on and on, driving my near-frantic pace as I walked toward Game On!, the local game store where my friends and I played after hours. Finally, the store appeared ahead of me like a beacon, a sign that this conversation, too, would pass.

While opening the door, I shoved my phone between my ear and shoulder, careful not to put the speaker too close. Hearing the words coming from the other end would do absolutely nothing to improve my mood. "Yes, Mom, I parked as close to the store as I could. Boston is perfectly safe. It probably won't even be dark by the time I head home. Would you prefer I took the T?...Well, moving back to Florida is not an option...I'll have one of the guys walk me to my car later."

I would do no such thing, but being my mother, she grasped at the straw unwittingly dangled before her. "Boys? What boys will be there? Tell me more."

"It's not a high school party, Mom." A deep breath masked my heavy sigh. "It's Gwen's husband and Holly's fiancé. You've heard me mention them a million times."

"What a shame."

"Actually, it's great. I'm happy for all of them."

Holly smiled and waved at me in greeting. Not for the first time, I marveled at how her belly completely swallowed her average-sized frame. The pregnancy also made her thick dark brown hair even more lustrous and shiny. Throw in her dancing brown eyes and massive smile, and pregnancy truly made my friend glow.

In response to her wave, I rolled my eyes and pointed to the phone. She came over and took the cookies out of my hand, which let me shift the phone into a better position.

"Shannon, we really need to talk about your love life," Mom said in my ear.

No, we really didn't. I'd explained why I didn't date much at least a hundred times. Sometimes I wished I hadn't bothered. She still seemed to think I chose a life of solitude rather than it being difficult to get to know someone in this age of swiping left and immediate gratification.

When I didn't reply, she sighed. "I just want you to be happy."

"I am happy."

"Why can't you settle down like your brother?"

"Sorry, Mom, I'm about to go through a tunnel. Gotta go!" Before she could say anything else, I hung up and shut off my phone.

"Tunnels in the store, huh?" Nathan asked as I walked into the back room where we played. Holly's fiancé looked every bit as excited about the baby as she did, with the same eager gleam in his blue eyes. Their happiness radiated out of them, making it impossible not to share their joy.

"A convenient tunnel is an excellent way to get off the phone," I said. "That woman would spend all night lecturing me on the importance of settling down with a nice man if I let her."

"She's your mother. She means well," he said gently. "We want the best for our children, even when we don't understand what it is."

"I know. I get it. And I appreciate her interest. I'm well aware that she could ignore me completely like Gwen's mom." I flashed a sympathetic smile toward my friend, who sat in the corner already munching on a cookie. "But I wish we could find the right balance between not caring at all and being obnoxious."

"It exists," Gwen said with a nod toward her dad. "Trust me."

"Well, we're unfortunately not going to become BFFs, either."

"She still bugging you to have babies?" Holly asked.

"That's the end game, I'm sure. For now, she's settled for insisting I find someone and, air quote, settle down," I said. "Sometimes, when I think of how much money my parents dropped on my brother's wedding, I want to tell her I'm getting married and take the cash. It would certainly help fund my game-making."

"She might want to attend the wedding," Cody pointed out.

"No problem. I'm sure someone would meet me at City Hall to get married for a percentage. I'd probably only have to pay a few thousand dollars."

"As someone recently accused of fraud," Holly said, "I'm going to recommend against that course of action. Let's start the game before this baby's born."

She wasn't due for a couple of months, but point taken. I stopped complaining.

Gwen said, "Thanks for the cookies. Did you bring your new game?"

A guilty twinge hit me, not because I hadn't brought the game but because at the moment, there was no game. I should be at home, figuring stuff out, instead of out here playing. "Um, well, I sort of hit a wall."

The bell over the front door jingled, and the final member of our group appeared in the doorway, carrying a bottle of whiskey. Tyler had close-cropped dark hair, a friendly smile with perfectly straight teeth, and such smooth black skin Gwen said he belonged in a skin care commercial. "What did I miss?"

"Shannon was about to tell us about her new game," Nathan said.

My intent had been to create a social deduction game, which technically wasn't a board game because it lacked a physical board. Social deduction meant most of the players shared a specific goal. They used visual cues and other clues to determine which of their friends secretly worked against them. Personally, I preferred purely cooperative games, but lots of people liked the thrill of outsmarting their friends and family. People like Gwen and Cody, but also a ton of others. The key to success in social deduction was largely theme: we'd played versions where you worked to find cannibals, Nazis, traitors, evil cultists, werewolves, and more.

"Uh-oh," Nathan said. "What happened?"

"I found another game with the exact same theme," I said. "Same name and everything. I don't want to be accused of copying."

Holly made a face. "That sucks. What was it?"

Quickly, I gave an overview. My game was set in the 1920s, inside a speakeasy. Players/mob members sought to determine which of their friends was secretly an undercover police officer, working to unmask that person before they turned everyone in for illegally drinking. Larger groups could assign additional secret roles such as the mob leader and the hitman. Each secret role had its own goals, which could affect the other players' strategies, whether they knew it or not. As the game developed, I found myself adding some surprisingly subversive elements.

Surprising because normally I didn't go for lying and being sneaky but in this game those elements added depth lacking in some of the other, similar games we played. Overall, I'd been proud of what I'd accomplished before discovering the need to shelve the project indefinitely.

"Hold on," Tyler said. "Has anyone here heard of that game?"

Everyone shook their heads.

"Maybe it doesn't matter," Gwen said. "Sounds like the other game isn't terribly popular if none of us have heard of it. Or maybe it's not that great, and you could design a better one."

"It's got less than fifty reviews on BoardGameNerd.com," I admitted. "And I thought of it on my own. I just hate the idea that someone might see it and think I took their game."

"Not to be that guy, but it's not *that* original," Cody said. "There are dozens of social deduction games."

"Yeah. The twist with this one–which I really liked–is that the players working together are the 'bad' guys, and they're trying to unmask the 'good' guys to win. Most social deduction games are the other way around."

"It sounds like fun," Tyler said. "You should see what you can do to make your game stand out. I'm happy to help, if you want to brainstorm or playtest. Or, um…even if you want some artwork for the prototype."

I cocked my head at him. "You draw?"

He looked away, grinning sheepishly. "A little. I took a graphics design course in college. It wouldn't be great, but it might help you put some life in the concept."

"He's just being modest," Cody said. "He's really good. Won a couple of contests in college."

"Wow. That would be awesome, thanks," I said. My phone beeped, drawing my attention to a text from someone responding to my ad. Since they opened with "I'm 420-friendly," I deleted the message. Not when I lived with my grandmother.

Seeing the lock on my face, Gwen asked, "How goes the roommate search?"

"Boy do I need a drink before answering that question."

"That good?" Cody reached for a cookie, pushing a lock of curly brown hair out of his eyes. It always cracked me up that Gwen, whose looks got many Anne of Green Gables comments over the years, wound up with a guy who resembled Gilbert Blythe.

"Umm…. No." I nodded at the bottle in Tyler's hand. "Thank goodness someone brought something other than wine and beer."

"Your other friends are all lightweights." He poured me a shot.

Accepting the glass, I sniffed it. Smoky, dark. A sipping whiskey. Gratefully, I tasted it, letting the warm alcohol roll over my tongue. A purr escaped me. "Thanks. I needed that."

"You're welcome. So what's the problem with the roommate search?"

"Well, apparently, everyone in Boston who needs a place to live is awful," I said. "One guy actually asked me if he had to wear clothes in the common areas."

Gwen laughed, and Holly shuddered.

"You know, Shannon," Cody said. "Tyler might have a solution for you."

"Oh, yeah? Do you know someone who's looking?"

"I do." Tyler hesitated for a second, glancing away before meeting my gaze squarely. "Me."

Huh. That gave me pause. I liked Tyler, always had. But he'd had a crush on me for quite a while, and living together could create an awkward situation. It didn't help that he'd kissed me last winter, while we were all in Mexico for Gwen and Cody's wedding. I'd had to explain that I couldn't feel sexual attraction for people before I formed a deeper connection with them. He claimed to understand, but something in his expression when I caught him looking at me from time to time made me suspect that, even though he respected my rejection, he'd change the situation if he had the option.

Speaking of awkward, this wasn't a conversation to have in front of our friends, even if they knew our history. "I'd love to chat, but I'm starving. Come with me into the kitchen?"

He must have sensed my hesitation. When we got to the other room, he said, "I know what you're thinking. I'm over you."

I wanted to believe him, but his request made no sense. Why would Tyler want to move in with me in the first place? "You've never even been inside my apartment. You live in Harvard Square. I'm out on the blue line. Why would you want to move so far away from everything?"

"Well, obviously, I need to see the inside before signing a lease," he said. "But my company opened a new office in Revere, and they put me in charge."

"That's great! Congratulations!"

"Thanks. It's a huge opportunity. But commuting on the T is a pain now, and I don't want to deal with Cambridge traffic in the mornings."

"You make good money. Why don't you get your own place?" A bit nosy to be sure, but sometimes curiosity made us ask rude questions.

"That's the plan. But you know how ridiculous Boston housing is. Especially when I work such long hours I'm barely ever home. Why pay fifteen hundred dollars a month to rent five hundred square feet I'm only sleeping in?"

He had me there. I lived on the top floor of my Nana's two-family unit. In exchange for doing her grocery shopping and running other errands—which I'd have done anyway—she gave me low rent on a three-bedroom apartment I could otherwise never afford on my own. Even with a roommate.

"Yeah, I get it." The kindest thing would be to tell him no, but we would be sitting in a room together for the next three or four hours, and I didn't have the heart to shut him down completely. Again. A possible out occurred to me. "I've got a couple of people lined up to see the place already. I'll text you later this week?"

"Sounds good. Thanks."

"Sure."

What I didn't tell him was that I absolutely, positively had no intention of letting a guy who had a crush on me anywhere near my spare room. Tyler was a nice guy, and I wished him well, but we couldn't live in the same apartment.

Not when I couldn't be attracted to him, and without that, our relationship couldn't be what he wanted.